THE TRUTH
&
ADDY LOEST

ALSO BY KIM KELLY

Black Diamonds

This Red Earth

The Blue Mile

Paper Daisies

Wild Chicory

Jewel Sea

Lady Bird & The Fox

Sunshine

Walking

Her Last Words

THE TRUTH
&
ADDY LOEST

KIM KELLY

Jazz Monkey Publications

First published 2021 by Jazz Monkey Publications

Copyright © Kim Kelly 2021

The moral right of the author has been asserted.

All rights reserved. No part of this publication may be reproduced, stored in a retrieval system, or transmitted in any form or by any means, electronic, mechanical, photocopying, recording or otherwise without the prior permission of the author.

The characters in this book are fictitious and any resemblance to real persons, living or dead, is purely coincidental.

Quotes from *The Lucky Country* by Donald Horne, which appear in this book, are reproduced here by kind permission of Penguin Random House Australia Pty Ltd, copyright © Donald Horne, first published by Penguin Australia, 1964.

A CIP record for this book is available at the National Library of Australia.

Design: Alissa Dinallo
Cover image: Shutterstock montage
Text dinkus: Kim Kelly
Author photograph: Dean Brownlee
Printing: Lightning Source, Ingram Content Group

Publishing services provided by Critical Mass
www.critmassconsulting.com

For love, and other acts of courage.

*My dear friend! Dearest girl! — Art! Who comprehends it?
With whom can I discuss this mighty goddess? How precious
to me were the few days when we talked together... I have
carefully preserved the little notes with your clever, charming,
most charming answers ...*

Ludwig van Beethoven, letter to Bettina Brentano, 1810

*And now good-morrow to our waking souls,
Which watch not one another out of fear;
For love, all love of other sights controls,
And makes one little room an everywhere.*

John Donne, 'The Good-Morrow', 1633

*I tell you: one must still have chaos in one, to give birth to a
dancing star. I tell you: ye have still chaos in you.*

Friedrich Nietzsche, *Thus Spake Zarathustra*, 1891

ADDY LOEST IS PROBABLY NOT GOING TO DIE TODAY

The house on Flower Street was one of those narrow, crumbling mid-terrace wrecks that hadn't seen much love for a hundred years. Its peeling paintwork and rotting floorboards ensured the respectable poor had moved out long ago, as they had across the whole of the inner-city suburb of Chippendale, and in their place a ragtag band of university students, artists and assorted dropouts had come to call it home.

And Addy Loest was one of them – she was all of them, in fact. She woke that morning, a Tuesday, the last day of April, 1985, queasy from a cocktail of last night's green ginger wine and a rapidly gathering guilt at the whole terrible load of herself. She had tried, she had really tried, but now, halfway through the first term of her second year of a combined bachelor's degree of arts and law, she had decided she might actually rather die than continue with the latter. She was not going to become a lawyer. She could not care for the offers or acceptances or considerations of contractual agreements; she didn't want to know one dot about civil and criminal procedure; the only dispute resolution she was interested in was how she was going to tell her father what she had decided.

I'll tell him on Sunday – I will, she promised the inside of her eyelids, not yet ready to face today, never mind Sunday, when she'd make the weekly train-trek home for lunch. Like a good girl. A good girl who respected and honoured her hardworking, self-sacrificing father with the truth.

She could already hear his fist slamming down on the dining table, the flinty remnants of his German accent sharpening with every syllable: '*What did you say, Adrianna?*'

Don't tell him, her lesser angel of self-preservation whispered. It wasn't as though he could easily find out: he was a hundred kilometres away, down the sand-swept sapphire coast that lay between Sydney and Port Kembla, where he worked six days a week as hard-headed, hard-hatted foreman at the steelworks there.

She burrowed further under her quilt, its midnight-indigo cover pretending darkness, but it was no use: she'd never get back to sleep again now. Outside, the city had begun to churn, the brakes of a semi-trailer wheezing up to the traffic lights along the main road beyond. It was somewhere around seven o'clock, she supposed, squinting out from under the quilt to find daylight struggling above the rusted tin rooftops of the row behind and through her grime-fuzzed window. She blinked at the pale grey sky, cotton-wool clouds blushed with the sunrise as though they'd brushed the rooftops on their way past. Her father would be getting himself ready for the day, she knew, combing his silvering hair, lighting his first cigarette, smiling to himself that his daughter would not only be the first lawyer in the family after a generation disrupted by war and intercontinental migration, but that she would be an industrial relations specialist of global renown forging once and for all the socialist utopia that was their birthright. Her brother, Nick, was only expected to win next Friday night's boxing match. Nick, two years the elder, would finish an unremarkable degree in economics this year and would probably go on to become a heavy-weight auditor for the taxation department, but for the time being, he was little more than a muscle-bound ape. They weren't very close, not these days, not like they used to be. Nick was indulged, spoilt, his way into the world of men paved with easily achievable expectation; while Addy's way was —

Her pulse began to thump. She sat up, her chest suddenly tight, aching, her mouth dry.

I'm going to die. She was certain, so certain: dread, a great wave of it, crashed about her and within her. *I'm having a heart attack.*

No, you're not, she told herself. *The doctors have said there's nothing wrong with you or your heart but existential angst and self-obsessed hypochondria – probably brought on by your own laziness and disappointment with yourself at not wanting to continue with law. Loser.*

She'd been to see a doctor again only a couple of weeks ago, this time at the Women's Clinic across from the university, a tank-tough matron peering disapprovingly over horn-rimmed glasses at her: 'You're not pregnant, are you?'

'No!' No chance of that. Addy didn't even have a boyfriend, not really, only Luke, whom she referred to as her boyfish, short for boyfriend-ish, just someone lovely she tortured regularly by not having sex with him – and she had no idea of the why of that, either. They'd had sex, of course – they'd been going out almost five months. They'd had sex three and a half times. She just wasn't keen to do it again.

The doctor had sighed as though she'd been told a lie; she told Addy: 'You're very thin. Try eating properly for a month, see how that goes.' With the unspoken suggestion: *Now, get out of my office and stop wasting my time.*

I am going to die. Addy was so certain, even as she was talking herself away from the dread.

Shut up, idiot.

Yes, she agreed. She got up, the thumping sensation beginning to pass, and she shambled to the bathroom. *I need a hamburger.*

The greasy Joe's up the road, on the corner, didn't open until nine, though. She turned on the shower and undressed, and as she did, she glanced over a bony hip at her bony knees and her bony feet, wondering if her diet was the problem. After all, hamburgers and coffee by day, fried rice and green ginger rotgut by night, and chocolate anything in between, wasn't exactly Pritikin, was it. When she was skint and practising the virtues of imposed frugality, she ate bananas and fish fingers and creamed corn on toast, sometimes with a slice or two of tomato. When she was drunk, she craved felafel. Her diet was indeed appalling. It also couldn't have been the problem, or not all of it, anyway. She'd been having these unfunny turns for more than a year, on and off; mostly few and far between; occasionally in clusters; occasionally waking her, shaking her in the night, gasping for air: *I'M GOING TO DIE!* Those last were the most frightening of the lot. The first had been more confusing than anything else: she'd been on the train, on the way to the first day of Orientation Week at the university, when she'd felt unable to take a full breath, as though the steamy, summer warmth inside the midday carriage was hampering the process. A nameless panic had prickled around the edges of her heart; her pulse had raced; but then the train had pulled into Central Station, and she'd forgotten all about it – until the next time.

Stress, that's all this is – stress-head.

That seemed to be the common thread, except for when it wasn't: like the time, just these summer holidays past, when she was home and sunbathing on Fisherman's Beach, alone and contented, blank-headed, listening only to the gulls calling, playing on the warm breeze; or the time she was making her father a sleep-in breakfast, a few days after Christmas, still celebrating her final High Distinction for English Lit, flipping eggs ahead of a long day of doing nothing but reading the poetry of John Donne, dipping into the texts for the academic year to come, this year, the lines of one of the poems she'd read the day before swirling through her mind like sweet-scented smoke:

Our two souls therefore, which are one,
Though I must go, endure not yet
A breach, but an expansion,
Like gold to airy thinness beat.

How beautiful, she'd thought. As the daughter of a metallurgical worker, she'd found that metaphor of the bonds of love expressed in beaten gold particularly romantic: stretched to a gossamer wisp and yet unbreakable, a tiny, tiny wire wound round the globe. And at that she'd found the notion bleakly sad: for she didn't think she'd ever feel anything like that for anyone, certainly not poor lovely Luke, whom she'd only just met then – and as she'd thought of him: *BANG*. Heart was thumping, bursting, not with love but with terror.

'What's wrong, Sprout?' her father had asked her, calling her by that name of deepest affection and permanent concern for her smallness. 'You look as if you've seen a ghost.'

'Nothing,' she'd said. 'No one.' She'd found enough of a smile to fool him, her focus on the burnt-orange kitchen tiles behind him: 'Just dreaming.' *Just fighting to keep my heart in my chest and my feet on the ground.*

She couldn't worry him with anything like the truth, whatever that might have been: *Dad, I think I'm dying.* She never let him know if she had the merest head cold; last winter, she'd sprained her ankle falling out of a pub on too-high heels, and didn't go home that following Sunday, so he wouldn't see the trouble it gave her: 'I have to study, Dad, I'm sorry – Legal Institutions exam on Monday.' *Liar.*

She'd seen seven different doctors so far, quietly, scurrying into their surgeries like an overgrown and underfed rodent, hugging her too-big shirt around herself, around her conspicuous nothingness, hiding her everythingness: 'Um, I'm not really sure if I'm sick or not …' She'd had two electrocardiograms done, and four doses of antibiotics in case it was an infection of some strange kind.

But it's just me, isn't it. Dying. Of non-specific dyingness. She stood there under the shower this bleary, weary morning, resigned, all beaten out in the post-panic settling of her nerves, with the hot water a blessing on the back of her neck. She tested her breathing in the quickly thickening steam: she was all right. She wasn't going to die just yet, unless perhaps a meteor speared through the tiny window above the shower and into her head, or unless the Soviet Union decided to commence the Nuclear Holocaust, or Ronald Reagan, in a fit of dementia, decided to conduct a missile test on Sydney, or the IRA moved in next door. All as likely as Orwell's dystopian nightmares becoming prophecy: *1984* was so last year. There were terrible enough real things going on in the world, she reminded herself: there was a famine in Africa, war in Lebanon, terrorists in Palestine, terrorists in Spain, contamination of Aboriginal land from atomic bombs dropped in the red desert after the last world war. Addy Loest had nothing to complain about.

She stood so long there in the shower she disgusted herself with the flagrant waste of hot water when so many had none, yet she stood there a little longer, anyway. *I have a hangover,* she groaned some justification. *You drink too much,* she growled back at herself. A flutter of panic followed that she might be running late now for her Contracts tutorial at nine, but then she recalled she wasn't going to attend it, and relief returned. That relief she felt meant withdrawing from law was the right thing to do, didn't it? Wasn't it the right thing to do? She didn't feel this kind of aversion to her other subjects: the thought of English Lit at eleven was one that made her want the clock to go faster, the quicker to discover what new revelation was waiting for her there. What new magic. Today would be the first lecture in a special study of the eighteenth-century poet Alexander Pope. What she'd read of Pope so far had seemed impenetrable, like a string of antique-Englishman in-jokes and allusions she'd never get, but that only dared her to want to know what the fuss was about. She wanted to know Pope's *story*. She wanted to know just about everyone's story: why people thought or felt or spoke the way they did; where they'd come from. Stories: they'd always brought her enlightenments and delights of all kinds, and fabulous mysteries that, on the page, seemed to stay still long enough for her to grasp, to brush her fingertips against at least. Language danced across her soul in shapes and patterns she'd only just begun to identify, not so much as grammatical parts, but as a dialect of truth. The real truth. She glimpsed a future of herself at a little desk by a window overlooking the sea, or a sea of trees, writing, and writing, and writing, though she couldn't yet see what truths she might tell.

You are fricken deranged, that's what you are. Need any more proof?

She turned off the shower, shying from this secret at the bottom of all her unreachable secrets, and dried herself – to the sounds of her housemate, Roz, awakening too, her bed just the other side of the bathroom wall. Moaning: 'Oh yesssss. There … There …' Roz had a new boy in there, there – the drummer in a band that had a Wednesday-night residency at their most frequented pub, the Harrington Inn, or the Hairy Egg as it was otherwise known. 'Fuck me!' Roz shrieked. 'Come on!' Roz was never shy. Roz was a voluptuously tousled, full-flame redhead, otherwise known as The Unmade Bed, and Addy was a little bit in love with her – more in love with her than she'd ever been with any boy. They'd known each other since Year Ten, having met during a junior high school public-speaking championship, held at Parliament House, in Canberra, and having been the only two from state schools to have made it through to the semi-finals – Addy from Wollongong High, and Roz from Caringbah High – they'd stuck like glue. They were practically from the same regional wilderness as well, south of the metropolis; to the natural inhabitants of the University of Sydney, anyone who hailed from anywhere south of Bondi was a foreigner, to be regarded with some suspicion. 'Don't slow down!' Roz slapped her drummer boy, possibly on the arse, and Addy heard him yelp: 'Jesus!'

Addy winced, and not only for him. It seemed the more hedonistically and flamboyantly herself Roz had become across the almost twelve months they'd shared this tumble-down terrace house, the more Addy had shrunk. Roz was a fine arts femme fantabulous, painting herself in large, loud splashes across any and all canvases she chose to inhabit; while Addy ... Addy seemed barely here at all. She hadn't even shown her face at a Young Labor meeting all year; couldn't imagine public speaking anywhere these days; it was hard enough to have to make the required contributions to tutorial discussions. What had happened to that girl, Adrianna Loest, who could stand on a stage and fill five minutes to brimming with all manner of guff, from the meaning of wealth beyond money to whether or not women could be heroes too, and make it fascinating, entertaining, words falling so easily from her tongue. She remembered the crowd laughing with her; she would float upon those drifts of laughter; she would thrill inside the spotlight stillness of their listening silences. That girl her father was sure would change the world. Where had she gone? A mouse-brown ghost in the misted mirror. Was she dead already?

'Yes! Yes! Give it to me!' Roz was off the planet.

Addy slunk back to her room, threw on yesterday's black jeans and flannelette shirt of blue-and-green checks, her usual student uniform these days, and she sat on the end of her bed. The digital alarm clock on her bedside chest said it was only a quarter to eight, but she didn't want to sit there waiting for hamburger-time, empty and too full, waiting on the end of a terrible play, staring at the blunt-edged numbers glowing emergency-red at her, like the Doomsday Clock set at three minutes to midnight, three minutes to terminal, global disaster. This was a long three minutes. She glanced around her room, not that there was much to glance at, the room being all of three metres by three-point-two; and she'd tidied the barely contained chaos of her wardrobe yesterday afternoon, her nocturnal-frock collection, her trove of most marvellous material things; she'd tidied her already tidy bookshelf as well. She tidied her bed now, straightening her quilt and folding her granny blanket neatly over it, lining up the colourful crocheted squares, so that she wouldn't look like a slob, in case —

Oh for God's sake – get a life. Seriously.

She grabbed her bag, her grunge-smudged canvas satchel, checked that her notebooks and her copy of Pope's *Selected Poetry and Prose* were there, as well as her unread library book, *The Poetical Career of Alexander Pope*, and Tacitus' *The Annals* for Ancient History, still faintly smelling of squashed banana, and *Gatsby* for American Lit, too, and then she crept down the stairs.

The lounge room at the end of the bannister was dim, windowless, but Addy could see well enough the remains of last night on the coffee table: the ashtray overflowing, sticky glasses ranged around the board game they'd played – Trivial Pointlessness, or something like that, it was called, a new game that their other housemate, Harriet, had brought back from somewhere expensive.

Harriet Rawley-Hogue, or HRH as she preferred to be known, was in fine arts with Roz, but that was about all they had in common. Harriet was the daughter of a judge, had gone to one of the country's most prestigious private schools, looked like something Modigliani might have framed, had a boyfriend who was in his final year of medicine, as well as being ridiculously handsome, permanently tanned, about to pop the question any moment, and no doubt this minute cradling her between sculpted arms as they slept in the front room up the hall – HRH's private parlour, complete with four-poster and silk drapery. Harriet was slumming it here with them, 'Learning a little worldliness,' she'd sigh conde-scendingly; Addy imagined that even Harriet's parents found her insufferable and had turfed her out. Still, the cast-off furniture, kitchen appliances and state-of-the-art stereo Harriet had also brought with her made the pain worthwhile – and made their place pretty cool, by comparison to most student digs. There might have been a hole in the floorboards under the chaise longue, but they had a chaise longue – plush powdery-lavender velvet, with scrolly repro Queen Anne legs. Eye-poppingly horrible, really, but cool.

They also had a piano, thanks to HRH, an elegant old upright, and Harriet's most redeeming feature – not just the piano itself, though. Sometimes, Harriet would play it, and she was very good. She'd play mostly Chopin etudes and Addy could listen to her all day. There was no piano at home, at Port, only the radiogram and her father's massive classical record collection. Very uncool out there in the Illawarra wilderness of steel and coal, where the only crescendos likely to be heard emerged from the rugby league commentary at a sneaky burst for the try line with three minutes to the full-time whistle, and any music that wasn't AC/DC was for poofters. Music, as in real *music* music, the kinds of music that gave Addy glimpses of who she really was and where she was really from, was something special she shared with her dad; Sunday afternoons listening to Beethoven paint seas of emotions into her she couldn't yet know; listening to the shushing of the surf, to the ripples of generations leading her back to a small town in central Germany she'd never seen. And at this moment, it all made her think of him again – her father.

His fist slamming down on the tablecloth, making the salt and pepper jump.

The instant ache of longing to know the truth of him – to understand – and never being able to ask. Because the truth hurts. The truth hurt him. Sometimes, if she stayed over on the Sunday night, after a glass of Riesling too many, he'd ask her to dance, and he'd look at her, there in his arms, and he'd let her see the tears in his eyes – not for her, but for her mother. They'd met in the dining-room hut of the Balgownie Migrant Workers Hostel in 1955 – he'd been nineteen, almost twenty, the same age Addy was now. Her mother, Elke, had been seventeen, a trainee machinist at the Friedelle Children's Wear factory. They were both orphans, washed up on these shores; they'd done everything properly: scrimped and saved for their marriage, for seven years they put away every spare penny until they had enough to put down the deposit on a patch of land on Gallipoli Street, living in a caravan there until they could afford to build their humble fibro home, made grand to them with its ocean-facing views, but none of their carefulness could stop fate from robbing Peter Loest of his Elke. She had just told him she was pregnant again, with what they'd hoped would be their third child; she died of an ectopic rupture the next day. Addy was only two and a half, and knew nothing more of any of it, except for her father's silent, stoic grief – a grief she supposed was only ever made worse because she looked so much like her mother, with her fine long nose and large eyes, which, she could only guess from the three black-and-white photographs she possessed, were the same crystalline blue, hair the same pale brown, too. Addy often imagined that if her mother had lived, they'd sit around complaining about their boring hair, and maybe talking about Germany.

'Germany?' her father would snort at any attempt at a question. 'No one wants to know anything about Germany – and neither should you.'

The war and every loss it had brought were still too close for him, forty years on.

I should get to my Contracts tute. How can I not finish law? How can I disappoint him?

Hamburger.

The resident cat – a stray called No Name – blinked at her from the top of the piano. He was a pretty thing, with an almost perfectly symmetrical marmalade splash across his otherwise grey face, making it seem as though his green eyes were peering through translucent butterfly wings. He yawned and curled back into himself.

She said aloud, 'You're no help,' reaching into her bag for the smaller of her notebooks, to leave a note, ostensibly for Roz, but really – what for? Just in case? She'd always been a note-leaver, just in case, and yet like the unfunny turns, her notes had subtly, although surely, increased in intensity and frequency lately. It seemed she couldn't leave a space without some explanation, some mark that she'd been there, some clue as to where she'd gone. She wrote now:

Am never drinking again, et cetera. Have left in search of early hamburger. Should I fail to return within a day or so, assume I have fallen into a vat of salted lard. Died doing what she loved – Addy X

She tore out the page and placed it under the paperweight between No Name and her telephone book. Then, just before she turned to leave, just as she was giving the cat a fleeting rub under his pretty little chin, something moved behind her: on the brown couch, the decrepit leather relic of indeterminate age that sat across from the lavender chaise, opposite in every way, with its lame disguise of pink paisley bedspread and assorted scatter cushions. And there was a body inside it this morning. She could see a mess of dark, shaggy hair at one end; black suede boots at the other. A foggy recollection that this was the singer in the band – musical relation of Drummer Boy upstairs. The band was called Elbow – *Who calls a band Elbow?* – and they were a post-punk, alternative folk-rock, jingle-jangle quartet, duelling guitars around an earnest baritone, like Elvis, but after too many cones, delivering dinky earworms like, 'She's a spoonful of blueness, so sweet and so dark, she's a moonbeam, she's a daydream, she is barefoot in the park' – that sort of wet nonsense. She couldn't remember his name, though, any more than she could Drummer Boy's. What had they talked about last night? Snatches of chat came back to her, voices raised over the current conversational standards: the looming threat of university fees and other evils of neo-conservatism; and then she'd won a piece of Trivial Pointlessness plastic whatever on the question: *Which race car driver won his third Bathurst 1000 in 1978?* She answered: Peter Brock. The singer boy had jumped up off the floor and shouted: 'How did you know that?' Slapping his thighs, he'd loomed over her, all tall denim stovepipes, fashionably threadbare, faintly accusatory. She'd shrugged and poured herself another drink; she didn't know how to say, 'My dad loves motor racing, and boxing, and rugby league, and Beethoven, so suck on that.' She didn't know how to ask: 'Why are you so shocked at a girl winning a piece of plastic whatever on a sports question?'

And she didn't want to talk to him now. She didn't want to talk to anyone.

He turned again under the pink paisley, squinting up at her, and she couldn't get out of there fast enough.

'With a little bit of extra beetroot, please,' she asked the man at the Olympia Café, the early-opener up on King Street, almost a kilometre away, in Newtown, a long strip of shops on the chipped pastel-plaster edge of western Sydney.

'More beetroot?' He looked over his shoulder at her from the grill and smiled. 'I like the beetroot, too,' he said, kindness in his gruff, rough voice; a nice man, presumably Greek and about the same age as her father, face lined with some similar boatload of cares.

Addy only nodded in reply. She was almost tearfully hungry now and a dull headache sat above her eyes.

'You don't get the beetroot in Maccadonalds,' he said, turning back to the grill.

Addy nodded again, out the window. She'd never set foot in one of *those* hamburger joints, franchises of which seemed to be springing up everywhere now. Their prices might have been a little cheaper than a greasy Joe's, but it wasn't real food, so her father would say; when he was drunk, he'd also say the whole operation was a front for the CIA in a way that left her wondering if it might be true. She watched the first spots of rain dot the footpath outside, cars whizzing by, a bus thundering past, rattling the glass in its tired old frame, and she wondered what this shop might have been, originally. One of the buildings across the road had the year '1895' inscribed on its facade like a block-type date stamp, but the ornate masonry around the arched windows of its upper floor looked somehow medieval and the decorative pediment above them seemed to have escaped from a Roman temple; the whole thing had been painted the colour of a lime milkshake, and at street level a new Thai restaurant had just moved in. All of the buildings up King Street were individually eccentric in this way – pub, butcher, fruit shop, pawn broker, record store, book emporium, second-hand furniture, bakery, pizza place, Chinese takeaway. All of them had been something grander once, or maybe people had simply cared more then, about the things they looked at – why not put a domed turret or a Juliet balcony on a charcoal chicken shop?

No such thing as a charcoal chicken shop in 1895 – idiot.

I just meant —

'Here you go, love.' The Greek café man brought her hamburger over on a plate, and oh God it was perfect: oozing barbeque sauce and fuchsia beetroot juice, burnt onions and sausage mince spilling from the sesame-seed sprinkled bun, this hamburger glimmered before her as something not quite real. Something magical. This could have had something to do with the blaring glare of the fluorescent lighting inside the shop reflecting at double strength off the mad yellow laminate tabletop on which the hamburger had been placed, but oh it was beautiful.

Addy looked up at the man and beamed: 'Thank you.'

'Is okay.' He smiled again, and reached behind him to the high, tiled counter, for another plate. For one horrific second she thought he was going to join her at the table. *No, no, no!* Hamburgers were best eaten alone, and this one – this one was special. She didn't want to share it in any sense. But he wasn't going to join her; he placed this other plate beside the one in front of her: it was piled high with hot chips. He said: 'On the house, for you, young lady. Eat up.'

'Oh!' The surprise caught in her throat. He was too kind; he probably thought she was starving, miserably scrawny and broke. She wasn't broke, though: she worked two long shifts a week in the toy department at the Town Hall Variety Store in the city – Thursdays from two until nine, and Saturdays from eight until five – all per the Shopworkers Union regulations and all above the hourly award rates. They were good to her there as well, the managers, always letting her juggle shifts if she needed to with a change of timetable at uni. She paid no tuition fees, not yet at least, her rent was low and she got a fifteen percent discount on stationery and basic comestibles at work. She had it damn easy, really. But this nice, kind man had given her an extra plate of pity. She must have looked like just another poor King Street dero, she supposed.

She hung her head over her food, pushed aside all guilt and self-loathing for the pleasure and privilege of hamburger, and ate every last mouthful as a moral obligation; she ate every chip, too; washed it all down with an orange fizzy drink.

That's better. She almost belched out aloud. She glanced at her wristwatch: it was a couple of minutes after nine now – less than two hours until English Lit. She supposed she might head for the library, read some more Pope before the lecture, but she wrote a note for lovely café man first:

Dear Mr Olympia Café,
That hamburger was superb, and your kindness will never be forgotten. I needed both this morning, very much. I hope you have a wonderful day. ☺X

She never signed her name on notes to strangers, just the smiley face and one kiss. As the man was now busy taking an order from a group of construction types wanting an industrial quantity of egg-and-bacon rolls, she tucked the note under the neat little stack she'd made of her plates and left without a word or wave, or a second glance at the half-a-dozen pairs of hairy legs crowding the counter, football socks pushed down above dusty steel-capped boots; didn't turn around when one of them gave her a leery, 'Why don't ya smile, sweetheart,' out the door. She knew that type a bit too well.

The rain was falling a little more heavily, giving her an excuse to pick up her pace, to get away from him, and to cross the road. Under the tin awning here, the rain crashed heavier still; she didn't fancy running through this downpour, all the way to the library – her books would get soaked, and so would she. It was mid-autumn cool turning cold and she was coatless; she hadn't brought an umbrella, either. Supposing she might pick one up for a dollar at the nearest el cheapo discount store, she backtracked to do precisely that, but before she got there, she passed an elderly woman letting herself into one of the shops along the way, muttering something under her breath, seeming to have trouble with her keys, grappling with them awkwardly, as she carried four sizeable shopping bags, those sort of roll-up nylon bags that fit half a cow in them once unfurled, two slung on each arm.

Addy instinctively slowed, and asked: 'Can I give you a hand?'

The woman frowned over her shoulder, but there was a smile in her bright blue eyes. 'It is all right, thank you, dear,' she said. 'I have fought with worse.'

An accent thickly, unmistakeably Germanic.

Addy laughed, with some warm reflex: 'All the same – let me help with your bags. Please.'

'That's very thoughtful, dear.' The woman smiled entirely now, a big, broad smile that seemed to comprise most of her face. She was quite elderly, perhaps seventy or more, and her hair, pulled back in a timelessly stylish chignon, was white, but there was something jaunty about her; spry. She wore a simple yet smartly tailored suit of plum-coloured wool, expensive-looking, European, and black shoes that appeared equally so. Addy immediately wanted to know her – know what a woman like this was doing letting herself into a shop in shabby old Newtown. What kind of shop it was Addy couldn't recall. *A haberdashery?* Although she found herself in Newtown once or twice a week, she didn't remember this shop at all; or perhaps it was only that the lights hadn't been switched on yet, making the window seem unfamiliar. Was that a zebra's head she could see within the sweep of a red velvet curtain?

She said to the old woman, taking two of her bags: 'It's no trouble. I just enjoyed a plate of free hot chips. One good deed deserves another, et cetera.'

'Good, good,' the woman replied distractedly, finally popping the lock, and giving the door a little kick with her fine patent-leather toe.

Addy was met with a draught of some sort of floral scent, as though the old shop exhaled. She took a couple of paces back, to check her bearings, asking herself again: *What shop is this?* In looking up between the awning of this one and the next, to try to see the facade above, she copped a face full of rain; her vision blurred, but she saw clearly enough: this was a building of bare brick, small colonial bricks, dark pink, almost the colour of the woman's suit, and unadorned in any way; it was perhaps the oldest building in the row. A bus honked – she was standing there with one foot on the road – and as she stepped back across the footpath, she saw the shop window now glowed, and so did the name of the place, in swirling cursive, quite unmissable gold lettering: *The Curiosity Shop.* There was the zebra, looking out from behind that red curtain, and the harlequin splash of a large tiffany lamp, a cave of wonders beyond: shelves of books and bric-a-brac, chandeliers and long-fringed shawls, and shoes, lots of shoes …

Once again, Addy looked left and right and back down the road at the Olympia, to check that this was in fact King Street. It was. Ali's Lebanese lay directly across the road: she'd had a felafel roll there last Saturday night. *This shop must be new,* she thought, following the woman through the open door. She placed the bags beside a glass display case here – one that was filled with brooches and bangles and beads, all glittering. The woman stood over the other side of it, pulling out frocks from the bags she'd brought in, shaking out a chiffon skirt speckled with soft gold sequins. This was a slice of heaven as far as Addy was concerned.

She asked the woman: 'Are you just setting up shop?'

'Setting up?' The woman was intent on smoothing frock-froth onto a padded-satin hanger. 'What do you mean?'

'Have you only recently moved in here?' Addy asked, still taking it in – embroidered corsets, lace-up boots, paste-jewel clutch purses – and calculating how much she could spend; the zebra seemed to smile approvingly, papier mache gatekeeper of all good things. 'Have you just opened?'

The woman chuckled, pulling out another frock, one of deep turquoise taffeta: 'No, dear. I have been here for eleven years. Twelve years in June.'

'How can I have not seen this shop before?' Addy couldn't keep the childlike wonder from her voice, as though she'd been flummoxed by a conjurer's trick.

The woman shrugged, not looking away from her work, continuing to plump out the bow on the back of the taffeta; she said: 'When we are young, there is so much to see, but we see what we must eventually, when we are ready to open our eyes to it.'

Addy's skin tingled at this cryptic crumb of wisdom, and at the beautiful sentence that delivered it. She asked, more to signal her respect than from necessity: 'May I look around?'

'Of course!' The woman chuckled again. 'Enjoy yourself.'

'I will.' All thoughts of getting to the library fell away. Addy glanced at her watch: subtracting walking time, she had an hour and a half to enjoy herself here.

The shop was narrow, perhaps no more than three metres wide, but it seemed to go on for the best part of forever. An hour and a half, Addy realised within moments, could only provide a mere reconnoitre ahead of many, many visits to come. There was too much she wanted to buy, everywhere she looked: a cut-crystal perfume bottle with a lilac tassel; a wall mirror etched all around with rambling pansies; a red net petticoat spotted with flock polka dots; a super-cute polyester shirt of purple cartoon petunias – *Only two dollars?* So said the tiny paper tag pinned by a thread to the wide collar. And rack after rack of amazing pre-adored frocks that appeared to be sorted by both colour and style. All of their prices were reasonable, too, it seemed, but Addy only had about fifteen dollars left until payday, two days away, and most of that would have to go on general sustenance. She had to buy *something*, though – a souvenir of first experience.

Hmmm. She entered what seemed to be the final section, a cul-de-sac of books, floor to ceiling. She could die here – happily. *Young woman found expired under a pile of barely scuffed near-new-release paperbacks, after suffering fatal attack of indecision at what to read next.* Some of the spines of the books hadn't even been cracked. And here, right at nose level, was what looked like a pristine copy of the latest great Australian blockbuster, Kathleen McAllister's *The Fire Flight*. Addy hadn't read it yet, nor had she seen the television mini-series it had recently spawned. Perhaps it was time. She opened the cover to check the pencilled price: *Fifty cents!* That was it, decision made.

She began making her way back to the front of the shop, book in hand.

And the purple petunia shirt as well – why not? She grabbed it from its rack on her way through.

'Success?' The old woman asked, adjusting a dress on a mannequin by the jewellery-display case.

'Success?' Addy repeated the question, all other words having left her at the vision of loveliness that met her here.

The dress – on the mannequin – she had to have it. Her heart pounded now with instant and unshakable desire.

This dress. It was made of pale-sky tulle over charmeuse, full-skirted, with a wide, round neckline and capped sleeves – the complete bundle of Addy's favourite shapes. But more than this, so much more, the tulle was appliqued all over with a shower of blooms – ruby-hued poppies mostly, true-blue cornflowers, too, tumbling among their leaves and stems – all of them falling into a garden that settled at the hem.

'Exquisite, yes?' The old woman pinned its price tag to the lining at the back of the bodice.

'Mmm,' Addy managed to reply, mesmerised. This was the pinnacle of womanly joy frockified.

'It is so small at the waist,' the woman sighed, patting it at hip height. 'It will not be easy to sell. But it is very pretty. Many will come to look.'

Addy nodded, placing the book and the shirt on the glass top of the display case.

The woman took them up to check their prices. 'Ah good, good,' she said, and smiled her broad, jaunty smile at Addy: 'Two dollars and fifty cents, please.'

Addy rummaged in her purse, taking out two scrunched-up dollar notes and some coins, but she could hardly drag her eyes from the dress.

'Why don't you try it on, dear?' the woman said, her gaze lively and knowing. 'You are a little thing underneath that boy's shirt, are you not?'

'I'm sure I can't afford it,' Addy mumbled, suddenly embarrassed at her flannelette checks and black jeans. She didn't like to draw attention to herself in the light, in the staring glare of day. It was only at night that her frocks came out to dance, only after a wine or a beer or three, and that now embarrassed her, too.

'It is twenty-eight dollars and seventy-five cents,' the woman informed her with Teutonic exactitude. 'A lay-by purchase may be arranged, should it be required.' The woman took up a feather duster, adding, 'I will leave you to think about it,' and she turned away to dust the shoe shelves behind her.

Twenty-eight dollars and seventy-five cents ... It was a bargain for a dress like that. Even if it was no doubt older than Addy was; 1950s, probably. At any age, this dress was one of a kind – absolutely priceless. Panic fluttered through her: *I have to have this dress*. For it wasn't just a dress. It was a story. A hundred stories she had to know; stories that could only be known by wearing them. She glanced at her watch: almost quarter to eleven. Where had the last fifteen minutes gone? She had to go or she'd be late for her lecture; she'd arrive a few minutes late now as it was.

She said to the woman: 'I don't have time to try it on. I ...' She was also reluctant to lay-by anything. She'd witnessed something of the perils of the system at the toy department of Town Hall Variety: women who'd get halfway through repayments for Christmas or birthday gifts they'd bought for their children, only to unexpectedly lose a job or a husband and – *whoosh* – money and toys would disappear entirely, no correspondence entered into. Interest-free but rough justice indeed – no consumer protections once you signed that kind of contract.

'I understand, dear.' The woman smiled over a pair of silver-spangled stilettos – *Oh dear God, I want them, too.*

'When you return, if the dress is still here, then it must be yours, hm?'

'Hm.' More wisdom. But when would Addy be able to return? Today, after English, there was lunch with Luke – *I can't stand him up again* – then there was Ancient History, then that *Gatsby* American Lit tute. She wouldn't leave campus until four-thirty today at the earliest. 'What time do you close?'

'Four o'clock.'

Of course you do.

The woman and her feather duster disappeared around a bank of tall shelves in the centre of the room.

Addy scribbled a note, surreptitiously, she hoped, tearing off a corner of *The Fire Flight*'s title page with the wish:

Wait for me. Please.
Addy X

Leaving her name as though they were already friends. She folded this scrap of frock-longing so that, to the untrained eye, it might have seemed less than nothing, a bus ticket discarded, a shopping docket lodged somewhere unlikely, waiting to be swept away, and she tucked it into the slim belt, a dark green band, buckled at the waist.

Please.

'Addy?'

That was the voice of a man, a deep voice promising authority, and she turned as if caught in the act of some petty crime.

It was the boy from last night, the singer in the band, last seen under pink paisley bedspread on the brown couch. Her stomach turned around hamburger and seventeen flavours of inexpressible shame. Now that she was giving it a moment's further thought, had they had some sort of argument about student fees over Trivial Pointlessness at some early hour of this morning? Had she really called him a 'frayed-denim fascist'? Or had she only thought it? She couldn't be sure. And for all that she didn't actually care, her heart had started thrashing about again. He was standing at the rack of men's jackets at the arse-end of the zebra. *What the frick is he doing here?*

She remembered his name now, too, half of it, anyway: Dan. Or 'Dolly', as his drummer-boy mate called him.

Dolly? Because his shoulder bones poke at his sleeve-seams as though his shirt is still on its hanger, and his thick dark hair curls at the hinges of his jaw, a frame for the blush of his cheeks.

Hers were scorching.

He looked like John Donne – that portrait of the poet as a young law student, or whatever that painting on the cover of her text was called.

She said, 'Yep. Hm. Hello. I'm late for English Lit.'

And she darted out into the street, into the rain.

ENGLISH LITERATURE & OTHER FORMS OF MIDDLE-CLASS INDULGENCE

Past the last of the shop awnings there was no cover from the rain whatsoever, all the way along the iron fence of the university grounds and across campus.

Shit. Addy said that quite a lot as she did her best to keep a steady pace, clutching her satchel to her chest and hunching her shoulders, in an attempt to keep her books from being soaked. *Shit. Shit. Shit.* The back of her shirt was completely saturated and she was shivering with cold as she skittered in through the entrance doors of the building where English Lit lived. Down the corridor, dripping and squelching her way towards the lecture theatre, she could already hear Professor Westbourne poshly droning into the microphone: 'Raight, then, where arhhh we ...'

Inside, she could see Professor Westbourne shuffling papers at the lectern. *Ha!* It appeared he'd only just arrived himself.

Addy's knees juddered with relief as she slipped into the nearest aisle seat, puddling everywhere, unbuckling her satchel to find that, while *The Fire Flight* had been spared, wrapped as it was in polyester petunia shirt, *Alexander Pope: Selected Poetry and Prose* was near to pulped with soddenness.

'Oh shitty, shitty shit.'

While her other books had soaked up a share, the one she needed most right now had sat at the front of her satchel, collecting the rain like a sponge. It trickled excess as she drew it out, making its own puddle on the bench before her.

'Don't let me interrupt your fiddling about up there,' Professor Westbourne glared over half-moon spectacles at her.

Heads turned; hers bowed quickly, trying to open the book-sponge to the poem they'd be reading today, but the pages tore like tissue as she did, her fingers clumsy, shaking with the chill at her back, with the faint remains of alcohol poisoning, and with humiliation.

She might have cried, if Professor Westbourne hadn't ploughed on.

'Now, "The Rape of the Lock", one of Pope's most studied works …'

The word 'rape' scraped at all her nerves as she sat staring at the woodgrains in the bench, varnish worn and scratched. She knew from her own reading that Pope did not mean rape in the modern sense, but an older definition, meaning theft – the poem was about a fellow stealing a lock of hair from a woman called Belinda, a trivial scandal blown up into epic proportions, meant to be funny, or something like that. She hadn't understood much of the poem – which was why she was here. She needed to know.

'In this special unit, I will attempt to illuminate for you some of the complexity of Pope's satirical genius,' the professor went on. 'What I will not do is bother to explain the many Homeric and other classical allusions and metaphors in the work, as they are too numerous for this brief study, and it is unlikely that many of you will be sincerely interested in any event. Do not waste my time or yours with questions on these. Most of you in this room won't even finish your degrees …'

Addy seemed to lose sight of all meaning at that; the edges of her vision dimmed; within a heartbeat, the sound of her own breath seemed to epically amplify. She was sure Professor Westbourne could hear that as well, just as he had apparently peered straight into her soul.

Adrianna Loest was a waste of space and time.

You're a nobody from nowhere – you're an idiot. How can you think you might know anything about stories, anyone's story? You don't even know your own. You don't even know who you are.

'Are you okay?' someone whispered beside her. A boy, sitting in her row, shifting closer.

She looked at him: a pleasant face, concerned eyes behind dark-rimmed glasses. She looked at his hand, there on the bench: long fingers, olive skin, somehow southern European, neatly trimmed nails, an outsider-ally of some kind. But even he seemed terrifying.

She said: 'I'm fine. Thank you.'

She pulled out her copy of *The Fire Flight* and began to read, to calm herself, to focus her mind around the shapes and sensations of the words.

'There is a legend of a bird that flies but once in its life …' the enigmatic prologue began. *'A beautiful bird that soars on one, lone magnificent flight before it bursts into glorious flame. For the height of freedom is only bought at the cost of great sacrifice …'*

Wow. Here was some fantastically muscular melodrama unfolding bold, golden wings from its opening paragraph. The professor's contemptuous drone disappeared to some place far away from these pages, taking time with it. By lecture's end, she'd read Part One.

'Next Tuesday, by which time you should have read "Eloise and Abelard", we will discuss …'

Guilt jabbed at the intrusion of his voice, and she closed *The Fire Flight* under the bench, smuggling it back into her damp bag. She'd essentially missed this lecture, anyway; she'd catch up without any problem, especially as there was to be no Homeric curiosity permitted; she studied past papers as a matter of course for all courses. But still … Guilt met a flash of resentment – and asked it out to lunch. As everyone around her lidded pens and folded notebooks away, she took out hers and wrote:

Dear Prof. ~~Westbourne~~ Wanker,
You are a pompous and utterly uninspiring bore. I spent this whole lecture reading The Fire Flight, *rather than listen to you. Did you know, Kathleen McAllister is an astrobiologist when she's not writing bestselling novels? (Or so Addy recalled from some television interview with the author she'd seen at home, at Port, watching the box with her dad.) You, on the other hand, don't appear to want to give anything good or amazing to anyone. And I bet the old Joe at the Olympia Café knows more about Homer than you do, too.*
Most sincerely,
☺X

'Excuse me, please.' The boy with the neatly trimmed fingernails was standing above her, wanting to get past.

Addy's face flushed through several shades of red – 'Oh, sorry' – she held her notebook close and swung her knees around to make room for him to get out, determined nevertheless to leave the note, this trace of her feeling, behind in the theatre. She carefully tore the soft, still slightly soggy page, the blue ink bleeding a little and somehow emphasising the sentiment; she stood up then and laid it boldly on the seat, for all to see – or at least for the next person to sit here. For a second, she wondered who that might be; she imagined them picking it up and nodding in agreement; she imagined herself, at that little window of her dreams, writing and writing some vast sprawling novel she hadn't yet seen.

You're going to stand Luke up again at this rate, you self-obsessed, screwy noodle.

Oh yes, she would; she checked her watch: it was nearing half-past twelve.

Her dread at seeing Luke was a slightly soggy bleakness all its own. She shouldn't feel this way about him – he didn't deserve her weirdness, her distance, her reserve. But it seemed she couldn't give him much of anything else.

Luke Neilson was such a nice boy, such a good boy, he was sitting by the big box heater in the campus cafeteria as though he knew she'd be in need of warmth.

'I'm sorry I'm late,' she said, weaving through the plastic tables towards him.

'Late?' He smiled and stood up on seeing her. He was so clean-cut handsome he looked like he'd stepped off the cover of a knitting-pattern book, blow-waved and air-brushed. Nice fair hair, nice clear skin, faultlessly nice all round, he was a walking sportswear advertisement, a cricketer and competitive cyclist; he was in his final year of vet science. He loved animals. He lived in a nice, semi-renovated terrace in Glebe but hailed from the nice, leafy North Shore, where his parents and two sisters worshipped him, not unreasonably, alongside their picture of the Queen on the lounge-room wall. Why he was interested in her, Addy could not fathom. He said: 'Don't worry, I haven't been waiting long.' He touched her on the arm in greeting, knowing better than to attempt a kiss; and with that touch, he added: 'You're freezing – did you get caught in the rain?'

'Hm, yeah,' she said, predictably shying, emptying the contents of her satchel onto one of the chairs in front of the heater's slatted vents, hoping to dry her books. She sneezed; she was somewhere beyond freezing, lost in the most frigid corner of a Narnian winter.

'Hey, Addy ...' He was bending over his own bag, its athletic logo glancing at her with the question of exactly how long it had been since she'd partaken of any proper outdoor exercise other than drunk-dancing. Luke was handing her his jumper: 'You should get that wet shirt off you. Here, why don't you go and put that on. I'll get us something to eat.'

'Thank you,' she said, taking the jumper. She tried to smile at him; she tried and tried; why couldn't she fall in love with him? Because he was too nice. Too good to be true.

She took the purple petunia shirt with her – *Handy, after all* – making her way to the back of the room, to the ladies' toilet, to change, wringing herself out over how much longer she was going to lead Luke on. They'd met last December, at the tennis courts of all places. She and Roz had been having a hit with a couple of guys, one of whom Roz was shagging at the time; Addy had been wearing her old tennis dress from schooldays, the grip on her racquet worn and sweat-soiled, falsely suggesting a sportiness she'd long since given away. When? She couldn't say. She simply didn't play anymore; and she hadn't picked up a racquet again since that day, either. Roz had decided after five minutes that that was enough vertical bit-jiggling for her, and they'd retired to the pub up the road, the Royal, for a beer. Halfway through her second schooner, Addy's eyes had met Luke's across the near-deserted Wednesday-afternoon bar, as he'd walked in through the glass saloon doors, with the sunlight behind him, glowing in his hair; her first thought: *How beautiful you are.* He'd just played a rather more energetic set; she smelt his salt at ten paces and was just beer-brave enough to think she might want to taste it, too. To dare herself; to try to be normal, cool, whatever. Four more schooeys and a bottle of cider later they were back at Flower Street and in her bed.

Irresponsible.

Yes. It was. Yes. It is.

It was lucky she hadn't fallen pregnant; they hadn't used any preventative, not that first time.

You'll break it off with him today.

I will.

She took a moment to repeat that in the ladies' mirror, eye to eye, and another to marvel at the fashion effect of Luke's brown jumper, khaki racing stripes down the sleeves, teamed with wide psychedelic purple petunia collar flopping out above the V-neck.

Hm. Interesting combo.

Outside the bathroom, some sort of blokey joking erupted from a group hanging about by the door. She recognised one of them straightaway, bang in the middle of the uproar: Chubs Keveney was his name, fellow arts-law undergrad, face of a renaissance cherub, halo of sandy curls, body of an adolescent sumo wrestler still stacking on the kilos, last seen lying gob-down in a pool of his own vomit at some otherwise forgettable party – someone had placed an empty chip packet on his head like a little sailor's cap, and apparently he'd stayed like that for hours, well into the next morning. Now, here he was simulating sex with a sausage roll to the thigh-slapping amusement of his fellow Neanderthals. All rugby players – rugby *union*, mind, not lowbrow rugby league – and mostly Young Labor acolytes swinging to the right, with their likeminded, unreconstructed fascist mates. All Student

Representative Council wannabes plotting out their pathways to power. *All dickheads.* Was it any wonder she'd not bothered with sport or politics lately? These were the nation's future leaders; these were the great white hopes meant to save them all from university fees, Liberal–National Party conservatives and terminal disaster. The steam rising off them here in the cafeteria stank like some fetid gas from the bowels of hell – they made her want to run home to wash.

'Addy Loest!' Chubs Keveney bellowed at her as she passed, deliberately mispronouncing her name as 'lowest', when it was a softer sound, 'luhrst', somewhere between 'lerst' and 'loast' – 'last', 'lest', 'list', 'lost', 'lust', she'd heard them all, but it was 'löst', if anyone could be bothered listening. Chubs kept his sausage roll poking out at groin level: 'Smile for me, honey.'

She threw an approximation of one over her shoulder: 'Fuck off.'

'Oooooooh,' the ape chorus applauded him, knuckling the plastic tabletops, a drumroll full of menace, full of unchallengeable masculine entitlement.

For all her chin-up dismissal, they frightened her.

'Dead-set dropkicks.' Luke could only offer a statement of the obvious, and a salad sandwich, as he met her back at their table by the heater.

Her inner child looked at the inch-thick layer of grated carrot and said: *Nah.*

She looked into Luke's super-nice blue-grey eyes, and she said: 'I'm so sorry ...'

'Sorry?' He smiled, so warm, so kind, so ... 'What do you have to be sorry about?'

She tossed between 'I'm not hungry' and 'I don't love you' for a hideously long time, with the sounds of the quickly crowded cafeteria scraping and shouting into her, with the sickly hot fumes of the heater gusting around her and Narnian shivers rattling from within.

I'm getting a cold, she told herself. *You can't make a decision to dump someone when you're in such an addled state.*

When are you not *in an addled state?*

Fair point.

Still, cowardice caught the words, and their truth, so that all she could say was: 'Um.'

'Addy ...' Luke finally took up the burden for her, like the gentleman he was: 'It's all right. If you want to break it off, I mean. I have sort of guessed already that you're not that keen. It's okay. We don't have that much in common. We're just kids, doing kids' stuff. No one got hurt, hey?'

Who was this excellent man Addy was letting go? She'd never know. She hung her head to hide her face again, to hide the forcing back of tears at how very, very hurt she was.

But why? Why was she so hurt and sad and addled and anxious all the time? Whatever the answers might have been, none of this was Luke Neilson's fault.

She raised her face to him, and, grasping a shred of her best, she told him: 'You're an absolute champ. My loss is going to be someone else's incredible gain. I hope she's wonderful.'

She began to return her books to her bag; they were not nearly dry yet, but she couldn't stay.

'If you ever need a friend ...' he said, as she stood to leave.

'Thanks,' she told him. 'Same.'

'Take care,' he said.

And she said, 'See ya.' Then she walked away from him, just like that, scattering shards of her heart with every step.

She'd left him no note, no souvenir of herself.

Perhaps that said everything.

Dragging herself home after her last class, she shambled in the front door and curled up on the brown couch with *The Fire Flight* and a family block of chocolate, sometime around five, with the house empty and the radiator on high. The last line she read said, '*Ray shut off the engine of the Cessna, thinking only of Sonia ...*' Addy wasn't sure about this mini-series-sexy farmer hero, and what might be in store for the heroine, a shearer's daughter who seemed to manage to be feisty, irritatingly passive and oddly familiar all at the same time, but she wouldn't find out this evening.

She fell asleep there and then with fictions mingling, visions of Kathleen McAllister's outback sheep station, Rowallan's Run, rolling away as Jay Gatsby's jazz band played a slow dance.

And then the phone rang, smashing through her warm, dark stillness like an ambulance on its way to a heart attack.

She sprang up off the couch. All was grey gloom but for a crack of yellow light seeping round the kitchen door.

And that damn phone: *BRING!! BRING!!*

She leapt at it, snatching up the handpiece, near knocking herself out with it as she smacked it to her ear: 'Hello?'

'Hello? Addy?'

Blood drained to her toes: it was her father's deep, dark 'hello'; she immediately expected to be told some terrible news: something had happened to her brother, Nick: he'd had a car crash, or choked on a fistful of his own arrogance, or needed help tying his shoelaces.

'Yes, Dad, hello,' she said, her voice croaking with alarm, recent sleep, chocolate-clag and, she supposed, a rapidly developing head cold as well: 'What is it?'

He said: 'What's wrong with your voice? Are you sick?'

'No!' Addy's brain swam in her skull. 'No, Dad. I just woke up.'

'You just woke up?' His own alarm shot down the wire. 'What are you doing asleep in the afternoon?'

'I was up late last night studying,' she gave him the automatic lie and fused it to some truth. 'I came home from uni only half an hour ago and I fell asleep reading a book.'

'Are you eating enough?' Her father's alarm did not abate; it never really abated at all. Was it any wonder she was so neurotic herself?

No.

'Yes.' She sighed, and then she softened. 'Dad, why are you calling?' She could feel his aloneness, there in the house on Gallipoli Street, the night-sky square of their lounge-room picture window looking out to sea. He'd probably just got in from work, the creases of his knuckles still grey with the coke-grime of his day, turning out sheets of steel, kilometres of steel, and ensuring no one died in the process.

'Why am I calling?' he said, bristling at the question, before reminding her: 'Your father can call for any reason he likes, Adrianna.'

'Of course you can, I was just —'

'I can't get to your brother's fight on Friday,' he spoke over the top of her.

Well, whoopee-fricken-doo, Addy's thoughts spoke over the top of her father's explanation. Boxing was boys' business – nothing to do with her.

'It's an important match,' he was saying. 'The opponent is ...' Addy couldn't care less who or what her brother was going to beat up next. 'If Nicky wins, this will mean he is one step closer to qualifying for the Commonwealth Games.'

All Addy heard was 'Nicky' – *Nicky, Nicky, Nicky* – until her father got to the point: 'I need you to go in my place.'

'What?' She was still dreaming, surely.

'I need you to go to the match – on Friday night. It's at South Sydney Juniors, the leagues club, at Kingsford. It's scheduled to start at seven-thirty, but my shift doesn't finish until seven and I can't get anyone to cover for me, or not anyone I trust, which is why I can't get to the match myself. Since it is on so early, though, it won't ruin your whole Friday night. I understand this is not your first choice of exciting things to do, Addy, but family must be there – for Nicky. For me.'

Family. The three of them were it, in the whole wide world.

Her father was going on: 'If he wins, he will go out drinking with his friends right away and he might forget to call me. If he loses, he won't call me until he is drunk, if he calls at all. I need you to get him to call me straight after the fight. I'm disappointed that I can't be there, Addy, I wish it could be otherwise, but it is not possible to change the situation. Please do this for me.'

Her heart strings didn't stretch to wisps of gold for her father – these were more like thirty-mil cables of galvanised iron. She couldn't say no.

'Okay, Dad. I'll be there, don't worry.'

'Thanks, Sprout.' She could hear the smile in his voice now; she could hear him opening the fridge door, and imagined him reaching for his pre-dinner beer, the curly cord of the kitchen wall phone just allowing that stretch. 'I will make apricot chicken for Sunday lunch, for you.'

Yum. Her favourite. The mere sound of the words 'apricot chicken' made her both homesick and proud – proud of her father. Finding himself so suddenly and tragically a single dad of two children under five, he'd done everything for them, over all their growing years – cooking, house-cleaning, clothes-washing, homework-nagging, arse-whacking – juggling it all between shifts at the steelworks and, here and there, night-school classes for his operating tickets for this piece of machinery and that, for his framed certificate of metallurgy. They'd had a couple of different housekeepers to help out when they were small, but Addy could hardly remember them; only her father, her amazing, self-sacrificing father, doing it all, leaning over his much-bespattered copy of *The Everyday Women's Cookbook* being quietly, everyday heroic.

'Thank you, Daddy,' she said. 'I'll see you Sunday, then.'

'You will call me on Friday night, yes?' he repeated the plea, the demand. 'Make sure Nicky calls me, yes?'

'Yes!' *As if I've ever let you down – that you know of.*

'Good girl, my good girl. You take care of yourself, hey, my Sprout. For me.'

'Yes, Dad.' *I'm so fricken good I'm drowning in a very large pot of anxiety soup, a special recipe by Pete Loest.* 'I've got to go, someone wants to use the phone, see ya, don't worry, bye.'

'Bye, Add—'

She left the rest of her name to roam for eternity in the small dark plastic hall of the handpiece as she returned it to its cradle. She stared through the hazy evening dimness at the dial: *Fricken Nicky.* She wanted to ring him now, tell him to think of their dad for a change, grow up and manage to make a phone call without having to be taken to a phone and shown how to use it. She'd like to remind him of every effort Peter Loest had made for his *Nicky Bratty-pants* – all the years of driving him to football matches and boxing training, pacing at the sidelines smoking seventeen packets of cigarettes for every game, every fight. What did Nick ever show in gratitude? Only his gorilla-sized pecs – and his thighs. Addy shuddered: her brother's thighs were so thick he couldn't even walk like a human. He hadn't always been so into himself, so remote; once upon a time, when they were kids, he'd been a champion big brother, a brother who could be relied upon to eat her peas when their dad had his back turned, a brother to save her a handful of her favourites from a mixed bag of lollies. But they didn't share much these days. They'd grown apart, so apart that although he lived not far away, just the other side of Newtown, they never crossed paths unless they had to. She'd only been to his place on one occasion, to deliver some new gloves from their dad; it was like stepping into a gym – an obstacle course comprised of barbells, skipping ropes and two different varieties of rowing machine, laid out where a lounge room should be. His was a world of raw eggs and cold showers for breakfast, plates of pasta the size of bathtubs, and beer kegs drunk straight from the hose. *Ug.* His housemate was a carbon copy of same, weightlifter, Dave Douglas. *Ug and Ug.* She didn't know how that concentration of testosterone hadn't blown the roof off their house.

Still, he was her only brother; she'd go to his stupid boxing match on Friday night and try not to think about it in the meantime. Try not to think about the fact that *Nicky* never had to go to any of her events of note, not when she won the district public-speaking competition, no school prize days or performances, not ever – he didn't even turn up to her birthday dinner last year. Why? Because he was at a training camp. *Somewhere in the jungle. Ug.*

She needed a beer herself – this minute.

No, you don't.

Yes, I do.

She turned to make her way to the kitchen, but as she did, her foot slipped on that copy of *The Fire Flight*, which had fallen to the floor, and now caused her left shin to bash into the edge of the coffee table, scattering a cloud of ashtray dust across last night's game of Trivial Pointlessness. *I need more than one beer.* She picked up her book and two of the sticky-rimmed glasses on the table. *Am I the only person in this house who can tidy or wash anything?*

A high-pitched whirring answered her from the kitchen. It was Harriet, HRH, doing something with her fancy food processor.

'Hello,' Addy said as she nudged open the kitchen door with an elbow: 'What're you making?'

'Hummus,' HRH replied, removing the lid of the gadget and peering into it, scraping down the sides of the clear bowl with a knife and an intent frown at the beige goo there – as though she were on the verge of creating some new artform with it. 'It's a Middle Eastern dip made from chickpeas and tahini paste.'

I do know what hummus is, Miss Condescension 1985, Addy immediately stiffened, but she kept that snipe to herself. She often wondered if she was being unfair in her judgements of Harriet, if class envy played a part in her dislike of the girl and her preposterously breathy, elongated vowels, such as those still hanging in the air – *taaaahiiini paaayste*. Addy was never sure if she was being the mean one, if she was rolling her eyes at another's otherness, like she was having a dig at someone with a speech impediment, rather than someone with a family trust fund, hundred-dollar-designer jeans and med-student boyfriend. *Be nice,* Addy told herself; she told Harriet: 'Mmm. I love hummus.'

Harriet, still poking at the sides of the food-processor bowl, as though the making of this hummus were a complex intellectual challenge, replied: 'I'm making it for a dinner party at Martin's tonight.'

Aaaaa'm maaaaaking it for a diiiinner paaaaartay at Maaaahrtin's tchoniiiight. Martin was the med-student boyfriend, and the *tch* on 'tonight' always gave Addy the snorts.

She turned away, placing the dirty glasses in the sink and letting the snort go there, under the running tap and down the drain; then she opened the fridge, beer-hunting. She was sure there was at least half a six-pack in here, but – *ah* – only one left. *Better one than none.*

'Would you like to share?' she asked Harriet, popping the ring-pull on the can.

'No, thanks,' she said, still at her hummus. 'I have a shoot tomorrow afternoon – no grog for me, I'm afraid.'

A modelling shoot, she meant – that's what HRH did for play money. And envy snicked at Addy again, for Harriet's largeness, not only in presence but in physical fact: the girl was near six feet tall, and yet impossibly graceful in her every move, her skin so perfectly white she looked like she'd been squeezed out of a toothpaste tube; with her thick black bob and her cheekbones so sharp they needed their own safety label, she was a walking fashion-magazine cover, made all the more glamorous in these dingy surrounds of stained, puke-hued melamine and matching lino.

'Oh well, more beer for me,' Addy chirped, not completely disingenuously. She took a sip and felt the alcohol go straight to her knees. She loved that feeling, first beer, first anything with grog in it: *Ahhhh*. She glanced at the bottle of ginger wine on the kitchen bench behind the food processor: only about an inch left after last night's effort; only about one drink; already she felt like consuming ten. The bottle shop up the road, at the Broadway Hotel, would still be open, and she only needed three dollars fifty – she had that in coinage, in her purse. She'd go and get another bottle of rotgut when she'd finished this beer.

Long day, she told herself and her shin, still throbbing from its argument with the coffee table.

Any excuse, pisshead, she replied to that self. *Can't you give yourself a night off?*

'How's that boysie-boy of yours, that darling Luke?' Harriet asked her, not really asking, only making chitchat as she continued to ruminate over her beige goo.

'We broke up today, I think,' Addy said, trying the thought out aloud, and it sounded about right. Sad and strange, but right.

'Oh nooo!' Harriet swung around to face her, knife poised with concern and with excitement at the prospect of juicy gossip: 'What are you going to do, Addy? Ohhh.' She sighed, as though auditioning for a daytime TV serial; and she sighed again: 'Ohhh, I thought you two were forever material.'

You thought no such thing – you only met him once, you marriage-obsessed bimbo. Faker. But Addy only shrugged: 'Wasn't meant to be.' She really did seem to feel all right about it now.

Harriet sighed yet again and leaned back against the bench. She gave Addy a wincing sort of frown, tinged with pity; she said with a tsk: 'What are you going to do with your life?'

As if you care. 'What do you mean?' *Heavy question from someone who does so very little with her own.*

'I mean, you seem adrift, Addy.' Harriet smiled, still wincing: 'You don't seem to have any ambition of any kind.'

That gave Addy's hackles cause to rise as her thoughts whirled: *I'm struggling to find my ambition after admitting to myself that the one my father chose for me is not what I want to do. I don't want to be a lawyer. I don't want to spend my life inside a labyrinth of negotiations and compromises, arguing points of law that don't translate into justice for anyone. I don't want to work inside a system rigged for the rich, and I'm too small to change any of it. There is only one way I really want to colour the world; only one power I aspire to have.*

She stood a little straighter and fired back an arrow of her most closely held truth. 'I want to be a writer.'

'A writer!' Harriet's laughter was as blithe as it was cruel; it rang around the tiny room. 'What would *you* write about?'

Addy was almost knocked backwards by the insult. She didn't know what to say, how to duck under the great wave of humiliation that had been forced upon her by so few words. She could barely hear herself as she replied: 'I'm not sure. Isn't being unsure an advantage when we set out looking for answers?'

Harriet ignored her question; she was still laughing: 'A writer! I'd never have picked you as harbouring those kinds of fantasies.'

I'd really like to punch you in the face – how's that for a fantasy? 'Why not?' Addy asked, angry but nonplussed. 'Why can't someone like me be a writer?'

'Well,' Harriet gave her another pitying look, 'you don't really *read*, do you.'

'Read? I've been reading most of the day.' Addy couldn't keep the bewilderment from her voice; she looked down at *The Fire Flight*, still tucked under her left arm. 'I have a book attached to me right now.'

'That thing!' Harriet's laughter just about put another crack in the kitchen wall. 'That's not a proper book. I mean *literature*. You need to read *literature* if you want to be a *writer*. And you need to *understand* what it is you're reading – *understand* the great masters. You need to travel, live on the edge, extend your boundaries, expand your mind. Speak French! *Parlez-vous? Read* French. Read *Madame Bovary en français.* Can you read French?'

Addy might have laughed too, and harshly, if she hadn't been so stunned. She tried to throw it back at Harriet: 'Can you?' But another wave of humiliation was crashing over her now: she didn't read in any language other than English; she'd won the German prize in Sixth Class, her last year of primary school, when she was twelve; it was the only prize her father had never made a deal of; he'd seemed somehow embarrassed or saddened by it and she'd hidden her little trophy under her bed as soon as they'd got home.

'*Naturellement!*' Harriet rattled off something in French then; it sounded false; brittle; untrue. She tsked again, brushing a wayward strand of glossy bob behind her ear: 'Never mind.' She stared at Addy for a moment, too long a moment; unblinking; horrible; before changing the subject: 'What *are* you wearing?'

Addy looked down at herself again, at the fruity combo of brown sports jumper and hippie-freak flower-power petunias. Regret flickered at seeing Luke there, on her, at having let go of Mr Nice – Mr Nice who had zero interest in literature of any kind unless it involved zoology or included photographs of baby animals. He especially loved kittens. She was going to miss him. She was going to have to get his jumper back to him – and, like the coward she was, she thought she might post it, rather than walk it the two kilometres down the road. Anger at everything flared – anger at herself mostly – but she gave the serve to Harriet, with the language she knew best, the salt-sharp argot of the Illawarra working class:

'What the fuck are *you* wearing, besides that stuck-up-bitch face of yours?'

Harriet Rawley-Hogue looked as though she'd been slapped with the flat end of a shovel – as intended.

'Addy!' That was Roz, behind her at the kitchen door. Appalled. They might have shared a lowly state-school education, but Caringbah was a long way from Wollongong – it was within the metropolitan bounds of Sydney, for a start. Addy Loest was a pathetic, stupid, lowlife outcast, or so said the shame that lay at the bottom of all her uncertainty. She wanted to run, to disappear, and would have, if Roz had not been in the way, blocking the exit with her ever-merry, ever-generous frame; her breasts cresting a snug crushed-velvet top, vibrant magenta clashing lavishly with fire-engine-red lipstick: 'Now, now, you two. Peace on earth, sweet creatures. We have tequila and lemons and …'

Addy didn't hear the rest of whatever it was Roz said about the Mexican fiesta she had planned; she shrank further from the 'we' Roz had also brought in with her: the Drummer Boy and Dan whoever-he-was.

'Hi, Addy.' This Dan character waved from the shadow cast by the door, tall, dark and more John Donne-ish than he was before. Even the shape of his beard stubble seemed somehow casually Elizabethan; the way he pushed back his hair from his forehead. A snippet of verse slipped through her like a fish:

> *My face in thine eye, thine in mine appears,*
> *And true plain hearts do in the faces rest …*

She gasped – as if winded – tried to form it into a return, 'Hello.' Probably failed. She looked away, grabbed the edge of

Roz's sleeve and whispered: 'I'm sorry – I don't feel well. I'm going to bed.'

'But I'm going to make nachos,' Roz said, although she was just as quickly sympathetic: 'You do look a bit peaky. Do you want me to bring you up some dinner?'

Addy shook her head; the air seemed to grow thick around her, slowing time and amplifying sound as though she moved through the dregs in the bottom of that bottle of ginger wine. She placed the half-drunk can of beer on the side of the sink, and the clunk it made seemed to shake her bones.

I'm dying.

Aren't we all?

'Excuse me, please.' Her voice was the smallest thing in the world as she made her way past Dan and Drummer Boy. She could hardly feel her feet, her hands; she could not think above the dread-heavy beating of her blood.

Upstairs, in her room, she lay down on her bed and tried to steady her breathing; tried to still the morbid thoughts that crowded and crowded like rats in her head.

You're not good enough.

You'll never be a writer – ha!

You're just a loser.

You're a sick, sad idiot.

You're trash.

You're nothing.

I'm going mad.

She pleaded silently, smaller and smaller still: *How can I stop this?*

But there was no reply. Only, eventually, an image emerging, suspended above the fray that was her mind: the garden frock she'd seen this morning. The spun-sky tulle, the splash of blooms: red poppies, blue cornflowers, leaves reaching each to each like outstretched hands. Beautiful. Instantly soothing.

She sat up and switched on her little red bedside lamp; opened her wardrobe doors: here, *here* was her place of peace, all her colours, all her best dreams. All of them unique: a ballerina-skirted evening gown in Monet-dot tones of lemon and amethyst; a cotton sundress spilling with blowsy scarlet roses; a swinging sixties cocktail sheath in lurid orange shantung silk; another more demure, navy blue, with a cream lace panel that ran down the front; a 1930s cabaret costume, all hip-hugging sequins, a shimmering madness of silver and cerise, and fringing that tickled the backs of her knees – not that she'd ever worn that one outside the house. How she loved them, and all the stories they contained, in every lingering hint of perfume, every trace of wear – every sense that she was *there*, once, whoever she was. None of them had cost more than five dollars, yet when she looked at the whole collection like this, it was clear she had a significant addiction: there were a hundred and three dresses in this wardrobe. There were far worse addictions to have, though, weren't there?

Her throat was sore, as if she'd been yelling, or sobbing her heart out. While she supposed that was only the head cold taking its course, she wondered if maybe she had been sobbing somewhere always. Sobbing for a hundred years.

She peeled off her jeans and her odd ensemble and chose a nightgown from the bottom drawer, a favourite: 1940s-style rayon, bias-cut and ankle-length, brocaded ribbons trimming the bust, and sprinkled everywhere with tiny forget-me-nots. It was slightly too big for her, but she felt like a goddess inside it: the stories it whispered took her from the ancient Temple of Apollo at Delphi and into a war-torn elsewhere with squadrons of Luftwaffe swarming overhead: it took her into the heart of a woman who actually did have something to worry about.

Addy was too tired now for worry of any sort; she was asleep before her head had met the pillow. She was dreaming of that gorgeous garden dress, the zebra waiting at the window for her, remarking: 'Ah, you're back at last. What took you so long?'

BEST INTENTIONS &
THE ART OF SELF-SABOTAGE

It's a truth universally acknowledged that a night off the grog will make the morrow a much better one than the day before, and so it was for Addy Loest. She woke a little after dawn, as was her norm, her internal clock set for consciousness as soon as daylight touched the tips of her eyelashes. This morning, a melody seemed to touch some remnant thread of her sleep. It seemed familiar but lingered just out of reach before disappearing into the sounds of someone flushing the toilet across the landing.

What was it? Addy tried to grasp the dream-memory. It had sounded like butterflies – or more like butterflies having an argument. It had sounded most like the third movement of the *Moonlight Sonata*. And this thought of Beethoven brought all warm thoughts of home to her now inside a waking smile: *Dad ... Apricot chicken ...* Which then reminded her of her brother and his Friday-night fight: *Ug. Let's not ruin the mood.*

She got up, her smile drifting back along a line of loveliness, to the garden dress, and the prayer she'd tucked into the back of its deep green belt: *Wait for me.* She sent out another: *You have to be mine. Please.*

Feet zinging on the cold old floorboards, she made her way to the bathroom, meeting Roz at the door, her wild red curls a luxuriant mess all over her head.

'Guh,' Roz croaked, but ever a friend she put aside her own troubles for a moment to ask: 'How're you feeling, Addles?'

'Better than you, I'd say,' Addy smirked, and mostly at herself: she barely had a sniffle to show for the misery of yesterday; she couldn't remember when she'd last felt so – so plainly all right. How odd. Squeezing past for the loo, she asked Roz: 'How was the fiesta?'

'Guh,' she croaked again, twirled a finger in the air and added greyly: '*Arriba*. Yahooey. Blergh. I hope we didn't keep you up.'

'No. Not at all,' Addy replied. 'I slept like a dead person.'

Roz smiled, sleepy-eyed: 'Well done. I don't think the music stopped until sometime after three.'

'After three?' Addy heard those dream piano butterflies in her head once more as she turned on the tap at the sink to wash her hands; not very Mexican butterflies; she asked: 'Did HRH get on the grog, after all?' She was thinking perhaps Harriet had got drunk and had a bash when she'd got in.

'What?' Roz squinted at Addy. 'No. Presume she stayed over at Maaaahrtin's. Guh.' Poor Roz held her head: 'I've got to go back to bed. See you at the WoCo meeting?'

'Oh …' The WoCo: the Women's Collective, subset of the Student Representative Council, and one which apes of the same cast as Chubs Keveney were determined to see cut out of the solidarity picture altogether: their mothers had burned their bras only for their sons to shove their sisters to the sidelines. Addy had barely shown her face at a WoCo meeting since term began; she hadn't had the energy or the inclination: the ladies were not all that much better behaved than the gents, in terms of blindness to their own privilege, at least. She could never see how she might begin to forge her father's socialist utopia from that base, where Karl Marx didn't mean all that much more than a badge worn on the breast pockets of shirts grunged not from hard labour but because their owners hadn't yet worked out how to operate a washing machine. 'Um …'

'Oh, go on.' Roz tugged on the front of Addy's nightgown, mock-moaning.

'Oh, all right,' Addy acquiesced. The idea wasn't totally repulsive, she supposed, didn't make her want to curl up under a rock as it had done every other time she'd tried to convince herself to go. Perhaps today might bring a better, more useful view of campus politics, too, with most of the weight of law studies lifted, and the complete absence of hangover. After all, it was important to get involved, be engaged, be the change you want to see, et cetera. She gave Roz her promise: 'See you there.'

'Fabbo.' Roz belched and shuffled off: 'Guh.'

Addy felt the warm, bright curve of her own smile as she watched her friend go, and it felt like sunshine spilling out from within: today seemed different in some other indefinable way. She recalled hurling her little snip of truth at Harriet yesterday: *I want to be a writer.* It was the first time she'd ever said anything like it out aloud, made such a declaration. And now, running the idea through her mind afresh, it felt good. Despite the awful things that Harriet had said, it felt really good. It felt right.

She stood there a moment longer, waiting for some kind of wrongness to descend, for panic to pounce, but it didn't; only No Name the cat meandered around the top of the stairs, winding his tiger-striped sleekness against the bruise on her shin, meowing up at her, green eyes blinking through their gingery butterfly mask. She picked him up and kissed him on the nose; she said: 'Come on, come and help me decide what to wear.'

For she didn't want to be invisible today; she didn't want to disappear anymore. She didn't know where this resolve had come from, but she wasn't going to argue with it, that was for sure. She felt sort of festive, somehow springy, something tingling in the air around her. She smiled again on realising it was the first of May today, so the calendar above her desk told her: it was May Day, and therefore International

Workers' Day as well, and that meant her father would have a slap-up dinner at the club with all his union mates tonight, he'd laugh and be merry, and not be lonely; and, as the world turned, somewhere in England, where it was actually spring, men would be festooning themselves with flowers and streamers and bells, dancing about. Perhaps she'd been somehow subliminally aware of all this.

She laughed to herself and chose her own most sunshiny dress: a pincord pinafore, tangerine ground with yellow flowers; a black skivvy for underneath, black tights and black boots; she looked smart, and somehow ready, though for what, she didn't yet know.

She wrote a note to her wardrobe, to all her colours there, a simple note of gratitude:

> *Thank you – all of you.*
> *Your comrade and friend,*
> *Addy Loest X*

When the autumn sun shone upon Sydney, even a crumbling gutter was transformed, its quartz particles sparkling under the wild blue sky; a rusty gate was rendered charming; an over-postered hoarding around a construction site became a work of art – even the one that Addy was striding past this minute, posters proclaiming every metre or so that Elbow would be playing at the Hairy Egg tonight.

She gave them all a glancing dare: *Can I go and have a dance without a drink? Without getting drunk?* She didn't have a great deal of confidence she'd succeed in that, but perhaps she'd try. She was quite partial to the support band, a jazz-funk quintet called Groovy Tuna, and she'd never seen them when she was sober. Who didn't love a bongo beat and a bit of screaming brass? Perhaps she'd even say hello to Dan Dolly Donne; he seemed an okay enough guy. She might at least make some gesture of apology, for having been such a bucket of weird whenever he was near. She might even attempt to make amends with HRH – *Or maybe not.*

Whatever the day might bring, she was heading for it at an easy clip. She was calm; she was cool; she'd eaten an ordinary breakfast of vegemite toast and tea; she'd even dashed off the introduction for her Fitzgerald essay, filling in the minutes until it was time to go.

She checked her watch as she strode on: a whisker after nine – excellent. The Curiosity Shop should be open by the time she got there. Unless, of course, she'd imagined the whole thing yesterday, and the shop didn't really exist. But she strode past this thought, too, chin high – each time it knocked on the lid of its box, she pushed it down again. Was there any better proof of just what a wonderful day this was? She was getting on top of her doubts. She was winning. Mr Olympia Café gave her a nod and a wave from his window as she strode past him as well, his spatula raised as though in confirmation.

And there it was, The Curiosity Shop, the bulb in the tiffany lamp flickering on as she crossed the road towards it, lighting up the multi-coloured diamonds of the harlequin glass and the heavy red curtain by it, draped like a sail at rest. The zebra seemed to grin, not at her, but – *Yes!* – the dress, her dress, was still there, exactly where she'd left it, too, on the mannequin beyond the jewellery-display case.

'Hello again!' she almost shouted on seeing the old woman, who was up on a stepladder, pulling the cord of another overhead light, a bronze chandelier strung with amber beads, that hung above the tall shelves in the middle of the shop.

The woman peered in the general direction of the greeting, until she found Addy there by her heart's desire: 'Ah! Hello, dear. You have returned.' She smiled with her eyes, with that glint of clear blue mischief: 'I thought you might. You have come to try on the dress?'

'Yes, please.' Addy almost bounced about like a child, she was so full of fizz at the want, at the thrill.

'Very well.' The old woman got down from the stepladder, folding it away, pushing it under the shelves with the toe of one of her patent-leather shoes, all one fluid movement; she wore the same plum wool suit, neat and trim, and she walked with such a straight back, such a precise placement of her feet, Addy wondered if she'd been a dancer or a gymnast once upon a time. At the mannequin, with care and gentle ceremony, the woman unbuckled the slim green belt at the waist, such a dark green, the colour of pine needles; the flowers, gathering and gathering below it, swished across the outer layer of tulle, floating across its pale patch of sky.

Addy held her breath, watching as her tiny note flittered to the carpet; the woman appeared too intent on the dress to notice, unzipping the side seam on the bodice. She didn't look up as she said: 'Another woman was interested in this one yesterday afternoon, admiring it very much. I talked her out of it. She was small, like you, but much older. She wouldn't have liked it once she got it home, I doubt she would ever have worn it.' The woman pulled the dress expertly up over the top of the mannequin. 'Not like you. You,' she looked at Addy now, raising an eyebrow somehow appraisingly, her German accent underlining her certainty, 'you will wear this gown many, many times.'

'Oh, I will, I will.' Addy laughed, taking the treasure of silk upon silk upon silk in her arms for the very first time: 'I hope she fits me.'

'She?' The woman laughed with her, delighted and wry. 'Oh, but I am sure she will,' she assured Addy, and waved her away. 'Try it on, try it on. The change room is down at the back – the door on the left before the last of the books.'

Addy almost ran.

It is also a truth universally acknowledged that a woman in a hurry to undress finds that it takes twice as long as usual, involves laddering her tights and near removing her nose with the thick, tight collar of her skivvy, but Addy got there in the end. She shivered in the dank, dusty old broom cupboard that was the change room, and not only because she was cold: even before she'd slipped the dress over her head, even before she'd zipped the zip, she knew it fitted her. The darts at her bust, the seating of the waistline, the sleeve-caps that cupped her shoulders: it was as though it had been tailored exactly to the fine bones of her frame.

The mirror on the back of the door said so, too. Addy raised her hands to her face, to the flush of her cheeks.

'Oh!'

Oh.

She buckled the belt and looked again.

This dress, this joyful garden that she wore, was perfect. Simply and intricately perfect. She stood there for some time in spellbound awe, taking in detail upon detail she hadn't quite seen before: the tiny black filaments ringing the stigmas of the poppies were crafted with such individual artistry it was as though the flowers were truly blooming there, somehow infused with life, each poppy unlike the next; the fluted pompom petals of the cornflowers strewn among them were each distinctly beautiful as well; and hiding in the clustering bunches of leaves around the hem, she found the delicate stars of camomile daisies here and there, golden centres smiling like specks of sun.

Yes, she would want to wear this dress many, many times. But could she dare? Would she dare? Where? Whatever, she didn't want to take it off right now. She'd have to, though: she had a tutorial for Australian History at half-past ten, and a lay-by to organise yet. She slipped back out of heaven and returned herself to ordinary. She tidied her hair and straightened her pinafore, preparing to make the biggest frock investment of her life. She checked the price tag again, dangling on its little safety pin: *Yep, still twenty-eight dollars and seventy-five cents.* A hundred disastrous scenarios swooped and squawked around her head, with all the possible ways she'd be prevented from paying off the lay-by, thereby losing dough and dress: she'd get fired from her job; she'd break a leg; she'd be abducted by aliens who'd wipe her memory; she'd be abducted by ASIO and accused of being a Soviet spy; Town Hall Variety would go broke after a devastating corporate embezzlement scandal and not meet the Thursday wages bill. But it would be worth all that and more for the chance to have this dress.

Yes.

Back at the front of the shop, the old woman was sitting on a stool behind the jewellery counter, reading a magazine. Addy could just see the cover: it was a German women's magazine, *Frau* something or other, with a photograph of Princess Di on it, wearing a silly hat and looking terrified. Addy wouldn't be seen dead reading any such gossip rag, but she'd have given anything to know all the words on the cover of this one. Or maybe not anything – she wouldn't forgo this dress for hell or high water now.

The old woman looked up from her magazine: 'So, you are happy with this gown?'

'I am, thank you.' Addy laid it down across the glass countertop and touched one of the poppies, smiling so wholly her cheeks stung with happiness. 'I'd like to arrange a lay-by, if I may, please,' she began, as though she arranged lay-bys all over town. 'I get paid tomorrow,' she explained, 'every Thursday evening, and I'd like to pay it off within the month, if that's all right. I have four dollars and seventy-five cents for the deposit, if that's enough, and then from tomorrow, I'd like to make four lots of six-dollar payments, if that would be acceptable to you.'

The old woman gave her a fond chuckle, light and kind: 'You are very organised. I would not be surprised if you paid it off sooner. Your suggestion is acceptable, of course, and very sensible.' She turned and reached for a small black ledger book that sat atop a narrow chest of drawers behind her. 'Now,' she said, taking up a pretty pen, its barrel enamelled with a cross-hatch pattern in white and gold, 'what is your name, dear?'

'Adrianna Loest,' she told her, and spelled out her last name, as she always did: 'L.O.E.S.T.'

The woman stopped still, pen to page, name as yet un-written; she looked up at Addy with a frown; a querying and somehow wary frown: 'I beg your pardon, could you please spell that again?'

Addy did, and with a near audible sigh: 'L.O.E.S.T. Loest.' Why was this always so difficult? Loest was not a common name, this was true; it wasn't even a common German name – she, her dad and Nick were the only Loests she knew – but it wasn't as though she was called Bhagwan Shree Rajneesh or Myfanwy Worcestershire, or even Kieran Keveney. It didn't deserve a frown – no one's name did.

The woman's frown only deepened, though, the furrow between her brows holding a story Addy wanted to know. Time stretched and spun around the globe, as the woman stared and stared.

Why is she staring at me like this?

The woman blinked then, cleared her throat and wrote Addy's name in her lay-by ledger book; she said, not quite meeting Addy's eye: 'You would like to make a deposit of four dollars and seventy-five cents, is that right?'

'That's right. Thank you.' Addy wondered what had happened, what was wrong. Had she been rude? Sometimes her oddness could be misinterpreted, she knew that. She took her purse from her satchel and the money from her purse, placing it on the glass between the book and the softly shimmering folds of the dress.

The woman took it, and without counting it, she opened the top drawer behind her and tossed it in a cash tin there, distractedly. She then pulled out a receipt book and scratched down the amount and lay-by terms upon it, firm strokes for the carbon copy beneath; she carefully tore the top page along its perforated edge, and offered it to Addy: 'Your next payment will be expected in one week from today.'

'Oh, I'll be in before then. I can't wait to return,' Addy was quick to say, and as sweetly as she could, taking the receipt delicately, trying to make up for how she might have offended the woman; she couldn't think what she'd said or done.

'Very well.' The woman nodded, gathering up the dress. 'I shall take your gown to the storeroom now, where it will be quite safe.' And with that, she left, disappearing into the depths of the shop.

Leaving Addy there at the display case, all alone.

I'm just being paranoid, aren't I.

She's an old woman – she's allowed to be inexplicably strange.

She's not even thinking of you. Do you have to be so self-obsessed even when you're happy?

Shut up.

Addy wasn't sure what to do. Time was ticking on – she had to make tracks now for that Aus History tute, but she didn't want to leave the shop unattended. Anyone could have walked in off the street and pinched the cash tin – pinched anything. There were plenty of dregs and druggies lurking about for Addy to know that was not a paranoid thought. She had another one of those nevertheless, sensing eyes on her; she turned, expecting a fellow customer. It was only the zebra, though, seeming to frown at her as well, as if to say: 'And who are you?'

On aimless reflex, Addy looked down at the receipt in her hand, searching for her name there, but found instead:

'ANNA LÖST'

Anna? Ö?

Oh. Addy felt the thought like a dull thud in her stomach: the woman was probably only getting doddery or didn't hear the 'Adri' before the 'Anna', going a little deaf. She looked at her watch again: she couldn't wait to find out – she really had to go.

Should she leave a note? A thankyou? She couldn't decide if that might compound the offence, if any were taken. If she signed it 'Addy Loest', that could appear as though she were correcting the woman; and if she didn't sign it at all, that would just be weird and useless. She could sign it 'Miss Loest' – or should that be 'Ms'?

You don't have to leave a fricken note everywhere you go. How about you try to keep that under control for the rest of the day.

Fair call. Good idea. I don't need to leave a note at all.
For fuck's sake, get on with it – get out of here!

She flicked the lock on the front door before she closed it behind her – that would have to do. Stepping back out onto the now brightly shouting, honking, growling street, she folded all these thoughts into the inside pocket of her purse, with the receipt; she'd be back again the day after tomorrow.

In the meantime, there was nothing like an Australian History tutorial to knock the gloss off the rest of the morning. The topic for this study unit was supposed to have explored the idea of this nation as the 'most peaceful democracy on earth'.

'Most lazy and complacent,' one of the boys in the tute-group dozen remarked five minutes in, and not without some factual basis, but the gloves were off in this contest of ideas from that point on.

There was the smelly guy with dreadlocks whose father was a merchant banker: 'Why don't you ask some Aboriginal people how peaceful this country is, hey, mate! Ask them about the massacres and poisoned waterholes that built this fine democracy.'

The first guy responded by leaning forward, knees splayed wide as they would go to show he was really an ape beneath his preppy crewneck: 'Why don't *you* ask some Aboriginal people if they'd like to return to life in the Stone —'

'No!' One of the girls, a high-pitched member of the drama society, joined in, straight from rehearsals for *Extreme Outrage*: 'You racist! Colonialism is murder. State-devised murder —'

'Go and take a cold shower, lovey,' young Mr Crewneck Crotch Display drawled, and gave her a scoffy, toffy tone of dismissal. 'You'd prefer a pre-Enlightenment existence, would you? Hand me the keys to your car, then. Walk home and put an axe through your TV.'

'Oh!' she gasped and mouthed the word: 'Arsehole.'

Behold the great brains of the future, Addy thought. Who were these people, so full of confidence in their own opinions, and seemingly so shy of questions, like they hadn't quite left their high-school debating teams behind? *How do they* know *so much? They talk like they know this stuff in their bones.* Addy hadn't read a lot of philosophy, only bits of Nietzsche and Schopenhauer, who didn't enlighten her with much more than the idea that the only thing that truly distinguishes us from the animals is our awareness of how terrible we are, but she wondered now if these philosophers' university tutorials might have been much the same, albeit without the present presence of 41.2% females. She wondered for a moment what the world might really be like if it hadn't been for the Enlightenment, the Age of Reason, that burst out of Europe in the seventeenth century, purportedly giving birth to Newton's laws of physics, modern democracy and, possibly, the harpsichord. Would there have been any less war or murder? Would colonialism have taken another form? Would we have continued to bludgeon and betray each other by some different means? Would rampant capitalism have manifested in a global desire for something other than Rubik's cubes? Would there have been no discovery of radium, no treatment for cancer, no nuclear bombs? No French Revolution, no Karl Marx, no *Les Miserables,* the novel or the musical, no International Workers' Day to be apparently entirely ignored by late-twentieth-century university students who'll never know real work or ever really need to struggle for anything in their lives? She decided only that she didn't know the answers to any of these questions, but that she could guess an alternative history would probably not have included Beethoven or Einstein, or cut-price paperbacks. Or chocolate. She was most certain that chocolate as we know it would not exist if it had not been for the Enlightenment – not the worldwide distribution of this human necessity, nor the technological means of its production. *And where would we be without chocolate?*

'What?' The dreadlocked merchant banker winced at her. 'Chocolate? What are you talking about?'

Addy felt the rush of blood to her face on realising she'd said that last thought aloud; she looked down at the yellow flowers on her too-loud, too-orange pinafore: *Why did I wear this today?* She needn't have worried about responding, though: no one was listening to anyone, anyway.

'Australia is starting to edge beyond its colonial beginnings,' another of the guys began an attempt at some kind of reason, but he had to raise his voice over the top of Dreadlocks. 'We're leading the way to the twenty-first century, as one of the most politically advanced nations in the world. Look at the industrial relations accord, entrenching goodwill between business and workers, and then there's universal healthcare. The Labor Party is —'

'The *Labor* Party?' Drama Queen shrieked. 'The *Labor* Party? There's no other party more steeped in racism – jobs for whites only. Jobs for the boys. Jobs for white scum.'

'Jesus Christ!' Crewneck Monkey Crotch bellowed back at her: 'What shade of white are you, then? White saviour?' And the room completely erupted at that: half falling about laughing; half protesting in dismay.

Addy didn't know where to look. She thought all the ideas that had been raised were worth discussing, worth unpicking sense from ignorance, but there was no discussion going on here. No one was really saying anything. It was all just noise. White noise; very white.

Round and round it went, until someone inevitably mentioned God – God in this context being the greatest, whitest Aussiest Labor hope of socialistic civilisation known to man, former Prime Minister Saint Gough Whitlam – which then prompted someone else to point out that he was a silver-spooned egomaniac who'd lately spent four hours at the United Nations being grilled for turning a blind eye to Indonesia's bloodthirsty invasion of East Timor: 'There's neo-colonialism for you – get a Third World nation to do your dirty work.' Then someone had to mention university fees – someone always had to mention university fees – in this instance, that Comrade Gough had abolished them and now his Labor successors Hawke and Keating were bringing them back in: 'Like the wolves in sheep's clothing they really are.'

'But I do love Paul Keating,' Drama Queen said, like a starstruck groupie. 'He's drop-dead gorgeous.'

And Addy ceased to hear much after that.

Dreadlocks was almost out of his seat: 'If there wasn't a law against it, mining companies would be poisoning waterholes in the Pilbara right now. You're kidding yourselves if you think —'

Words, words, words swirled around her, entwined with that shadow-shame of still not being able to remember if she'd actually called Dan Elbow Whoever a 'frayed-denim fascist' the night before last. Hypocrisy was a tricky fish, wasn't it? And so was Addy's mind: *I'm never drinking again. I wonder what Donne would have made of*

Nietzsche? In an alternative history, maybe they're having a chat and a beer at the Hairy Egg right now, talking about God. Waiting for Einstein to turn up and explain the space-time continuum to them. Maybe I should switch to science? Not unless I'd really like to feel out of my depth. I'm hungry.

'The National Union should be doing more to stop it – this is insanity.'

'But the rich *should* pay.'

'Yes, but the poor *will* pay.'

'Raise taxes!'

'You're dreaming.'

'This is ludicrous!'

Yep. Addy looked over at their tutor. His name was Ned Needham and he wasn't much older than them, maybe late twenties; he'd only recently finished his PhD – not in class-room control. Their eyes met; they exchanged wan smiles; he looked at his watch, then raised a hand in the air as though he wasn't the teacher at all. He said, with excruciating hesitance: 'If we can get this back to the topic, please. You've all read *The Lucky Country*, I take it.'

It was one of the texts that had been set as additional reading. It was one of Australia's most famous books, by Donald Horne, probably Australia's most famous intellectual. No one had read it – except Addy. Everyone else just *knew*. But they shut up at last.

'Right,' said Ned; Addy could see how hard he was battling his nerves as he pressed on: 'Might I suggest the chapter, "Nation Without a Mind"?' He picked up his copy from the stack of books on the floor by his chair, and began to read:

'… one can learn something about happiness by examining Australia – its lingering puritanism. The frustrations and resentments of a triumphant mediocrity …

'On it goes,' Ned let the text do the talking:

'… to a sophisticated observer the flavour of democratic life in Australia might seem depraved, a victory of the anti-mind.'

Of course, Addy was the only one who laughed – and Drama Queen shot her a look, as if the outburst was inappropriate.

She listened to her stomach rumbling for the rest of the tute, wishing she hadn't told Roz she'd meet her at the WoCo over lunch. It was only going to be more of the same there.

And it met her before she'd even got in the door of the Women's Room.

'Ew, is that raw onion?' The one called Zondra didn't even say hello. She was one of those tall, willowy, tie-dyed hippie-crites, who proselytised veganism with one hand and stabbed you in the back with the other. Two years older, she was in her final year of sociology. She was also one of the exalted – an elected official of the WoCo.

Addy smiled, holding up her sandwich bag: 'Yep. Onions – and beetroot.' She was going for health today and going hard. 'No animals were harmed in the making of my lunch.'

'Except me.' Zondra crossed her legs, holding court from her moulded plastic throne, turning away from Addy as

though she were an irrelevance. No one else said hello, either;
and Roz was running late as usual.

I don't belong here.

Wait for Roz.

No.

Yes.

Another soon came through the door, but it was only
Drama Queen. Her name was actually Jane Buckingham, and
in she strode now, breasts outthrust like a pair of ballistic
warheads.

'Hi, Jane!' just about the whole room chorused.

That's it, I'm fricken going.

Most of these women, some two dozen in all at this
meeting, were members of an old girls' networking pool from
Sydney's top private and selective schools, daughters of diplo-
mats and bureaucrats, doctors and lawyers, all of a sort
proclaiming Australia a classless society – for them. Bourgeois
feminism would save the world from itself. All they needed
were tambourines and temperance badges and they could
proclaim themselves New Age Wowsers, so Addy thought.
Smash the patriarchy and replace it with rich-lady totalitarian
maternalism. But she would wait for Roz nevertheless. Besides,
from the hubbub around her, she picked up that this meeting
was taking a show of hands to protest funding cuts planned
for women-specific services – such as advice on sexual health,
abuse and abortion, and rape crisis counselling. Numbers were
important for things like this: taking it up to the baboons who
held the purse strings of the Student Representative Council.
It was an outrage that 'men' like Chubs Keveney even had a
say – but there was democracy in action.

'Child care?' One voice cut through all the others here:
it was Claudine Claymore, Zondra Smythe's chief rival and

fellow elected fem-official. Claudine had angelwing hair-flicks to rival Princess Di's, high-waisted tartan slacks and a bunch of expensively tailored prejudices to match. She was saying, in her clipped, impatient, bound-for-the-judiciary way: 'Subsidised child care is all very well for the very unfortunate, but I am of the general opinion that a woman unable to care for a child should not have one.'

'Are you suggesting forced abortion?' Zondra turned in her chair. 'Are you suggesting women must choose between family and career?'

Whoa. Addy bit into her sandwich. *Might as well settle in for the show.*

'I am suggesting good sense.' Claudine mock-shuddered. 'The Women's Collective should not waste time and resources on issues that do not affect the majority of women on campus. The vast majority are not mothers. Child care is a non-issue.'

'It's an issue for those women who drop out of university each year because they've fallen pregnant,' one of the quieter members spoke up at that.

Claudine shrugged: 'There aren't many of them.' And she hardened further still: 'It is not the business of the Collective to encourage women to place their children in state-sponsored baby farms. We should not enable any child to be made so motherless.'

'Motherless!' There was Drama Queen Jane, shrieking like a siren. 'What about the men! The bastards – aren't they somehow responsible, too!'

The corner of crust Addy was chewing turned to sawdust in her mouth; she shrank into a vision of her father at the stove, cooking dinner night after night; her father tucking her into bed, his beery kiss on her forehead a statement of love marking the end of each day; her father tying the ribbons in her hair, getting her ready for school, straightening the collar of her uniform, his knuckles never quite clean of the work that put food on the table and a roof over their heads. Not all men were bastards. Only some. Only —

'Sorry I'm so late, chicky babes.' It was Roz, rushing in, bangles clanking, her big red hair the biggest idea the WoCo had ever known; she held her belly and rolled her eyes: 'Got me curse, didn't I. And I must warn you I have been farting like a foghorn all day.'

And they all laughed; everyone loved Roz. She was all class, no class, class of her own.

Addy shrank further at the fact.

'Here, pet.' Roz thrust a bag of chocolate freckles under her nose.

But it was too late.

Addy only wanted alcohol now.

NOT GERMAN ENOUGH, HEART TOO BROKEN

She was determined to hold off the grog for as long as possible. She went home, to Flower Street, thought about watching the afternoon soapie serials on TV, but their TV had the crappiest snow-storm reception, and would only make her feel like drinking. So, in pre-emptive atonement for the drinking she would certainly do later, she sat at her little desk in her room and wrote most of the rest of her *Gatsby* essay, though it wasn't due for a fortnight. She then began a bit of additional reading for Ancient History, though the text she turned to hadn't been suggested in the lecture notes: *Tacitus on Germany*, a monograph included in the back of her copy of *Complete Works*. It wasn't any kind of conscientiousness that led her here, rather a yearning to know where she was from – *really* from. The same yearning that saw her on other odd occasions searching the words of *Beowulf* for traces of German in the Old English, traces of her own long-ago and far-away beginnings within tales of monsters and dragons and impossible valour, within runic code etched into stones with swords. Her yearning to solve the puzzle of herself. To work out why she seemed to sit on the edge of every circle, never quite finding the right place to be.

'The Germans, I am apt to believe, derive their origins from no other people ...' so said these words of Tacitus, the Roman, written almost two thousand years ago. Where did they come from, then? Out of the earth between the Danube and the Rhine? Describing the tribes of the Germanii as nobly savage in some slovenly, thuggish way, javelin-wielding warriors emerged from the page, from 'gloomy forests and nasty marshes', their unshockable women going with them into battle to tend their wounds. They were a 'pure' people, never intermarrying with others, their 'eyes stern and blue', all with blond hair and huge bodies – exactly like her brother, Nick. She blinked at seeing him so solidly here, and her private jibe that he'd have made a perfect poster boy for the Third Reich rippled chillingly through time, across empires. There didn't seem to be anything of Addy in these Germans, though, except that the women were partial to wearing a bit of purple, and that everyone possessed a herculean capacity for getting pissed: 'day and night without intermission'.

Maybe it's a genetic thing? Maybe I'm designed to drink. A lot.

Maybe you're just on the road to boring old alcoholism.

I want a beer now. It's been a long day.

It's always a long day with you.

Shut up.

It was only half-past five, though – she would try to hang on a little longer. She didn't want to be drunk before it was time to go to the pub – she'd mistimed the beverage regimen too many times before, passing out with her head on a table, fast asleep while the music crashed and jangled around her. She read a little further:

Frequent then do they fight amongst themselves, as usual for men intoxicated with liquor; and such broils rarely terminate in angry words, but for the most part in maimings and slaughter.

Nice. That only made her think of Nick again and the fight on Friday night – and how much she did not want to go. She was definitely not genetically German enough to enjoy the sound of fist meeting flesh. She hated it. She didn't want to go to a leagues club to witness it, either – although she'd never been to this particular one, South Sydney Juniors, she knew what it would be like. She didn't want to be alone among all those men, all shouting and carrying on, with the only other girls there being wet t-shirt contestants with enormous boobs, all hairspray and fake tan. Nothing bad would happen to her, she knew that, too – Nick's coach would be there, and probably so would other acquaintances of her father's, as well as one or two of Nick's friends. She'd be all right.

She would *not* be all right.

And she could not hold out anymore.

She grabbed her purse, heavy with extra coins she'd scrounged from the bottom of her satchel, from pockets and drawers, then she thumped down the stairs and out the door.

Flower Street was just about dark now, its terrace rows and long-abandoned warehouses colourless under lamplight that didn't quite reach to the alleyway that would take her up to the Hotel Broadway. Whether alone or with Roz, she always felt like a pathetic wino sneaking up to this pub and its el cheapo-est bottle shop – the haunt of Chippendale's most dedicated, deadbeat drunks. *If the shoe fits* ... But economy was necessity. As the house had been completely drained of grog at last night's fiesta, she thought she'd get a six-pack of beer – limit herself to two of them for now – and a bottle of ginger wine to share later, when they'd return home after the gig at the Hairy Egg. With the extra coinage she carried, she had a little over twelve dollars – enough for the alcohol and a felafel on King Street as and when required. She'd have to go hungry tomorrow, until she got her pay from Town Hall Variety, but so be it.

'Got a smoke, sis?' A dark shape emerged from all the other dark shapes in the alley, dark skin, dark eyes, long dark hair curling out from under a striped football beanie – a woman – and Addy startled, just an ordinary startle of surprise.

'Sorry, no.' Her breath was ragged at the question, tight inside her steady stride; she smoked only occasionally, mostly bludging off others; she kept walking, eyes on the streetlight at the end of the alley, by the pub; she was nearly there.

'Fucken white bitch,' the voice helped her quicken her pace, another voice telling her: *you don't belong here*; and being an Aboriginal voice, it came with a fair whack of authority.

Addy ran the last few steps to the pub and didn't look back; her own voice shook at the counter of the bottle shop and so did her hands as she fumbled at her purse; she walked the long way home, back around towards the uni, her pulse banging in her ears, her breath charging like a train, and the blackening night closing around her shoulders, closing around the edges of her sight. She wasn't frightened of the woman harming her, stealing her bag of booze or the money she had left; it was something worse than that. It was guilt at being a *fucken white bitch* that had Addy by the throat, and the way that guilt played with every other guilt she carried around with her every *fucken white bitch* day. Guilt at struggling so relentlessly with phantoms that didn't exist, when others had real struggles to contend with. Guilt at walking on stolen land that she could do nothing to return. She was nothing – really. She was not a real Australian; she was not a real German. She was not a real Illawarra surfie chick; she was not a real Sydney University student. She fell between the cracks of everything, and it was desperately lonely there – everywhere.

The house was still empty when she returned, and she opened a can of beer unaware she'd even done it until she felt that first-beer relief swimming in her knees.

That's better.

It wasn't, and yet it was.

She stared hollowly at the kitchen bench for a moment, until the remains of her housemates' cooking sprees came into view: Roz's crockpot 'soaking' by the sink, nachos pond scum festering across its surface; and HRH's food processor bowl lined inside with globs of hummus that had set like concrete.

Do not clean it up – you might be a trash load of frick all, but you are no one's housemaid.

She compromised, giving Roz's crockpot a scrub and rinse, while leaving the royal hummus as it was, a small monument to the super trash that was overprivileged ignorance.

No Name meowed, leaping up on the bench at her elbow, rubbing his butterfly face on her wrist; she opened a can for him, too, of kitty-mush, and spooned out a little onto his china dish on the back step. She finished her beer out there on the step, listening to the traffic ease off its end-of-day rush; watching the last of the evening's indigoes fade into space; missing the bright splash of stars above the ocean at home, at Port; missing her dad. For a second she considered calling him, just to say hello, but she thought her heart might break if she did that; she couldn't ever cry to her dad; his heartbreak was real and hers was —

She cracked open another beer instead and called the cat: 'Come on – come and help me choose what to wear.'

Something purple?

Up the stairs she went, No Name following as if in obedience; she smiled at him, his tiger tail high in the air. He leapt up onto the bed, onto the crochet squares of her blanket, where he settled and watched her choose from two possibilities: arty-tarty violet lace, sort of Madonna doing heavy metal; or a pretty vintage late-50s-ish A-line, fine-paper taffeta with actual violets on it, violets floating over a musky-pink ground.

'What do you think?' she asked No Name, only to find he'd lost interest, circle-curling into sleep. She'd already decided on pretty, though – she wasn't drunk enough for Madonna.

'Hello! Anybody home!' There was Roz, keys jingling, bangles clanking up the hall. Addy heard the thump of her bag at the bottom of the stairs: 'That you up there, Addles?'

'Yep,' she called back, rummaging for lipstick in her desk drawer.

'How're you feeling, pet?' She called up again, concerned, as Addy had led her to be, having left her today after the vote at the Women's Room with an excuse of stomach ache – only half a lie.

But Addy called back, now restored, or so it seemed: 'Great!' And she gulped down the remains of that beer – belching a further assurance: '*Ja – wunderbar!*'

When she danced, there was only joy. The music and the movement, and joy. It didn't really matter what music it was or how the dance came, it was the play of sound and spirit: she was large and free and minuscule, something atomically, intrinsically hers flying between and around every note. She was the choral burst, she was the famous ode's kiss for the whole world, the blare of brass, the thrum of bass. And she was apparently incapable of achieving this sober.

Groovy Tuna slid into a smoky, jazzed-up cover of 'Play That Funky Music', and Addy was the sax, carving the air with her hands and her hips. She was the little girl who would, once upon a time, dance in the back yard, whirling around under the rotary clothesline, making herself dizzy, falling down to watch the racing clouds. She used to sing, too, all the time. When did she stop?

Where are you, Addy? Where have you gone?

I'm making funky music, white bitch.

'Here y'are, pet.' Roz sloshed another schooner at her, and they grooved together between band and bar, small women, big beers, among the Hairy Egg's cool but never-too-cool crowd of young funsters all out to have a good time and to maybe get shagged later.

'Hey, spunk bubble.' Drummer Boy joined them, bending to give Roz a kiss. His actual name was Kendall Clarke, so Roz had told Addy on the way here, an economics law dropout, and he was exceptionally tall and reedy thin, unusually affectionate, too, for an option-enriched boy in a band – one whom Roz would no doubt subject to some affectionate bondage and discipline later. Addy watched them kiss, the crowd thickening behind them, all herding in for Elbow, and most of them girls, looking breathless already, and at least half of them wearing tutus teamed with fishnet stockings and striped gondolier t-shirts. They crammed for prime position in front of the stage, and Addy slumped inwardly: forgetting herself in a dance-trance would be impossible now, fending off the flailing limbs and smouldering cigarettes of these diehard Elbowettes.

She'd already decided she'd spend half her felafel money on a further schooner, even before Dan the Man appeared out of the tobacco haze. He waved, an index finger raised, from across the room, above the Elbowette horde, as though he'd sought her out, and only her, with that mild, sweet-boy, Elizabethan smile.

Don't be deceived, Addy Loest – he's a pothead.

While she might not have remembered much about that first night they'd met over Trivial Pointlessness, she recalled most distinctly now that he'd rolled and lit at least three spliffs in the course of that evening: he kept his stash in a black silk pouch embroidered with blue-and-white stars that had fallen from the sky along the road to Marrakesh. How was it that she could remember this detail but not the insult she'd hurled his way? Maybe he'd been too stoned to notice, anyway; hopefully. She'd have bet all her felafel money he was stoned right now.

He said: 'Hi, Addy.' He was so cool, guitar case in one hand, pushing back his shaggy long hair with the other, he didn't appear to notice the room around him; he might have been approaching a bus stop. *Definitely off his face.*

'Hello,' Addy finally replied like a normal person, although she swayed slightly on her feet.

'Gee,' he said. *Who the hell says 'gee'?* He looked her over with a sort of awed nod-shake of the head, then he said: 'Great dress.' And he walked on, towards the stage.

Then her heart did something very strange: it just about leapt out of her chest, wanting to skitter after him.

How drunk are you?

Not nearly drunk enough.

She skulled the rest of the beer in her hand and turned back to the bar for something a little stronger: 'A schooner of Riesling, please.'

As they say in the classics, don't mix the grape and grain – but Addy Loest hadn't read that book. After her schooner of Riesling, which was near half a litre of the nastiest cask wine imaginable, and four further beers, followed by three generous glugs of green ginger rotgut and a shot of whatever shit Drummer Boy had in his hipflask, Addy Loest was as smashed as was possible for a human her size to be and still remain on her feet. As she had not eaten a thing since that beetroot-and-onion sandwich at lunchtime, it was astonishing that she hadn't lost consciousness.

There were, however, several important things that Addy would not remember from the run of events that night in anything other than a surreally juddering collection of disparate pictures and emotions.

Among them, lurching back along King Street, getting jostled by a skinhead girl with a safety pin through her nose and shouting after her in reply: 'If you're the face of white supremacy, sweetie, we're all fucked.' Roz dragging her away: 'Jesus, Addy, you're going to get killed one day.'

Then home again, at Flower Street, at about one in the morning, she hijacked the stereo, 'My turn! My turn!' and, standing on the coffee table, with an audience comprised of various Elbows and Tunas and their attendant tutus, she started belting out the choral section of Beethoven's Ninth Symphony, punching the air: *'Freude! Freude!'*

The gathered lost interest quickly, as Roz had begun cutting up a little baggie of speed on top of the piano, on the back of Addy's telephone book there, but one devoted audient remained: Dan the Man. He sat on the floor at Addy's feet, head down rolling another spliff, and at first she thought the stereo was playing tricks on her when a baritone seemed to stray from the choir, the voice drifting rather close. Except it was Dan, joining her at the song, looking up at her, smiling: *'Freude, schöner Götterfunken, Tochter aus Elysium, Wir betreten feuertrunken, Himmlische, dein*

Heiligtum!' And so on: words whose very sounds translated into hardcore, insistent joy, the joy of everyman togetherness, of friendship, of the better angels of western civilisation, of getting drunk on the best wine there was – love. She gave herself over to the rapture of it, the fantasy of singing with the Berliner Philharmoniker; the crazy delight that someone else was sharing this with her. She was Beethoven's *Tochter aus Elysium* – she was his Daughter of Bliss. She was the *Ode to Joy*.

Until the needle jumped and skidded along a scratch on the old record, hissing and crackling into the blank black vinyl grooves at the end. But she was too distracted now to bother trying to get the music going again, too curious to be disappointed; as the sounds of the party closed back around her, she asked this boy at her feet: 'How the frick do you know the words?'

He stood up, laughter in his stoned-sleepy eyes, and those straight white teeth smiling and smiling: 'Oh, I don't really know the words. It's just a family thing. Just something stupid we do at parties.'

She thought: *You are stupidly handsome.*

She thought as well: *Addy, be careful. You are too stupidly pissed to judge.*

She wasn't a good judge of anything in any state, she decided on realising that although she stood on the coffee table, he was still eye level with her. How could that be? He hadn't seemed so tall before; had she shrunk, or had he grown?

He asked her: 'How do *you* know the words?'

She didn't tell him she used to sit by the radiogram at home after school, before her father returned from work, playing it over and over again, her brother, Nick, yelling at her: 'Would you turn that fucken thing off, you idiot!' She only told this Dan boy: 'I just like it.'

'Righto.' He chuckled, lighting his spliff.

She stared at him then, swaying a bit more than slightly there on the coffee table, remembering that they really had just sung a good portion of the choral section of the *Ode to Joy* together, in German, or thereabouts; she said, testing the reality: 'Are you German?'

'No.' He took a deep drag and exhaled. 'My grandfather is, sort of.'

She asked, like an idiot: 'Does he drink a lot?'

And Dan laughed fully, a loud, round sound: 'Shit no. He can't sing either. He's just nuts – he's almost ninety-one. He's amazing. I'm named after him, the youngest grandkid, and I don't drink either. I just get fried, a lot. Don't tell him that.'

'I won't,' she replied as though it might be a possibility that she'd meet this grandfather in the next five minutes. She found it amazing that she was talking to someone who didn't drink, and that she hadn't noticed this before, when they'd first met, possibly because she'd been drunk. Indeed, she couldn't recall when exactly they *had* met. She asked him, inside this wonder: 'What's your name?'

'Dan,' he said, with a questioning frown, the sort of frown that suggested surprise that she didn't know his name; he made it plain: 'Daniel Ackerman.'

'Hm,' she said. The name meant nothing to her, but tears sprang, sudden and brimming: drunken tears, yes; tears that this boy had a German grandfather, an *amazing* grandfather – a live grandfather of any kind – and that he was just cool and normal about it; tears that the only grandfather of her own that she knew anything about had been a lawyer, a small-town solicitor, who died when her father was little, before the war, and was nothing more now that a grunt across the dining table, a wordlessly heartbreaking reason to work and work and work harder; tears that she was such a freak by comparison to the boy in front of her – to anyone; and so damn stupidly, embarrassingly drunk.

He said: 'Are you all right, Addy?'

'No,' she said. 'I'm going to sit outside for a little while.' She had to get some fresh air, try to stop the world from spinning, lurching. *Oh, holy frick.*

She jumped down off the coffee table, grabbed a cigarette from Roz's packet there, half squashed from where she'd trodden on it, and then she went out through the kitchen, trying not to stagger too much, feeling like a football tottering for the touch line; she swiped the gas lighter from the stove on the way through, and slumped down on the back step between No Name's dish and the beaming moon, nearing full. The gas lighter was nearing empty, though, and try as she might, she couldn't get that cigarette lit.

'Here.' Dan sat on the ground below her, holding out his lighter, cupping the flame. It was a Zippo flip-top, silver and solid. *So cool.* And the smoke bit into the back of her throat as he said: 'I ... um ...'

She managed to locate and focus on his eyes; they were brown, warm brown, like his hair that now fell across his forehead, a tangled wave; she wanted to brush it from his face, only she'd never done anything like that in her life; instead, she said: 'Um?'

'Yeah.' He looked away, and the light from the kitchen caught the flush of his cheek; he said: 'Ah ...' He looked away at the weed-sown patch of bricks that passed for a yard, and all his shadowed angles – jaw, cheek, knee, boot tip – were a jumbled elegance, a bundle of Apollo's arrowheads at rest.

She thought she'd try for a witty quip at his present inarticulacy: 'You might look like a poet, but you're not much of one, are you.'

'Oof.' He turned to look back at her, sleepy smile pained: 'You don't hold back on an insult, do you.'

'Oh, I didn't mean —' She didn't mean to insult his song-writing, not out aloud. She'd never criticise another's attempts at creative expression so cruelly, no matter how woeful. The chorus of one of Elbow's best examples rang in her ears: 'The stars in her eyes scatter at the graveside of my desires. She cuts me and I bleed her lies.' Awful, but not so awful the author should be punished for it.

He said: 'I know what you meant, Addy.'

Addy. Her name ricocheted around the high tin fence and pounded into her chest; regret stung with whatever other unremembered insults she'd chucked at him the night before last: 'Really, I —'

'Really. I am a shit poet.' He grinned, as if proud of the fact. 'I get fried, very fried, and see what happens, see what crap comes out of my head. But someone's got to do it. I don't think we'd pull much of a crowd if we went instrumental. And if we played covers, you'd find out what bad musicians we are as well.'

'You're honest,' Addy said, impressed, surprised, staring at him, searching for other words herself.

'Best policy,' he said, and then he looked away once more. 'Um …'

Idiot. 'Did I just insult you again?' *He's such a sweet guy and you're a mean bag of spiders, aren't you.*

'No. Hm …' He took another deep drag on his spliff and asked the fence: 'What are you doing on Friday night?'

'Ha!' The thought of what her Friday night would bring eclipsed any understanding that he might have been about to ask her out. 'Friday!' She smacked her knee and dropped the cigarette she'd forgotten all about, anyway: 'On Friday night, I am going to a boxing match, believe it or not.'

'What?' He squinted at the incongruity of the idea.

'Yep.' She nodded, and wished she hadn't: the world sloshed around, bouncing off the inside of her skull; she groped at the words, enunciating slowly: 'I am going to a boxing match and I am going against my will. My father is making me go – and boy oh boy, I don't want to go. But I have to. I have to go and watch my brother beat up some other guy. *Biff. Biff. Biff.*' She pumped little fists at the night. 'I have to catch the bus out to Kingsford, too – that's just as bad. I hardly even know where that is.'

She didn't understand Dan Ackerman's reply at first; he had to say it twice: 'I'll drive you, if you like.'

And that made her tearful again; she had to put her hands flat on the concrete of the step so that she wouldn't fall off it: 'You'd drive me? In your car? You have a *car*? Which you would *drive* me to Kingsford in? You'd do that for *me*?' *How drunk am I? Oh my God, totally rat-arsed.*

'Yeah, of course,' said Dan, still smiling, smiling. *Such a sweet, sweet smile.* 'No worries. It's not far from my parents' place – in Coogee. We could have Chinese at the club – I always take a girl to the classiest places.'

'Really?' She could feel her bottom lip begin to tremble, overwhelmed by his sweetness. 'You'd do that for *me*?'

He laughed, so loud, so free, and she clung to the sound as though it might keep her upright.

She stared at him again, wanting to talk more, wishing her brain wasn't so incapacitated; eventually, she found a question, her least ridiculous uncertainty: 'Are you at uni?'

'Yeah,' he said. 'Electrical engineering. Final year.'

'Get out of town!' She smacked her knee again; she hadn't picked him as science-minded at all; she hadn't paid enough attention to him as a fellow human to imagine much about him at all, apart from being the ghost of John Donne sent to taunt her with the fraying cuffs of his denim jeans. 'Really?'

'Really.' He flicked his spliff end against the back gate and it made a soft *pling* on the corrugated tin. 'Got to get a real job one day. Maybe in a studio or something, if I'm lucky, but working in sound in some kind of way, hopefully.'

She looked at his hands and imagined them twisting and fixing wires: working. He seemed so suddenly real and perfect, she couldn't help letting a simple truth speak for itself: 'That's so beautiful.'

'Beautiful?' His laughter was gentle, querying.

She wasn't sure what she might have just said; she scrambled at the nearest thought that didn't have anything to do with how she might have wanted to kiss him; she attempted to say something that sounded intelligent: 'The way electricity goes down the wires and round and round. It's beautiful. Magical.' *What the frick?*

But he said, 'Yeah, I think it's magic, too.'

Inside the house, at their backs, the music blared, someone turning up the stereo, The Cure plunking and scratching at the night with the song, 'Let's Go to Bed'. Addy could have said, 'Ah, now there's an example of poetry that's just as awful as yours, and they're raking in millions.' But at that moment one of the neighbours stuck his head up over the fence, yelling down at them: 'Turn that fucken music off or I'm calling the cops.'

Fair enough. The people on that side had only moved in a few weeks ago, and they were yuppies – young urban professionals – husband-and-wife actual lawyers who must have wondered what they'd done buying in to Chippendale. Addy sympathised with the man's upset, not that she could move to do anything about it.

'No worries,' said Dan. 'Sorry, mate.'

'I'm not your fucken mate.' The neighbour was beyond annoyed.

But Dan laughed at him: 'Keep your fucken hair on. Mate.' Then he left her and went inside; the music died.

She stood and held onto the door frame for a little while. *What am I doing? Why am I here? I hope the police don't come and find me this wasted.*

You should be locked up. Thrown in the bin. Trash.

She made it as far as the brown couch, where she lay down, curled in a corner of it under the pink paisley bedspread. HRH and Maaaahrtin returned from wherever they'd been; Roz made toasted cheese-and-tomato sandwiches. Addy could have done with a sandwich of any kind, except she was too far past it to eat. She fell into a doze as a pair of deep voices duelled, close by her, arguing about the treasurer's plans for a broad-based consumption tax, Dan Ackerman sounding not very stoned as he said, 'It's an evil idea, hitting those who can least afford it the worst. What does Keating think he's doing? It won't fly.' Addy opened an eye, smiling straight into the back of his head as he sat on the floor, against the seat-edge of the brown couch, his hair curling down around the collar of his shirt, his shoulders broad and ironing-board lean: *He's not a fascist at all, frayed denim or otherwise. Maaahrtin's the fascist. Of course.* Martin Chalmers, HRH's med student, was such a clean-cut, bloodless conservative, he thought universal healthcare was a bridge too far towards communism and the annihilation of western civilisation. She must have got their voices somehow mixed up the other night – they were quite similar in low-note resonance, if not quite the same level of poshness. There it was, mystery solved, more or less.

Order was restored to Addy's understanding of the world now, at least temporarily. It had even stopped lurching about so furiously.

She would remember the drape of her arms around Dan Ackerman's neck as he carried her upstairs.

But she wouldn't remember what happened next; she wouldn't remember a thing.

A POTENTIALLY LIFE-CHANGING DISASTER & OTHER SMALL, EPIC EVENTS

Addy woke in a galloping panic at the usual hour around dawn, wondering where she was, how she got there, and why she was in so much pain. Her head was throbbing, and her stomach was clenched so tightly she thought she'd been stabbed – before she realised this was just a bad hangover and she was, in fact, in her own bed, safe and warm and —

Naked.

Or at least naked from the waist down. She looked under her quilt to see what she was wearing: an oversize yellow-and-white-striped singlet top she only ever wore to the beach, over her swimming cossies. And no underpants. Addy always wore underpants.

What have I done?

She sat up – far too quickly – so that she now felt she'd been stabbed in the head, multiple times. It's never easy to distinguish a natural anxiety from the kind inspired by alcohol abuse, and Addy was as yet naïve to the idea of just how much the latter had begun to hurt her mind, but in this instance she leapt with the full force of both to the worst conclusion possible:

You stupid, stupid slut.

That then catapulted to calculations of time-of-the-month: *Oh my God.* She imagined legions of sperm streaming through her, hunting for their target; she imagined that conception was occurring right this moment, seed spearing the tender little globe of her shame. Disgust and fear pummelled into her.

You stupid, stupid slut.

She scrabbled through her memories of the night before, and all she saw was Dan Ackerman, like flash cards charting her laughable desire for him – from the moment he began making love to his microphone on stage at the Hairy Egg, if she was honest with herself. *Oh my God*: singing *Ode to Joy* in the lounge room – had that really happened? *For fuck's sake, really?* Really. She saw his long fingers rolling another spliff; his beautiful smile; her arms around his neck; his hair brushing the tip of her nose.

She wanted to die. But she had to get up to pee, and the acid sting she felt at doing so seemed only further evidence that she had surely done the deed.

And where was he? This great, sweet guy? Nowhere to be seen. She was just another groupie-whore now, used by the boys in the band, and discarded afterwards without a care.

I'm never drinking again.

Sure.

I mean it this time. I'm never drinking again. This hurts too much.

She went straight back to bed. She had an Aus History lecture at nine-thirty, on Australia's relationship with China, and an Ancient tute after that, on the reign of Nero … she was not going to get to either of them. She was too sick, and too ashamed. She set her alarm clock for twelve forty-five, to wake her up for work – she couldn't miss that. She had to pay her rent, her share of the gas bill; her lay-by on a dress too pretty for an idiot like her to ever wear.

She plummeted back into black sleep along visions of having to confess pregnancy to her father, his angry fist shaking the walls of the house. She would not be a lawyer; she would be a single mother instead.

When the alarm went off – *BLERT, BLERT, BLERT* – she was in the middle of a dream, in stuck-to-the-spot shock that Dan Ackerman was demanding that she pay for his Chinese meal. She was pretty sure that didn't happen last night; nevertheless, she spent a good few minutes hoping she was right about that, for the idea she might have gone to a restaurant in such a blithered state was almost too much to bear.

Her vow returned, and firmer still: *This is not going to happen again.*

A decision was also made, that she wouldn't be getting that lovely garden frock from Newtown, not only because she didn't deserve it, but because she'd have to hold onto as much money as possible so that she could plan for an abortion, if necessary, and in secret – even with the Medicare rebate, the termination itself would cost almost half a week's wage, and she'd no doubt have to take time off work as well. She could see herself in the waiting room of the Women's Clinic, with Mrs Doctor Horn-Rims telling her: 'I told you so.' At least she'd be able to pinpoint precisely when the conception occurred: in the early hours of May 2, 1985: the moment Addy Loest ruined the rest of her miserable life. The day after May Day. *MAYDAY*. She couldn't drag a child down with her. She couldn't disappoint her father with such a terrible load of clichés, either. She would be pragmatic and sensible about this, if nothing else. She would protect her father from this worst of herself.

With her hangover reduced to a dull gungy blear, she showered and changed into her work clothes: a plain blue uniform that zipped up the front, a muted mid-blue that on a man said 'air force', and on a woman said 'tea lady', 'cleaner' or 'lower-order retail'. While she didn't particularly like working at Town Hall Variety, up in the toy department or, on occasion, down on the ground-floor cash registers or stacking shelves in the grocery aisles, she did like going to work. It was the only time she never felt out of her depth or hopeless: she'd go to work, do her job, get paid: it was a simple and dignified transaction. Predictable, mostly. It was also good for her soul to know that in this small corner of humanity she was needed, even if it was only for a price check on a teddy bear – she was necessary. And useful: dusting, straightening the displays, or helping a customer choose a gift for a special little —

Oh fuck, oh fuck, oh fuck, oh fuck, oh fuck.

Stop being hysterical – you know very well that the chances of you being pregnant are statistically negligible. You're just a stupid slut, nothing more, nothing less.

And a hungry one. She went downstairs to put the kettle on, make some toast, ignoring last night's detritus in the lounge on the way: the sticky glasses, empty beer cans, a sad plate offering a hash of sandwich crusts and cigarette butts; there was worse waiting for her in the kitchen, though. As if the uncovered, dried-out slab of cheese wasn't enough, such a waste of good food, with chunks of tomatoes splattered around it like they'd been attacked by a blunt chainsaw, Harriet Rawley-Hogue's food-processor bowl remained on the bench, still unwashed, its hardened globs of hummus glaring at Addy, the pièce de résistance of careless, callous, middle-class contempt.

And there was no bread.

Fuck you. Fuck you all – especially fuck Harriet.

Addy would never be proud of what she did next but would always consider it something unpleasant that simply needed to be done. She opened the cupboard under the sink, put on her rubber gloves; she picked up that food-processor bowl and marched it through the house, up the hall to HRH's bedroom door. She knocked – no answer – and, with a wave of guilt that was no match for the anger pounding over the top of it, Addy entered the regal sanctuary. She'd never crossed its threshold before, not in the whole time they'd lived here, almost a year, only seen it from the door: the four-poster bed sumptuously hung with one decadent length of rose-tinted silk above the head board, the cheval mirror in its gold-dusted frame, the richly carved antique 'armoire' by the window that looked like something from the last days of the Raj. There was a vase of ivory dahlias on the bedside table. There was crisp white linen on the bed. And it was here, between the plump featherdown pillows, that Addy placed the dirty food-processor bowl for HRH to find when she got home. No note required.

You can't leave it there. You're angry with yourself, not HRH.

HRH is a pig, and I am angry with the world.

She slammed the front door as she left the house. Her black sandshoes thundered at the footpath as she made her way along the backstreets towards the city centre. Town Hall was a little over two kilometres distant, but she usually walked it unless it was raining or scorchingly hot; the bus was a slow, hideous press of men in suits and women with wailing strollers this time of day, and the train at Central Station was halfway to her destination, anyway. She was so hungry, so near to eating-her-own-hand starving, that when a newspaper seller whistled at her as she passed through stinking, honking Railway Square, calling after her, 'Helloooo, baby,' she snarled back at him: 'Paedophile.'

Once through the swing doors of Variety, her sandshoes squeaked across the linoleum under the *ka-ching* of the registers and the PA yelling, 'Code 54 to Men's Footwear. Code 54 to Men's Footwear,' as she wove her way among the towering shelves of Confectionary and Stationery towards the escalators. Ascending, she paused there momentarily to think of that Code 54 and the poor bastard who was about to be sprung thieving a pair of shoes he no doubt desperately needed but could not afford: the shoes here were so crap you'd have to be desperate to steal them. She imagined this nameless, faceless man and his story: he needed that pair of woeful polyurethane business shoes for a job interview; to look respectable for his child's christening; for his mother's funeral.

Fuck the lot of you.

With the last of her energy, she prepared to summon a smile for the Pay Office lady, Pearl Piccolino, up on the first floor, at the rear, behind Ladies Underwear. Addy knocked on the closed roller shutter of the window there, knowing she would be spied through its peephole: 'Sorry to pester. Addy Loest here. Is my pay done up, please?' *If I don't get something substantial in my stomach soon, I'm going to pass out.*

'Not done till after two,' came the response.

Fuck you. Addy's shift began at two – in fifteen minutes. 'Please? I'm in genuine need.' *And I've never done this before.* Unlike many of the other student-casuals. She needed a lie; an appeal of hardship would not work with pitiless Pearl; she'd have to come up with something more urgent than mere starvation, so she gave her the most desperate excuse she could think of: 'It's a matter of feminine hygiene.'

'Ew.' She heard Pearl recoil behind the shutter at the idea, but it worked. Up came the drawbridge, and there was Pearl herself: lovely in name and in appearance, her fingernails always impeccably varnished, lipstick to match – today a vivid coral – her hair a cloud of titian ringlets so perfectly permed Addy often wanted to touch them, or snip them into a topiary to make a love heart of her whole head above her fairy-princess pointed chin. That's where any loveliness stopped, however.

'Employee number,' she said, like an android deprogrammed of all personality.

'One zero five nine seven,' Addy replied; she never usually minded reciting it – 10597 was a prime number, and although she'd never found any other concepts of mathematics beyond arithmetic particularly useful or appealing, she found primes mysteriously pleasing, as if their indivisibility by anything other than themselves and one could make her own aloneness slightly less abnormal – but on this occasion she felt like adding: *And would you please hurry up?*

Pearl Piccolino turned to her wooden box of yellow pay envelopes as though tranquilised. *Flick. Flick. Flick.*

For frick's sake – PLEASE! Addy looked at her watch: twelve minutes to two.

Flick. Flick. Flick. 'Here.' Pearl finally smacked Addy's pay onto the counter, and with it the pay book: 'Sign and date.' A coral talon indicated the line, but Addy didn't have a pen. She'd forgotten her pen and the small pocket notebook she always brought with her; how did she forget that? *I am out of control.*

She asked, barely containing her distress now: 'Have you got a —'

'Pen?' Pearl rolled her eyes and turned again, so slowly Addy thought she must be doing this deliberately. How a little power can corrupt so mightily.

Hurry up, you sad cow! Addy imagined Pearl's husband spending long hours at the pub to avoid her; and caught the thought: *Maybe he gives her a hard time, and that's why —* she caught that thought, too: *Oh, who the fuck cares!*

'There.' Pearl smacked a pen on the book.

Addy scribbled as required, grabbed her pay, and back down the escalator she flew. Outside, she fought her way through the heavy traffic against the lights – she'd die for something to eat now; she'd push cars aside; rip sheet metal with her bare hands. But she made it alive and unscathed: to the greasy Joe's takeaway across the road.

'Small hot chips, please.' She rushed at this counter, tearing the pay envelope in her pocket, pulling out a two-dollar note.

'Small hot chips, yeah girlie.' The man at the grill here leered, pervy, a cruel snarl on his lips, shrinking Addy to such a scrap of nothing, she couldn't stop her tears any longer.

She hung her head to hide them; she turned to the fridge behind her and took out a can of orange fizzy. She stood there waiting for her chips, and she cried.

'Cheer up, girlie,' the man said as he took her money; if she hadn't been so crushed, she'd have spat in his eye.

She stood on the footpath and ate her chips there, scalding her mouth as she stuffed them in, to the sounds of a hundred jackhammers refurbishing the derelict Queen Victoria Building on the corner opposite, the great big statue of that HRH there looking unamused. Addy told her: *I hate this place, too.*

I want to go home, to Gallipoli Street, to Dad. To safety.

I want to grow up again, undo whatever mistake I made – the mistake that made me this way. So confused. What did I do?

She wouldn't answer that question soon: it was two minutes to two; she chucked the remains of the chips in the nearest bin, glugged down the fizzy and ran back across the road; composed herself on the escalators up and up to the second floor.

Maybe it's just me. I'm just a freaky fuck-up, and this is just the way I'm meant to be.

'Hi, Addy love.' There was Cheryl, her floor manager: plump and motherly and with a melancholic, resigned cheerfulness that recent immigrants from northern England seemed so often to possess. 'How are you going?'

It was all Addy could do not to run to her bosom; she straightened her back, tightened her ponytail, and said: 'Great! Thanks!' *Wunderbar.*

Eight o'clock marked the start of ghost-ship hour in the toy department of Town Hall Variety. Cheryl, like the rest of the full-time day staff, had knocked off at five, leaving Addy on her own, apart from Kevin over in Electricals, who didn't have much conversation beyond the features of the latest Walkman headset or multi-cassette deck ghetto blaster; and apart from the night manager, Slavenka, who roamed across all three levels of the store hunting for malingerers, her square jaw and eagle eyes promising a spell in an Eastern Bloc re-education facility for anyone caught at a lazy smoke or idle chitchat. Slavenka Markovic was friendly to no one – except Addy.

'Hello, darlink.' She waved now from the top of the escalator, keys clinking from her belt as she walked. 'How has it been tonight?'

'Oh?' Addy closed the stock book she'd had open on the shelf between rows of army combat and superhero dolls she'd been pretending to be checking; she'd really been scratching down some thoughts in the new pocket notebook she'd bought on her tea break, writing and rewriting a few lines of her own awful poetry: *I am a sightless bird tossed between slipstreams, burned by the blue, too huge and too tiny.* It had seemed somehow a plagiary of something, naggingly derivative somehow, as well as stupid. Pointless. She smiled wearily at Slavenka: 'It's been very quiet.'

Other than practising bad verse, she'd been thinking how odd it was that she'd studied only English or American poets when she'd never been to England or America, and maybe hadn't even visited those countries genetically by any ancestral tour. Would she write better in German, if she could try? She'd made a note to read some Goethe or Schiller, do her own extracurricular compare and contrast; then her thoughts had loitered back to John Donne, anyway, to how universal his words seemed, themes of love and death, the beauty and terror of atom-stretching change; transformation. She wanted to transform into something, anything, yet she wondered, deeper still, if perhaps her DNA, her cells, all our cells, were somehow marked, fixed, not only by the material of heredity, but by time, and memory, and ... wisps of a larger thought she couldn't quite grasp.

Slavenka nodded, and said in her no-bullshit, no-prisoners way: 'You look tired. You have been studying hard, hm?'

'Hm.' Addy nodded. Studying was one word for it; life-wasting was another. She only needed to look at the traces of tired disappointment in Slavenka's own eyes to be reminded that life was not meant to be wasted. Slavenka was actually an industrial chemist. She'd been a leading researcher for a pharmaceutical company in Dubrovnik, until her husband, a physicist moonlighting as a Croatian separatist agitating for independence from Soviet Yugoslavia, had got them into such political hot water, they'd had to flee. Once here, though, her qualifications weren't recognised – which was why she was roaming the ghost ship of Town Hall Variety these days, while her husband drove a taxi, because 'Croatian physicist' sounded too much like 'Commie terrorist' to the white-bread Australian ear. Addy wasn't going to disappoint Slavenka further with any of her own petty truths, so she gave her the easiest lie now: 'I think I'm getting a cold.'

Slavenka clicked her tongue: 'You are probably not eating well. Have you had any fruit today?'

Addy shook her head and said facetiously: 'Not unless you include the orange fizzy I had for lunch.'

'Ah!' Slavenka clutched her heart: 'That stuff is chemical weapon. Nazis invented the recipe to make all the people mad, America buys company then and sells it to the whole world. Don't drink it.'

Addy felt a small, warm smile curling on her lips, not only for Slavenka's jagged-edged joke, but because she was the only person Addy knew who seemed to be able to say the word 'Nazi' without suggesting every German dead or alive was to blame for them and their evils. Addy hated that word, every time she heard it; she hated it because it upset her dad, this word, 'Nazi', that was forbidden from being spoken in his presence, although she didn't know the precise details of why, or what they might have done to him personally, apart from ruin his childhood. She seemed to know more concrete facts about Slavenka's history from their fleeting chats than she did her own father's. She wished she could tell her something of all she was feeling now; talk to an older woman who knew life was complicated. She had so many questions, she didn't know where to start. How could she begin to ask what she most wanted to know: *Who am I?*

Whatever, Slavenka was on her way now, no time for further chat tonight. 'You go and buy some fruit at Grocery before closing,' she instructed with a brusque do-as-you're-told nod. 'I won't notice if you leave five minutes early.'

'Thank you,' Addy said as she watched her disappear behind the bank of toasters and electric kettles that flanked the far side of the escalators. She would do as she was told; she'd certainly purchase a couple of bananas tonight – she could feel her body pleading for the nutrition – but what she was really hankering for was a large fried rice from Mr Lim's, the Chinese takeaway on Broadway, which she'd pick up on her way home, and wash down with a bucket of orange fizzy. Her hangover had mostly dissipated now except for this craving for sugar, salt and fat; she'd treat herself to a family block of peppermint chocolate, too. She'd probably eat the whole thing, and that pre-emptive shame brought a bucket of self-disgust with it. She seemed to be made of shame and self-disgust, secrets and dead ends. She caught a glimpse of herself home alone at Flower Street, loading her Kraftwerk cassette tape into the stereo, crouching forward, pressing 'play' and 'rewind' and 'play' again, not only because the moody experimental Krautrock was cool – she'd listen to Nena's new wave '99 Luftballons' just as intently, inwardly, covertly – but because she was —

Oh.

Suddenly breathless, her chest tightened; her lungs ached as if she'd been running uphill, as if she'd been thumped from behind. She clutched at the shelf beside her, to steady herself. *This is only an unfunny turn*, she was sure she recognised the sensation. *There's nothing wrong with me. I can breathe*, she told herself. *I can breathe.* Oh, but how it hurt; how the ground beneath her seemed to warp and heave. She knocked one of the combat soldiers off its row with her elbow, and the plastic box containing him thwacked onto the lino with such a force she seemed to hear it through her bones.

A phone rang somewhere, over in Electricals; a woman in a tan raincoat stood at the central display of plush toys, inspecting a blue gnome – one of the most expensive and the most pointless, its popularity was as inexplicable as Addy's condition, and should have come with a label declaring it a harbinger for the End of Days. She tried to focus on the woman and the gnome, to still the tide of panic, but just as she was beginning to calm, the piped music sent her the first tinkle-tankling guitar bars of Simon & Garfunkel's 'The Boxer'. Normally, this was a song she liked for its simple, proletarian elegance, one which could even make her feel a fondness for her brother; now, it only brought her a reminder of tomorrow's match and a foggy recollection of having mentioned it to Dan Ackerman last night. *Why would I have done that?* Questions swarmed and images flickered. *Why was I dancing on the coffee table?*

She wanted to be sick.

'Hi, Addy.'

She turned, and it was him. It was Dan Ackerman. Of course, she didn't believe it at first, preferring to think him a figment of post-alcoholic psychosis – rather than have to face him.

She blinked, but he remained: Dan Ackerman. He was wearing grey overalls, and he was holding a box of fuzzy-felt, the circus set with the prancing horse, ballerina pirouetting on its back, none of which made any more sense.

He laughed: 'Sorry. Didn't mean to spring on you like that.'

'Oh? That's all right,' she replied, defaulting to polite, obliging, still not trusting he was real.

He explained: 'I've just finished work – at my uncle Evan's factory, over in Beaconsfield. He makes gates and railings, you know, fancy ones. I sweep the floor, do as I'm told and all that. One of my nieces is turning three next week and I nearly forgot to get her a birthday present. She's in Brisbane. I'll have to post it tomorrow.' He held up the box of fuzzy-felt. His knuckles were grimy. He was tall, taller in work boots, she smaller in her sandshoes, yet she didn't feel small in front of him. He was far too perfect to be real. He added: 'But I … um … I just … you know.' He laughed softly again, at himself: 'I just wanted to say hi.'

You are the most beautiful man I've ever met.

He said: 'And also, to see what time you need me to get you to Souths Juniors tomorrow night, for your brother's fight – that is, if you still want me to pick you up. Or whatever …' His smile lost all certainty; he frowned as though he might have got this all wrong.

And well he might, for Addy was only just cottoning on that she'd accepted Dan's offer of a lift – and a Chinese meal, at the club. How this had come about was no longer relevant; she wasn't going to put him off now: despite every complication, real and imagined, around any and all further interactions with Dan, Addy did not want to catch the bus out to Kingsford, at night, on her own: it was only six or so kilometres away, but it was a foreign country to her.

'Yes,' she said quickly. 'Thank you. I'd really appreciate it.' That's not what she'd meant to say, or how she meant to say it – like he was a taxi driver offering to help with her shopping bags. She offered him the best thing she could: a bit of honesty: 'I'm so sorry to sound like such a flake. As I'm sure you noticed, I got very drunk last night.' *Slut.* 'I'm not feeling so good this evening.'

'I bet.' His smile returned. It was the smile of a boy who wrote earnest, dope-fuelled love-rubbish; and it was as perfect as the rest of him. He said: 'I'm no one to judge. I smoke too much. I get nervous all the time, especially before a gig – love the music, hate performing – before I know it, I'm having a smoke every time I have to get out the door. It's not good. But I promise you, I'm not stoned right now.' He grinned; it went straight to her knees; he said: 'I'm going to give it away. Seriously. Did you hear, there was a massive bust at the Jay Club last night?' The Jay Club was Sydney Uni's marijuana club, where the coolest of the cool hung out collectively growing their hair in lieu of doing anything socially useful. She shook her head; he explained further: 'Seventy arrests – my usual dealer was one of them. Much as I love a smoke, I don't want a criminal record. Dad would kill me – for all kinds of reasons. He's a doctor, and dirty on any of that stuff. And my grandfather – well, it'd kill him. The cops were pretty heavy-handed, and I don't really blame them. If I was a cop, I might want to give some of those wankers at Jay a bit of a hard time myself. Anyway, all I mean is that I'm not stoned now, and I won't be tomorrow night, either.'

She didn't know what to say to that; it didn't seem her business whether he smoked dope or not. She was sure, absolutely sure, that her own wrongdoings were far more deplorable. He was a doctor's son, a beloved grandson, a young prince of the world of men; she was no one; she said: 'And I'll try very hard not to behave like a whore on turps.'

She'd hoped he'd find the quip witty; he didn't. He frowned: 'Um …'

She tried to make it better: 'Apologies for anything and everything I did last night that was inappropriate.' *And which might yet be leading to consequences neither of us is prepared for.*

He said: 'It's not a crime to get drunk, Addy. It's not good for you, and it's not my thing, but it's not a hanging offence.'

'I know. I don't mean that.' She felt her face flush, but she had to say it straight, get the words out in the air. 'I mean whatever happened in the bedroom.'

He looked quite plainly horrified at what she was suggesting; he paused for a moment, a long moment, before saying it straight himself: 'I carried you up to your bed. You were asleep, mumbling something about the Industrial Revolution. Roz came with me – to help you get undressed. I left her to it. I went home. I might be many things, but rapist isn't one of them.'

'I didn't mean —' *Oh, can I manage a conversation without insulting him?*

'Yeah, I know you didn't mean that,' he said, and so gently. 'But that's what it would mean. And I'm not like that. Never.'

'Okay.' *Wow. How much of a shitbag can I be?* 'I'm sorry.'

'Don't be sorry, please.' He tilted his head. *How impossibly lovely can you be?* 'What time do you want me to pick you up tomorrow?'

'Time?' Time. The fight was scheduled to begin at seven thirty; if they were going to eat before it, then they should allow half an hour for that, plus, say, fifteen minutes in case of any delay with the meal; then there was travel time from Chippendale to Kingsford – maybe allow twenty minutes, at least, to account for Friday-evening traffic. She was usually quick at this kind of everyday arithmetic, but it seemed to take her half of forever to work it out. *What's twenty minutes plus thirty minutes plus fifteen? Sixty-five? What is sixty-five minutes? Are you fricken demented? Yes. An hour and five – let's call it an hour and fifteen, to be safe.* 'Um. Six-fifteen?'

'Six-fifteen it is.' That smile, that squinted smile, was like something from a real-man, can-cracking beer commercial. She half expected him to wink; he didn't. *Don't think about beer. He doesn't drink beer. You're not having a beer tonight. You're not having a beer ever again.* He said: 'Do you need a lift home tonight? What time do you knock off?'

'Oh.' *What? No!* This was too much. 'No. Thank you.'

'It's raining outside,' he said, in a way that suggested he'd considered she might not have been aware of the fact, stuck as she was up here in a windowless discount variety box. 'I'm happy to wait until you finish.'

'Wait?' *NO! PLEASE! FREAK! I just want to get my chocolate and my fried rice and be alone.* 'I don't want to put you out.'

'You wouldn't be putting me out.' His warm, dark eyes were laughing, loving, generous: *so beautiful. WHAT?* 'You know I only live up the road, not even five minutes from you, Shepherd Street – stumbling distance from the engineering buildings, too.' Although she knew the street he was referring to, he might as well have said he lived on Jupiter. 'But I don't want you to think I'm a creep, so I should cut my losses now and see you tomorrow, yeah?'

'Yeah.' *FUCK! WHAT?* 'No. Creep? I wouldn't think you were —'

'But hey, what's your phone number there at Flower Street?' he asked, words racing over and into her own. 'In case I'm held up or I get kidnapped by a gang of ninja koalas or something.'

Who are you? She was too stupefied to laugh.

He'd made a sensible request, however; she should respond to it sensibly. She turned to the shelf behind her and opened the stock book, retrieving her own little book from it, flipping past the pages of her scribblings with her well-practised secrecy. She wrote:

Addy Loest – 318 0407

Another prime number and one she liked the look of, except for the way she often slightly misjudged the second 0 so that it could have been mistaken for a 6; this one was all right, though. Her pen hovered by the number, wanting to add more, leave more, a smiley or —

Just give it to him.

She tore off the page and handed it over, and the warmth in those warm, dark, thoughtful eyes of his was something a bit criminally lovely as he took it, folding it into the hip pocket of his overalls, confessing: 'It's pretty creepy that I stole the note you wrote the other day, the one you left on the piano, and then I followed you, up to Newtown. That was a bit nuts, sorry. But you know … I just … you know. Now I've got two – of your notes, I mean.' He shook his head at himself, laughing and not laughing at all; he was awkward, boyish: sincere. 'I should go before I make a complete goose of myself. If you're not at home tomorrow night, that's cool, I'll understand. I – yeah. See ya.'

Some heartstring seemed to slip from her after him as he walked away, some glimpse of something golden. She watched him disappear down the escalator, glancing back at her once, a small wave with the box of fuzzy-felt; and she apologised again, silently: *You are way too beautiful for me.* She picked up the combat soldier that had fallen to the floor, and she put him back on the shelf.

'Good evening, my young friend,' Mr Lim greeted her as she stepped into his small, bright takeaway. 'Large fried rice for you?'

'Yes, please.' Addy smiled the smile of nearly fried rice, nearly home; it no longer mattered that she was exhausted and freezing from the rain and the gale-force wind outside.

Mr Lim shouted through the kitchen hatch to his invisible cook, words she couldn't understand but which were part of the comforting ritual as well.

He turned back to her, and then shouted again on seeing her more clearly: 'Look at you – you are all wet! It's a cold night, you wait by the fire.' He pointed at the large radiator on the floor beside the counter, behind the two tables that comprised the eat-in option. 'You get warm – here, here, get warm.'

She did as she was told, sitting down on the chair nearest the radiator, careful to keep her shopping bag full of chocolate and bananas and fizzy away from the heat, and while she waited, he told her about his two sons, as he always did if it was quiet like this, one of them having almost finished medicine, the other just begun; he said: 'You make your father very proud, too, yes?'

'I try,' she lied, but still she smiled.

Mr Lim brought her order over to her, in its blue-and-white-striped plastic bag; he said: 'Here, you have some chicken soup tonight with your rice. From one father to another. Don't tell anyone I give to you for free.'

'Thank you,' Addy told him, with the instant happiness that only another's true good wishes can ever bring. 'I'll be warm for a week on your kindness alone.'

She was already toasty warm, warmer than she'd ever been. She was falling in love, for the very first time. In love with a boy called Dan Ackerman. She melted now every time that heartstring wrote his name across the vast page of sky that was her soul.

But through every beautiful feeling, every new hope and dream, an evil whispered steadily: *You're not good enough, Addy Loest. You're not good enough for him.*

LOOSE BALLOONS &
THE TELLING OF UNTOLD TALES

Happiness is never whole, ever tinged as it is with longing, or sadness, or worry of some kind, and only more so as time goes by, but the following morning, that Friday morning, Addy was as contented as it was possible for a semi-permanently distraught almost twenty-year-old to be. She even slept in a bit. She didn't even panic when her internal clock screamed: *You have a Dispute Resolution lecture at nine!* Because she was no longer a law student. And that was fine. Or it would be, once she found the courage to tell her father, and today she felt capable of even that, sort of.

No Name stretched in a patch of milky sun behind her knees, and she imagined Dan Ackerman, one day, there, somewhere, possibly not behind her knees, but in that general space. At her back. *With* her.

And now it's time to get up. She rose quickly, leaving that thought there in the bed; she'd never actually had sex sober, except once, sort of, and she could never let herself think about that. It was too awful, the unsafest place she knew. She also knew Dan Ackerman wasn't like that. She knew he was a person of genuine tenderness, as though she could smell it and touch it, but the thought of any intimacy was still too overwhelming. Too difficult.

She luxuriated in a long, long shower instead, uncaring of the water usage, thinking about the day ahead. Fridays used to be a mad squeeze of most of her law subjects; now, she realised, she'd be able to take on an extra shift at Town Hall Variety; she could start to put some money away, save for a plane ticket. Everyone was saving for a plane ticket, but she had no yearning to follow the pack – to London or Los Angeles or Paris or Jaipur. She wanted to go to Berlin: she could see her little desk by a window overlooking the River Spree, writing and writing and writing there, like Brecht or Kafka, even Mark Twain. But would it be too sad today, she wondered, with half of its city patrolled by Stasi death squads, trapped beyond the Iron Curtain, and all its old grandeur pocked with bomb craters? Would it be too sad for words? She knew the town in which her father had been born was not far from Frankfurt, but Frankfurt had been bombed to smithereens. She knew the town he was from was called Lindenfels – and that was just about the extent of the information she had eked from him, when she'd lied about the faculty of law needing his place of birth on record when she'd first enrolled at uni. She knew where Lindenfels was in every geographical sense, from maps she'd looked at, but she didn't know what she might see there today, if she could go there. To Germany. Deutschland. *Das Land der Dichter und Denker,* land of poets and thinkers. Was that where she belonged? Would her father be too sad if she left to go and look?

'No – I will not allow it.' She could hear him forbidding her from mentioning it again, as if the very thought was cursed.

She sighed: *I'll just go to London, then. Sneak across while I'm there. He'll never know.*

And it wasn't a possibility that could eventuate anytime soon: it would take her at least a year to save the fare. Less the twenty-four dollars left on the lay-by for that garden frock. She smiled from the inside out at that thought, for a new frock was as good as a holiday – especially a new old frock like that one. This was what she would be doing today, primarily: putting another six dollars down on that masterpiece of tulle and applique, and then probably spending the rest of it worrying about what to wear that night, to the boxing —

Don't spoil the morning with all that.
Don't spoil the morning with anything at all.

'I can't work you out sometimes, Addy.' Roz was standing at the kitchen bench plastering a piece of toast with raspberry jam, and Addy was standing at the kitchen door in not a small amount of astonishment. The whole kitchen was as spotless as could be; when she'd crept in last night with her plastic bags full of comfort, she'd not turned on the lights before grabbing a fork and spoon from the drawer and skulking dozily up the stairs to her room, but now, here was the fruit of her anger and resentment, the sweet and the bitter, Roz telling her: 'Harriet's making noises about moving out, and you know what a pain that would be – she owns more than that food processor. The TV, the stereo – the cutlery. Why couldn't you have just talked to her?'

The echo of Harriet's dismissive laughter returned, her condescending disbelief that Addy should have any ambition to be a writer; and so Addy could only shrug at Roz with the most basic defence: 'Harriet and I don't speak the same language.'

Roz replied with a heavy, both-sides sigh, those creamy crests of her bosom spilling over the cups of her black bustier – the costume of her Fridays and Saturdays, her days of hard labour at a theatre restaurant called Fancy That, playing a bawdy wench, where the tips alone sometimes paid her rent. A penny dropped for Addy here, though: no matter what costume Roz put on, no matter her company or her circumstance, she knew who she was: she was a suburban girl with the world at her feet; she wasn't especially pretty or clever, but her zest, her embrace of all life through thick and thin and every weather in between, made her far more than merely attractive. She was the kind of girl other girls wanted to be: confident. Even her heritage was forthright, cheerful and clear: her parents were modest yet irrepressibly hopeful shopkeepers, with a hardware store at Miranda Fair shopping centre, having emigrated here from Devon when she was three, wanting to raise their children under a brighter sun. Roz Watkins was an English rose – she was, in fact, a bawdy wench.

She said to Addy along the tail-end of that sigh: 'I'm worried about you.'

'Worried about me?' Addy prickled with all her own complexity; she didn't like to worry anyone, and she was determined not to worry about it herself. *Not this morning, please.*

'Yes,' Roz said, cutting her toast straight down the middle. 'You're like a balloon cut loose at the moment, and I don't know how to yank you back.'

'I'm all right.' Addy prickled only more: *Do you need further instruction on why you should never drink again?* She still couldn't remember Roz helping her undress the night before last; Roz would have been drunk, too, drunk and speeding like a bicycle without a chain, but she was never drunk the way Addy got drunk. Roz only ever enhanced who she always was; while Addy – what had she been doing? Only replacing one confusion with another – one that was, at least temporarily, a little less awful.

'Guh.' Roz waved away bad feeling as though it were a blowfly. 'Not for me to be yanking anyone anywhere, unless they'd like a taste of my own mayhem. I just want you to know that if you need to talk, you can talk to me. You know I love you, Addles.'

'Aw.' There was a blast of brightest sunshine. 'I love you too, Rozzie. I'm sorry I'm such a freak.'

'We're all freaks.' Roz rolled her eyes and bit into her toast: 'Nothing too special about you, Loose Balloon. Except …' She chewed and Addy moved towards the teabag tin by the stove. 'Dolly Ackerman is full-on mad for you.'

Sunshine glittered up the back of Addy's neck and through her hair; she hid her smile in her armpit, reaching into the cupboard for a mug. *He's not 'Dolly' to me*, she held the thought so close, she was cheek to cheek with it: *He's Dan. Dan the Man. The beautiful man who came to see me at work, after his work, came to buy fuzzy-felt for his niece.*

'Try not to break his heart, won't you?' Roz said over another mouthful.

'I'm no heartbreaker.' Addy filled the old stovetop kettle; she filled her head with the cool rush of the tap water whooshing around inside the steel.

'Ha!' Roz snorted. 'Don't mention that to Luke. I've heard he's no happy chappy at his newfound freedom – crushed since you broke up with him.'

'Crushed? Come on, Roz.' Addy wasn't buying any of that. *Just kids doing kids' stuff*, that's what he'd said. *No one got hurt, hey?* 'We weren't really ever on. Not seriously. He hardly seemed devastated by the breakup.'

'Yeah, well.' Roz shrugged. 'How someone seems and how someone is can be two different things. And it takes two people to have a relationship, you know – you don't get to decide what the other person feels.'

The wisdom of that struck Addy: how very true it was. It was also perfectly reasonable that he'd said one thing to her, to save face, and another thing to some friend. *Don't we all do that all the time?* She also realised she still hadn't washed and dispatched Luke's jumper; she would do that this afternoon; she would send it off with a kind and loving note; not too loving. Just kind. The thought that she might actually have hurt him — *Oh*. It didn't seem possible but — *Oh*.

'And that extends to HRH, Addles.' Roz returned to the central concern of this kitchen-sink chat: 'She's been having a hard time the past few weeks herself – Maaahrtin's got an offer to do some graduate exchange thing at Haaahrvard for next year, and he's going. Who wouldn't? But he told Harriet – just over Easter, at dinner with her parents – that any plans for them getting engaged would be delayed indefinitely. And then last night – whammo – he says to her that he wants to be free to "explore other options" while he's away. How brutal is that? Selfish shit of a man. Yes, yes, I can say, boohoo, good riddance, get another one. She's really suffering, though, Add. It's all relative, hey? She can't help who she is. Do something nice for her, will you?'

Addy knew this was about more than Roz not wanting the hassle of Harriet moving out; this was about not being a selfish shit. For all that Addy had her reasons to despise HRH, for all that HRH had deserved and would always deserve that dirty food-processor bowl in her bed, the one German thing Addy could never do was Schadenfreude. She could never take any pleasure from someone else's upset. She'd get Harriet a bunch of nice, apologetic sunflowers or something on her way back from Newtown today; she'd make peace; she'd move on.

More than a promise, she felt something shift within her as she strode up to King Street, a lightness in her feet, an unusual clarity of mind. As she passed those tatty band posters along the hoarding of the building site, she might have blown them and all the hard-hats beyond them a kiss, if she'd been that kind of girl. Instead, she thrilled at the idea that the next time she'd see Elbow, she really would hear Dan's songs sober for the very first time.

How romantic! She laughed at herself, out aloud, and the sky seemed to laugh back at her, with her, from today's crisp, cold blue.

Small steps were required, she knew; small, careful steps were needed before she could even imagine kissing him without the assistance of alcohol; but by the time Addy got to The Curiosity Shop, she had already rented them a cheap apartment in West Berlin and gone shopping for bread and milk. He'd go travelling with her, wouldn't he? Of course he would. She would spend her days writing; he would spend his days being an amazing sound engineer for the Berliner Philharmoniker, and in the evenings, he would come home to their flat and read her words back to her, cherishing every one of them. They would make music that no one had ever heard before. And then … And then everything would be unimaginably perfect. She almost waved an assurance of this at Mr Olympia Café, sweeping the front step of his shop; she almost ran across the road, as though she ran towards this destiny, and not from the onrush of a westbound bus.

She could have sworn the zebra winked as she approached. She was so excited, so ordinarily, justifiably excited, that it didn't even really trouble her that the lay-by receipt for frock heaven had seemed to have disappeared from her purse, sometime since Wednesday morning, about a thousand years ago. The old woman in the shop would remember her – hopefully. *Hm.* Addy remembered only now that the woman had been a little doddery, having got her name wrong – writing Anna on the receipt, instead of Adrianna. *Never mind. It doesn't matter*, Addy told herself, feeling so capable it was uncanny: *We will work it out.*

As it was, the woman appeared to recognise her immediately. 'Ah. Good morning,' she said, from her perch behind the jewellery-display case, closing her magazine to do business. There was, however, a wariness in her clear, sharp gaze as she added, unsmiling, 'You are looking very pretty today.'

Addy looked down at her happy-morning outfit: she wore a white ruffled broderie blouse sashed with a red scarf over a soft grey peasant skirt. She'd thought it romantic; present second thought suggested she probably looked like a reject from a Duran Duran video clip, dismissed for boring hair. She felt suddenly untidy under the old woman's stare; she felt as if this woman could see that she was only ever playing dress-ups, bereft of her own style. But Addy said, 'Thank you,' nevertheless, and after another stretch of strangely loaded silence, she added: 'I've come to pay some more off my lay-by. Please.'

'Yes. Of course.' The woman turned to pick up the ledger book on the little chest of drawers behind her, but she didn't open it when she placed it on the glass top of the display case in front of her. She held one hand, her left hand, upon the cover of the book, as though to keep it there, prevent it from floating away. Stories drifted around them like slow motes from every curio in the shop, from its shoes and chandeliers, its tiffany panes and the zebra's mane, the books and bric-a-brac, its racks and racks of clothes; Addy glimpsed a real romance in the woman's plain gold wedding band; real style in the set of her hair, the cut of her collar and the fabric there – dark green today with a faint turquoise check – pinned mid-lapel with a brooch, an abstract splash of pearl and marcasite. The woman was a study in dignity and grace; dread whispered at the edges of all Addy's wonder, for how she might have displeased her.

The woman seemed to take her own deep breath before she spoke again at last, asking Addy: 'Is your father's name Peter?'

'What – I beg your pardon?' Addy wasn't sure if she'd heard her correctly, if her accent hadn't tricked —

'Your father,' the woman repeated her question. 'Is his name Peter Loest?'

'Yes.' Addy's heart raced with excitement of a different kind, another new kind: no one knew her father, not outside his small circles of steelworks, union, pub and boxing ring. He didn't have any German friends, apart from Beethoven, not close friends, or not that she knew of; his mates were Dutch, Hungarian, Italian, Yugoslav, Polish, British all-sorts and general, white-bread Aussie; he never went to the German Club at Wollongong, either, said it reminded him too much of happy times when he was young, going to dances there – presumably with Elke, her mother. Addy could hardly believe she was asking the question in return: 'You know my father?'

The woman shook her head slightly: 'No.' She reached behind her into one of the drawers, taking out an ashtray and a packet of cigarettes, and with her face still turned away, she said: 'I knew your grandmother, Anna, and – well, that was a long time ago. I have not seen your father since he was a small boy. He is well, your father?'

He is an overworked, overbearing stressed-out chain-smoker, was the description that came to mind, swirling around and into the coiled chignon on the back of the old woman's head, but Addy nodded: 'Yes.' *You knew my grandmother?* Addy was too awed by that idea to say another word.

The old woman seemed somehow stricken as well; she lit a cigarette, and then turned to Addy once more, offering the packet to her with a nod, but Addy shook her head.

The woman took a deep draw on the cigarette and said, exhaling: 'You look a little bit like her – Anna – your grandmother.'

Addy remained mute at that, too; she'd always thought she resembled her own mother, and that was that, from those few photographs she had; there were no photographs of anyone from her father's side, nor her mother's. Life had begun for the Loests at Balgownie Migrant Workers Hostel, and that was that.

'Do you know much about your grandmother, your father's mother?' the old woman asked her, cautious at the question.

Addy shook her head. She hadn't even known this grand-mother's name – nor any of her grandparents' names. All she knew was that her father had been born in 1935 and had been orphaned – his father dying just before the war, and his mother during, and her father said he couldn't remember either of them. He spent his childhood in an orphanage, too young for too much Sieg Heiling – a bitter joke told to snip off any further inquiry. After the war, by the age of fourteen, he was on his own, digging latrines in a displaced persons' camp waiting for a ship out of there – anywhere. America, Canada and Australia, the only options, wanted children under seven or young men as labourers; or, for obvious reasons, Jews who couldn't or wouldn't return to their homes; he'd had to wait another four years, and then took the first ticket on offer – Australia wanted lots of ditch-diggers for the Snowy Mountains Hydro-Electric Scheme, but when he got here, a recruitment officer from the steelworks bagsed him first.

He was strong, thick muscled – still was – though never as strong as Nick, because of his years of malnutrition. That was all she knew of his Germany; a brief, fragmented chapter of a thousand sorrows; a story of how precarious life could be, even for a small-town solicitor's boy. Addy told the old woman: 'I only know my grandfather was a lawyer, from Lindenfels.'

The old woman looked as if she might choke on that cigarette; she swallowed hard; her voice rasped: 'A lawyer from Lindenfels?'

'Yes.' Dread now rocketed through Addy as she waited to be told her grandfather was really an SS officer, on the run for war crimes; she didn't want to know; she wanted to turn around and run away herself.

But when the woman asked her: 'Would you like to know about your grandparents?'

Addy could only nod once more and whisper: 'Yes. Please.'

Whatever the woman was going to say, it would be her own story that Addy would hear, one answer to the everywhere, every-moment question that sat in the centre of her heart like an empty room: *Who am I?*

The woman got up from behind the display case to shut the shop door, turning the 'closed' sign around. She said: 'I think we had better sit down together, dear.' She picked up her ashtray and cigarettes and beckoned with a jut of her chin: 'Come.'

Addy followed her down through the shop, past the shelves of shoes and handbags, to a tapestry chair, its faded zigzag pattern making it almost invisible there between the colourful racks of skirts and blouses. 'Sit down, sit down,' the woman told her, disappearing behind a bookcase Addy hadn't noticed before, either, one filled with encyclopaedias and other weighty-looking hardcovers. When the woman came back a moment later, she was carrying her stepladder, unfolding it as she approached, and appeared to be about to sit down on it herself.

'No – please.' Addy stood. She couldn't take the comfortable chair ahead of an elder.

'Sit,' this elder insisted.

Addy sat, and the woman sat too, even managing to make her stepladder seem stylish, knees to the side over the pointed toes of her shoes; and so she began:

'You look quite a lot like her, really, your grandmother – your colouring, the gold tint of your skin, your small frame. Your grandmother was like a sister to me, a little bit older. And you are probably wondering who I am, hm?'

Naturally, Addy was, but she could not so much as nod to indicate it.

The old woman explained, mostly to her cigarette: 'My name is Frieda Stevenson – that's who I am now, a grandmother myself. Then, when I was young, I was Elfriede Falke – Elfie. Your grandmother was Anna Engel. We were Elf and Angel – she was the good one, I was the bad one. We were inseparable. Our fathers were partners in a law firm in Darmstadt, which, if you don't know, is a city not far from Frankfurt.'

Addy knew precisely where Darmstadt was, having pored over the map of Germany in her *Jumbo Family Reference World Atlas*, among others, so many times the locations of most major towns and cities were imprinted on her retina, but still she did not move to nod; she did not want to move in case this woman, this Frieda Stevenson, stopped talking.

She went on: 'Your grandfather, Adam – Adam Loest – came to work at the firm as a clerk, in 1922, after the first war. I was only a little girl in plaits, thirteen years old, but Anna was sixteen – and she fell in love with him instantly. He was much older, about twenty-four or twenty-five – a *man* to me – and he had been a soldier in the war. Of course, it was a war that Germany had just lost. It wasn't a good time for many. There were a lot of angry men in the streets, gangs and fighting, that sort of thing. There were food shortages and not enough jobs, and much confusion about how to fix things. Your grandfather had been much more fortunate than most. He was from an ordinary family, from Lindenfels, yes, a small town, not far from Darmstadt, and his father was only a saddle-maker, no one in particular, but Adam had distinguished himself in the army, as brave and very intelligent, and so he had been given the chance to better himself.'

The old woman ashed her cigarette as carefully as she delivered every word, continuing: 'Adam and Anna were completely in love with each other – so much that I wanted to push him under a train. I was so jealous, such a silly child.' She gave a little shudder of regret at the memory. 'Anna's parents felt even less happy about it. They were, to say the least, quite snobbish, and did not think Adam was a suitable husband at all. Adam had to work very hard to win them over, and even so, it took him almost ten years. He was under the nose of his would-be father-in-law every day, and still he managed to hide his true colours. Most of the firm's clients were factory owners and other kinds of businessmen, and Adam would spend all day working for them, then in the evenings, at a café near his apartment, he would go and have his meal and give free legal advice to poor men who needed it. Not even Anna knew what a good man he was, not then.

'It was only after they married, in 1931, that Adam confessed to her he was a member of the SPD – the Social-Democratic Party of Deutschland. Anna was terrified of anything political. Anyone who was comfortable was terrified of anything political. Just as things had started to get a little better, the Great Depression then destroyed any peace – destroyed the economy, destroyed everything. The whole country was a ship with no rudder. It felt like anything could happen. But that was also why Adam refused to give up his work with the SPD. He wanted a better future for everyone – where the men who had sacrificed so much for their country as soldiers would be rewarded with good jobs and good wages, education and opportunities for advancement. He presented himself as proof of this logic – a simple case of justice and quiet perseverance.

'He wasn't any radical, not at all, but he defended some of those types when it was becoming more and more dangerous to do so. First, Anna's parents disowned them, which was terrible enough for her, but she knew something worse would happen. She always said that's why it took her so long to have a baby – so long for her Peter, your father, to come. When she did become pregnant, Adam moved them back to Lindenfels, so she could feel safer. It was only thirty kilometres away, and such a pretty town, a postcard town. The streets and houses wind around two hillsides, covered with linden trees, and one of them has an old castle on it. And it was safer, for a time. She had her mother-in-law there, who was a good woman, even if they didn't have so much in common, and I stayed with her often, too – I could do as I pleased. I wasn't interested in marriage myself, and certainly not with any member of the Nazi Party. By then, the Nazis had banned everything except themselves, and I was – no one needs to know what I was. Anyway, Peter was born, he was healthy and perfect, and Adam was in love with his little son. They were very close, your father and his father, from the first moment. They are like a photograph in my mind of how a man and boy should be. Such happiness together, that little boy would laugh and laugh.' She shook her head.

She told her cigarette: 'I don't know what Adam was doing with the resistance. For his family's sake, he had pretended to distance himself from any political activity, but I can only imagine he was continuing to stand up for those less fortunate in his quiet, persevering way. Perhaps he was organising against the slave treatment of workers under the Nazis, from all the unions being banned. Perhaps he was standing up for the Jews that had remained in Darmstadt – their circumstances by that summer of 1939 were unbearable. The district was one where there was a lot of resistance feeling, and not only from socialists, even if it could not be openly expressed. We were civilised people.'

Frieda Stevenson looked away, far away; she put out the cigarette.

'Anyway,' she said so plainly, too plainly, into the ashtray: 'He was killed.'

'What happened?' Addy couldn't stop the question from charging out of her, and immediately regretted the rude, harsh sound. 'I'm sorry, I —'

'Are you sure you want to know?' Frieda Stevenson looked across at her, her hand hovering over the packet of cigarettes but deciding against another. She sat there on her stepladder, hands clasped on her lap: 'It is not pleasant.'

Addy found a few more words, urgently: 'I'd be very grateful, please.'

'Well ...' Frieda Stevenson looked down at the carpet, into the lines of tiny fleur-de-lis there, lines and lines of them like spent stars dotting a tired, old darkness: 'They wanted to make a show of it. They had seemed to wait for just the right time, when we were all together – Anna and Adam and little Peter, me and Adam's mother. There was no warning, only a knock at the door. There were three of them, Gestapo officers – they dragged Adam out into the street. Two of them beat him and the other one made us come out to watch. No one else came out of their houses to witness his humiliation – that's how much your grandfather was respected. But no one could save him. He was beaten to death, right there in front of his little son. They beat him while Peter screamed – everyone in the town would have heard him. Then they pushed me into the back of their car first, and next Anna as well. We never saw Peter again. I survived what they did to us afterwards. Anna didn't. I will not describe to you what they did to us – I don't want to. You must know that your grandmother fought them, she fought very hard. She was always timid, always easy to bend to the demands of others. But she wasn't then. She fought so hard, and she paid the price.'

The two women stared at each other, shocked: the younger for the first time, the elder for all time. And then for Addy, the layers and layers of realisation began crashing down around her; the first of them: *He knew – Dad knew.* He might have only been a small boy, but he saw them kill his father, he saw them take his mother – it was all written on his soul, whether he remembered or not. Her heart at once shattered for him and remade itself with understanding. No wonder he was always so worried, so racked – so *intense*. She wanted to find a phone, call him, get on the next train home, just to touch him, hug him. *Oh, Dad.* He wouldn't break from work for a scene like that, though. Someone might get killed – there could be a fall from a high gantry, a scalding from a gust of steam, a fatal shower of molten steel; a coke oven might explode – if he wasn't watching, carefully.

Every emotion crashed then, too: love, grief, anger – anger so sharp and vastly wheeling, she had no word for it at all.

'So yes,' Frieda Stevenson sighed from some place beyond sadness, 'your grandfather was a lawyer from Lindenfels, and your grandmother was my dearest friend.' She picked up the packet of cigarettes and put it back beside the ashtray again, resisting yet another as she asked, carefully: 'And your father, he is happy in his life?'

No. Addy ached all over at that question. *Dad is permanently shattered because, on top of that total sackful of arsehole sandwiches, when he finally found happiness with the love of his life, she died as well. I don't know how Dad gets up every morning, if you want to know the truth.* She wasn't going to further sadden this woman with anything like that, though, so she told her the other, better half of the truth: 'He's the best father in the world. He's a foreman at Port Kembla Steelworks. Everyone loves him there.' *Except when he shouts, but he only shouts because he's permanently terrified something bad will happen if he doesn't.* And then, like her father's daughter, she quickly deflected further conversation on the subject, mostly because she thought she might start crying for about a thousand years if she didn't: 'It seems like some kind of miracle that I've met you – now, here – doesn't it?' she blurted inanely. 'Something good? A little bit of something magical?'

'Magical?' The old woman chuckled, nodding, somehow smiling to herself before she replied: 'It can only have been a little bit of magic that brought me here. He was a ship's mechanic, in fact – an Australian. We met in Hamburg, when I was —' She waved the thought away. 'Anyway, I didn't know a thing about Australia. I wasn't sure I even liked him for the right reasons, at first – I wasn't sure I would ever like any man. But he was a wonderful person, and he made me laugh every day. We had twenty-four years together, two sons, and now, five grandchildren. I lost him in 1973, to lung cancer, and I thought I would die then also. One of my sons told me I should have a shop, because beautiful things that remind me of more beautiful times stop me from being depressed – a good book does, too – and so here I have been since then. A lot of magic, yes.' She chuckled again. 'A lot of magic has brought me here.'

They sat there smiling at each other like old girlfriends for a moment, kindred spirits meeting in the preloved dusty air between them, before Frieda Stevenson said: 'Stay where you are.' She got up and disappeared around the far side of the bookcase again; a door hinge creaked and a draught swept in, eddying around Addy's ankles, before the woman returned, rustling, with the dress over her arm – Addy's lay-byed garden frock. She said: 'I want you to have this now.'

'Oh, but I couldn't. I've only paid —'

Frieda Stevenson shook a finger to shush her. 'And I have only been clearing out my wardrobe of old favourites I will most definitely never wear again. I must be honest. My husband, Derek, bought me this dress in 1955, from a very expensive boutique in the city, far too expensive for us at the time – it was a surprise, for our seventh wedding anniversary. And it was in every way inappropriate. I had not recovered my shape from having my second baby a few years before, and I had been feeling frumpy and old. I *was* old, so I thought – I was forty-five, almost forty-six. So, my husband buys me a dress I will *never* fit into – that is how stupid men can be. I had thickened around the waist – there was no going back. I've never worn this dear, dear gown. Someone should. And it should be you. *This* is magic.' She held out the dress and the folds of tulle swished as if within a spell she had woven herself.

'I …' Addy touched the poppies where they tumbled down to the grass at the hem; she didn't know how to respond, and couldn't in any case, as another emotion rushed in: that here was something of her own mother, too, that in that same year, 1955, she was dancing into Peter Loest's arms for the first time.

It was as if the poppies spoke themselves as she was told: 'I only ask that when you wear this dress, you remember that you are perfect and important, just as you are – no matter your burdens or blemishes. Live well, enjoy the best of life, especially for those who are no longer here.'

Addy looked up at Frieda Stevenson not at all confident she could promise that, but she said, at last: 'I will. Thank you.' *For everything.*

'And most importantly, come back. Come back to the shop. I …' The woman frowned as though distracted by some thought of her own.

Addy was keen to make this easy promise, though, frock addict that she would always be: 'Of course I'll come back. I think we can be sure I'll pop in at least once a week.' She would also have to try to find out what Frieda Stevenson herself did during the war – what she meant by *no one needs to know.*

'Good.' They smiled together for a moment once more, some heartstring mended, some long-lost friends separated by life and death and somehow bundled together again, before Frieda Stevenson turned and began marching the dress up to the front of the shop in her straight-backed, spritely way: 'I will put this in a bag for you, dear. Hang it up immediately when you get it home – it is impossible to iron.'

Addy felt she was being ushered out of the shop, as if Frieda Stevenson had such brain-stopping exchanges every Friday morning and this one was over. 'You have a busy afternoon ahead, I have no doubt,' she said, 'but do take care with this gown, please.'

'I will,' Addy said; she didn't have anything else to do except take it back to Flower Street and hang it up. She glanced over at the zebra, hesitating. She didn't want to go; she wanted to ask something else, but she didn't know what. She fumbled at it: 'By the way, what's the story with the zebra?'

'Ah!' Frieda Stevenson laughed, a light laugh, high and bright, like a tinkling of small bells, as she handed Addy the bag, ballooned now with frock. 'That was another anniversary present from Derek – for our thirteenth. He and one of his old navy friends stole it from a travelling circus, at the showgrounds. It lived in our dining room for as many years again. I was so sure the police would come for it – and Derek. Only they didn't. Zebra is not for sale, of course – he *is* Derek, for me. I need him every day.'

I want that kind of love, Addy made a wish for it there and then.

'Enjoy the rest of your day – Adrianna, isn't it? Such a pretty name for such a pretty girl.' Frieda Stevenson had her hand on the door; she added, an afterthought: 'You're at the university, yes?'

'Yes,' Addy replied, but she didn't get the chance to elaborate.

'See you again soon,' Frieda Stevenson said, the bell on the door jingling as it opened, giving Addy another less-subtle suggestion to be on her way.

'See you, then ...' She could only leave it at that and step out onto the street, back into the day. She could barely believe it was the same world here, shining grimily under that high sun, as though nothing had happened, nothing had changed. She crossed the road through gridlocked, mad-busy traffic, and at the kerb opposite, she glanced back, but the lights had been switched off in The Curiosity Shop; the door was shut once more; the 'closed' sign remained there, too; a shop unseen, a shop to walk past.

What was Frieda Stevenson doing now? Addy wondered. Probably having that second cigarette. Addy thought about getting herself a hamburger, with extra onions, but she needed more than the comfort of food. She quickened her step: she needed to write all of this down – find the words, chase them down, catch them, before any could escape.

SPECIAL FRIED RICE &
TRUE ROMANCE

By the time Addy's key met the lock at Flower Street, however, she'd decided three and a half times that she had no choice but to forget any foolish ideas of writing – *Writing what?* – and return to studying law. How could she not? It was a matter of honour. This was more than merely a need to please her father in light of all the happiness he'd been denied. She was destined to take up her grandfather's fight. Wasn't she?

Fight? No one was going to beat her to death for wanting to take up the workers' struggle here; no one would murder her for wanting to cure the causes rather than the symptoms of poverty, not in sunny Australia. Socialism wasn't illegal here. She'd just be ignored – derided for her left-wing bleeding heart, especially by the right wing of the Labor Party. The worst that would happen was that she'd have Chubs Keveney sliming up to her in Manning Bar, the uni's beer barn, wanting to know why she didn't want to suck his sausage roll. This was the eighties: God had been reborn in the form of greed. The welfare state was being cheerfully dismantled by those it had raised up from the dustbins of empire and the rubble of war: *We've enjoyed our free university fees very much, thank you, and now the next generation must pay, because we've decided the money should go to tax cuts for business and top-earning white-collar workers, such as lawyers, who are good, deserving people that can't be expected to be always giving handouts to those who are lazy and dirty and poor – ew, poor people.* Last year, at a Young Labor meeting, Addy was told by an older, recently graduated know-all, that there were no 'real' poor people in Australia. There was no fight to be had. It was hard enough trying to have a sensible conversation about it with anyone, never mind consider making it her life's work.

And yet, she had just been informed that her grandfather was more than a little bit extraordinary – that small-town lawyers and their otherwise timid wives could be brave and noble and true. Pride alone should carry her through law school.

And yet ...

I don't want to be a lawyer. I'm so sorry, Dad. She imagined herself in court, pleading a worker's compensation case for an injured non-union concrete-layer against the solid travertine edifice of a carpark property developer: *Excuse me, Your Honour. Hello? Can you hear me?* All she could hear in response was the spooky, space-station synth of ELO's 'Telephone Line', and no one answering with anything except for eternal loopholes stacking justice in favour of the rich. *I can't make a difference there. I'm too small to stand up for myself, let alone anyone else. I'm too crushed. Too —*

'Oh, it's you.' It was HRH, her head in the hall as Addy came through the door.

Oh, fricken hell. Addy realised only now she had forgotten to buy her that bunch of apologies. She'd sailed straight past the florist without the slightest thought. *Think now:* 'Harriet ...' she began. *Be a big girl, Addy, and suck this one up.* 'I wanted to talk to you, about the food processor – I'm so sorry.' *Make it unconditional, even to her smug, hoity face:* 'What I did was uncalled for.' *Lie:* 'You didn't deserve that.'

Harriet raised her nose in the air and said, with an imperious shake of the head: 'I wouldn't expect anything else from a little guttersnipe like you.'

Guttersnipe? Who the fuck says that? Miss Edwardian Parody 1985?

Harriet had worse to deliver, though: 'It's one thing to be ugly on the outside, but ugly on the inside is a form of self-mutilation.' And she closed her bedroom door on Addy's stuck and steamrolled frown.

Fuck you. Addy knew that Harriet was only offloading, only indulging in some pot-calling-kettle-black; she knew that Harriet was undoubtedly suffering some truly if only relatively dreadful anguish at the hands of Maaaarhtin Arseface; nevertheless, the barb made its mark.

I'm not ugly, Addy told herself as she trudged up the stairs. *I'm not ugly.*

You're a fricken horror show and you know that best of all.

Shut up. Please.

She laid the garden frock across her bed.

You don't deserve anything so lovely. And you didn't even pay for it – you should take it back to the shop.

Shut up. Please.

She opened her wardrobe to find a spare hanger, but the first thing she saw as she parted the wall of frocks was Luke's jumper, abandoned and lonely beneath their hovering hems.

Is there anyone you've ever known that you haven't disappointed?

Please.

When she turned back for the garden frock, No Name had pounced upon it and had begun to knead. 'No!' Addy shrieked, scaring the poor cat, and giving herself only more proof of her ugliness.

She hung up the dress, trying to concentrate on doing as she had been instructed, carefully shaking out the tulle and the charmeuse beneath, placing the folds of the skirt neatly between the press of all the other frocks.

You're too ugly for such a pretty dress.

She called back the words of Frieda Stevenson: *Such a pretty name for such a pretty girl.*

That old lady was lying – people lie about that sort of shit all the time. Making small talk, making ugly girls feel fine. She only felt sorry for you.

No, she didn't.

Keep telling yourself that – loser. She couldn't get you out of the shop fast enough, could she?

That was undeniable; it was also utterly implausible that Addy had been hurried from the shop for being too ugly. Or for being a loser. It was much more likely that the woman had been upset by the retelling of those bad memories. Hideous, heartbreaking memories which Addy had brought forth. *Good on you, idiot.*

In a whirl of frustration and need to put right all her imagined wrongdoing, she gathered up her dirty clothes for washing – her jeans and Tuesday's shirt, Wednesday's tights, sundry undies; Luke's jumper as well – and she took them downstairs to the laundry.

It wasn't really a laundry so much as a cupboard off the kitchen, behind a sliding door by the fridge, room enough for the machine and tub and not a lot more. She shoved her washing in around the agitator, then fished out Luke's jumper again, to check the label. Although she knew it wasn't wool, she had to be sure – yes, it was thirty-five percent cotton and sixty-five percent polyester, fully machine washable. It was just a posh sloppy joe, all told, but the last thing she wanted to do was destroy it. Soap powder in and dial pushed on, she left the washing to itself and returned upstairs to her desk, clutching at words as she went, trying to gather every skerrick of story she'd hoped to scribble down – for her grandparents, for her father and her mother, for the too-real bravery and sacrifice that had made her own life possible, whether she was an idiot or not.

From the drawer, she pulled out one of her large, foolscap notebooks, and from her bookshelf she took her *Jumbo Family Reference World Atlas*, opening it at the map of West Germany. She scanned the web of red roads for a moment, until she found what she was looking for: Darmstadt. Of course, Lindenfels wasn't on this map – it was too tiny – but she knew from other maps she'd found in various libraries that it was approximately equidistant between Darmstadt and the town of Weinheim, and slightly to the east of another town called Bensheim. She also knew from her research so far that Lindenfels had indeed been a pretty, postcard town, nestled in the Odenwald, a range of picturesque subalpine mountains, in the state of Hesse; it had been a tourist resort before the war, a favourite of hikers and city holidaymakers, and afterwards, a Jewish refugee camp was set up there. All facts that had seemed so disconnected from her, until now.

Darmstadt, she wrote the name at the top of the page, and beneath it the year, *1922*; beneath that she wrote: *Grandfather – Adam Loest (Löst)*. Her fingers tingled at the shapes of his name, as if her cells were responding somehow to memories not her own, but his. Tears stung as all the stories, their stories, spun and settled in her heart.

Oh, Dad. Daddy. She wanted to call him again, wanted to run home to him. What would she say, though, if he were right here with her now? She couldn't say anything. She would never say anything. She would never tell him she knew.

What he had seen. What he so obviously did not want to remember.

How it had wounded him.

How his wounding had wounded her.

She had so much to say. But what? And to whom? She turned the page with all her yearning, burning need and saw at last that here was a place where she could say whatever she wanted to. She stared at it; it stared back at her. And now, finally, she dared to begin:

> *The first war had been kind to him. Adam had survived. He had also distinguished himself on the battlefield with courage and quick wits enough that he rose through the ranks. Not bad for a lowly saddle-maker's son. But then, as the war had worn on, there were fewer and fewer courageous and quick-witted young men to choose from.*

Addy paused and looked at her pen, wondering how those words had come. They didn't seem her own. Because they weren't, not completely. They were Adam's first, she supposed. They were words that belonged to her family. And not only to her family: she would want these words to belong to any wounded heart. All hearts. These were words that had been brewing through every story she'd ever longed to tell, and through every story she'd ever heard or read. They were fresh-cut words that sprang straight from forever and always.

She wrote out her heart on the page. Pages and pages, one after the other. A view of a Darmstadt street she'd never seen; a sketch of face she'd never met; lines and lines of garbled notes she hoped she'd be able to decipher later. She wrote without stopping, until hunger brought her back into the here and now.

What am I writing? She didn't know. She looked out her window, which, in this imperfect writing room, she had to bend back a little in her chair to do, set as this window was just above the middle of her bed – the only configuration of furniture that worked, given the size of her wardrobe. She stared a little numbly at the rusted rooftops of Chippendale, as if her brain had been emptied out. Relieved. And yet she fizzed inside with – what *was* this? The roofs and chimney pots were gold kissed in the —

Oh fuck. Oh frick. Oh fuck. What's the time?

She looked down at her watch. It was almost half-past five.

It's all right – I have forty-five minutes. He won't be here until six-fifteen.

He? Like Dan Ackerman picked her up every Friday evening for club Chinese and a ringside seat to watch her brother punch another man in the face. *What?* Truth would always be stranger than fiction. *And I have to wash my hair – my hair is disgusting. What will I wear? What will I wear? WHAT WILL I WEAR?*

She hurled herself into the shower and mentally ran through her wardrobe, with the story of Adam and Anna Loest tugging at the edges of everywhere. She didn't want to leave them; she even considered catching the bus to Kingsford alone, just so she wouldn't have to talk with Dan, or anyone – except her grandparents. After all, Dan had said, 'If you're not at home tomorrow night, that's cool,' hadn't he?

Stop that thought right there. I will not be standing up Dan Ackerman. I can't wait to see him – his lovely face. His warm, dark eyes. His smile. His very cool suede boots – I hope he wears them.

God, what a load of superficial observations they are.

What? I'm not supposed to find him attractive?

You pay too much heed to meaningless details. A real writer —

Shut up.

Apart from wanting to discover every detail about him there was to know, she could not possibly no-show him or he might think she thought he was a creep for stealing her note from the piano. That was the most romantic thing that anyone had ever done, as far as she was concerned.

WHAT WILL I WEAR?

It doesn't matter – you're going to a leagues club. Just get dressed.

She skittered back to her room, trailing drips all over the cruddy old floorboards as she went, thinking she should sweep up here one day – no one else ever did. She made another mental note to unload the washing machine down-stairs and get those clothes on the line before they stank. *So much for sending Luke his jumper today – how self-absorbed are you? Please, shut up.* She opened her wardrobe doors, and the first frock she saw, of course, was the garden dress, its poppies and cornflowers beckoning: *You know you want to.* And she wasn't going to. Apart from being entirely inappropriate for the occasion, she didn't want it to get wrecked: many of her dresses were marked here and there, scorched by careless cigarettes in crowded bars and parties. She never wore a favourite anywhere like that; in fact, there were at least twenty dresses here that she'd never worn at all, because they were too beautiful.

Once she'd discounted all the purples, reds and oranges as too attention-seeking and all the pale colours as too dangerous an invitation to spill sweet-and-sour pork or curried prawns all over herself, she was left with black, brown or pink.

Wear pink – show him you like him. Be pretty.

Wear black – don't show off. It's your brother's night, not yours.

Fuck off.

So, she compromised, choosing a black dress splotched all over with big pink camellias. It was a nice cut: early 1960s-ish demure, with a high, squared neckline and bell-shaped skirt, full but not too full, not too long, not too short. As for the camellias, they were so pink the New South Wales Amateur Boxing Association could use her as a beacon in a storm should the weather turn bad again. There was no time for further mucking about, though.

My hair is still wet!

She raced back to the bathroom, flapping and crashing a hand through the contents of the cupboard below the sink – to find no hair dryer there. She raced then into Roz's room, hoping to find it on her dressing table, which was where it usually otherwise lived, since Roz had the most hair of anyone Addy knew – and there it was among her empty paint tubes and rolls of film, wedged between her camera and a black lacy bra. As the dryer was already plugged in, she turned it on and got to it, trying not to worry about how boring her hair was. There was no internal argument to be had about this: it was a simple fact. Her hair was mouse brown and dead straight; it didn't even glint in the sun; once, during the school holidays at the end of Year Eleven, she'd tried to streak it blonde with peroxide, like all the other girls did, and hers went green – and not even an interesting green, but kind of a sickly, phlegmy green. *It doesn't matter*, she reminded herself: she'd ponytail it, pin it up and forget it was there.

'Urghhhh …' Something groaned behind her on Roz's queen-size, unmade bed – and it wasn't Roz, who would still have been out wenching it at Fancy That. It wasn't the abstract nude on the easel by the balcony doors, either. Two king-size feet were sticking out the end of the giant heap of quilt, almost invisible among its explosion of wine-red batik lotuses, only seen now Addy was looking – and they belonged to Drummer Boy Kendall, she could only suppose, going for a world championship medal in sleeping all day. Addy would have envied his effort, if she hadn't been standing there in her undies.

'Oops.' And she raced back out again with her half-dried hair.

It was now almost ten minutes to six.

Breathe.

What are you panicking for?

I don't know – everything.

You are crazy.

She tried to stop her brain racing, tried to focus on the only important thing – getting ready – and she was almost there, having chosen her jacket, a cropped black gabardine, understated, neither cool nor uncool, and her shoes, ballet flats so she wouldn't have to worry about snagging a heel or falling over, and her lipstick, not too pink, not too showy, and she was just applying a little mascara when there was a knock on the front door. At which she just about poked out her left eye with the brush.

'F—ouch!' she couldn't help shouting out, as the door creaked open downstairs, HRH drawling breathily: 'Oh! Dolly, hello.'

Dolly – like she knows him – fuck, my eye. Is it bleeding? Why are you early? You're ten minutes early! Fuck, my eye. Fuck, fuck, fuck.

'Are you looking for Kendall?' Harriet was asking him.

'Ah, um. No,' Dan replied, his voice sliding up the bannister and through Addy's ribs to fizz there with every other strange excitement of this day. 'I've come to pick up Addy.'

Addy – that's me. She forgot all about her weeping eye.

'Oh?' Harriet sounded surprised. 'Adrianna, it's for you,' she called up the stairs, and Addy caught what she imagined might be a note of sadness in it, one that stilled the giddiness. She didn't have to like Harriet to feel sympathy for her: rejection wasn't any fun, even for stuck-up cows.

Don't look too happy, she schooled herself, looking in the mirror of her wardrobe door again. *Don't rub it in.* She checked the mascara damage: it hadn't smudged too badly; she never wore enough for it to make too terrible a mess, anyway. She was as ready as she'd ever be.

'Coming!'

She closed her notebook and quickly stashed it back in the desk drawer; she checked her purse for money and keys and down she went, not too fast, not too slow.

Breathe.

He was leaning against the piano when she saw him; he looked up and said: 'Wow.'

Wow. He'd had a haircut, just a normal, tidy haircut; he didn't look like a frayed-denim Elizabethan poet now: he was wearing a tan corduroy sports coat with a plain grey, collared shirt, absolutely appropriate for an evening at a blue-collar leagues club, where you didn't want to make any particular statement, raise any eyebrows, cause any trouble, get kicked out; he was also wearing those suede boots, those delicious boots. Whatever, he looked just – *Wow.*

She said: 'Hello. You're a bit early.' *Why did I say that?*

But he laughed, 'Yeah,' offering no explanation. 'Do you want to go?'

'Okay.' She thought her ribcage might burst open with the flutter of a thousand startled birds as they stepped down the hall and out onto the street, into the night.

Parked under the light near the end of the terrace row, his car was old and small, aquamarine faded by the sun, and as he held out the door for her, for a moment, she couldn't make sense of the scene: no one had ever held open a car door for her before; chivalry was dead and gone; boys didn't do that sort of thing anymore, certainly not boys where she was from, certainly not boys in bands, either, not even Luke Neilson, with all his North Shore niceness, and most girls didn't want that kind of patriarchally charged attention in any case – not educated girls, at least. It felt awkward, and she put her hand on the top of the door as though she didn't know what to do next – *Just get in the stupid car.* She did and, thankfully, he left her to it, going around to the driver's side.

He got in and pulled his door closed with a wheezy thud; long legs hinged up under the steering wheel, he paused there for a moment before he turned to her and said: 'You probably think I'm stoned, don't you?'

She shook her head. Her excruciating self-consciousness had not allowed for any such wonder about him, and most of her mind was now consumed with how she was going to avoid looking like an idiot putting on her seatbelt, it being of an unfamiliar, old-fashioned style.

He said: 'Well, I'm not. I promise you. I'm just, um …' He smiled and bit his bottom lip; and he winced, scrunching up his nose – *Unbe-fricken-lievably lovely* – before he confessed: 'I'm just a bit nervous.'

And that was the moment, right there, that Addy Loest stopped falling in love. This was the moment those bonds of gold set like solid steel between them – not that she quite knew it yet. There was too much, far too much, going on in her head.

She wanted to say, *I'm probably more nervous than you are*, but the thought remained trapped, with several others, including: *I need a drink*, and, *How the hell does this seatbelt flap-doodle thing work?* It was one of those across-the-lap seatbelts with a levered catch, and the last time she remembered seeing one she was about seven years old and her father had put it on for her. She said to Dan now, scrambling for something pleasant and non-idiotic: 'Your car is very cool.'

'You think so?' He grinned; she'd said the right thing. He told her: 'It's an Imp, 1965 – she's tiny but she's tough.'

I'm tiny and made in 1965, but I'm not tough, just minuscule, and I don't believe there's any such car called an Imp. Seriously – am I even here? Addy looked back down at the seatbelt catch and asked the easier question: 'How does this work?'

Dan said: 'It's just the same as on a plane. Just lift up the ...'

She didn't hear what he was saying; she'd never been on a plane; and the side of his hand now brushed the top of her thigh as he clicked the catch closed.

'Yeah, go on, pull the belt this way ...' He was obviously repeating whatever it was he'd just said.

The noise inside her head was relentless, almost painful. She stared into the pink camellias splashed across her knees.

He leaned on the steering wheel and asked her: 'Addy? Are you all right?'

The question snapped her back with the usual shame of not being all right, as well as the new shame of not being all right in light of everything she'd learned about her grandparents this morning. She said to Dan Ackerman: 'I'm fine. Sorry – had a long day, um, writing. I'm a bit mad.'

'An essay?' He seemed to buy that well enough; he put the key in the ignition.

'Yeah,' she lied. *Why did I just lie?* 'American Lit – *Gatsby*.'

As he drove, heading south with the bumper-to-bumper stream of evening office escapees, they exchanged some rote small talk about the literature they'd studied at school. As he was two years older and the texts alternated every other year, it turned out they'd been set the exact same ones for their final exams: *King Lear*, *Pride and Prejudice*, Philip Larkin, Sylvia Plath. But could Addy remember a single interesting thing about any one of them? No. And so she shifted the subject, asking him: 'Where did you go to school?'

He pointed out the window; by no spectacular coincidence they were passing his alma mater right that second: 'There – Sydney Boys.'

Of course you did, she shrank again, and just as baselessly. Sydney Boys was a huge public school, here on the edge of the city, and was academically selective in a way that made it, and the girls school next door, the kind of school you sent your children to if you were a bit posh but didn't want your kids to be prats. Sydney Boys was where all the cool boys went, and tribes of them continued through to Sydney Uni, generations of them. Addy had been the only student from her whole class at Wollongong High to go to Sydney Uni at all. Everyone else who'd gone on to further study went to the universities of Wollongong or New South Wales. Her father had wanted his children to go to the best and most prestigious – if it was free, then why not? Sydney Uni was a ticket that would take you through many more doors; while Wollongong Uni was, to Peter Loest, hardly much of a step up from the technical college where he'd earned his certificate in metallurgy; it was an institution feeding graduates to the steel industry – not one that would see his children reclaim their rightful place in the world. She felt her mind drifting away again – loose balloon, so Roz had called her, and that's precisely what she was. But as she drifted, her heart began to pound, not with any happy sort of excitement; only lead-dread fear, a thousand nameless fears.

Please, not here. Not now.

She fought it; she fought it harder than she ever had, changing the subject again: 'What's your favourite Chinese?'

'Mmm …' He turned right, following wide white arrows marked on the road. 'I eat anything that's not nailed down, but at Souths Juniors, the honey chicken is pretty amazing. It's a good restaurant.' He glanced at her with *that* smile, and she forced herself to keep her focus on it, on his sweetness. She was safe with him; safe here; even if her lips tingled with the panic and her mouth had gone so dry she was sure he could hear her swallow.

I'm all right. I'm all right.

She touched and grasped the string of that loose balloon, re-found the conversation and asked him: 'You've been to Souths Juniors before?'

'Heaps,' he said, accelerating as the traffic began to clear a little. 'My folks come here all the time. Well, when Mum has a night off the tools, which isn't all that often. Dad's almost always on call, with the hospital, so he doesn't like to be too far away or be at any place where he can't just take off.'

'What sort of a doctor is he?' *Listen to the answer. This is interesting – be interested.*

'He's a general surgeon,' Dan told her, frowning at the road, changing lanes. 'He's one of the guys that gets to have the first look at accidents and emergencies that come in, to assess the damage, stop the bleeding, prevent imminent death and all that.'

'Wow. Action man,' Addy tried for a joke, and joked to herself at the same time: *If I do have a heart attack, then I'm in good hands, aren't I?*

'He'd say it's just fancy mechanics, putting the bits back together,' Dan replied. 'He wanted me to follow in his footsteps, his last hope from four sons. But no thanks. I want to have a life. He's set a bad example for us.'

She wanted to ask him if he had an intense and overbearing father like she did, if it might be some quirk of Germanness, but she couldn't ask him something so personal and presumptuous as that; she asked him instead: 'You've got three brothers?'

'Yep. All older, though, in their thirties,' he told her, eyes on the road. 'All over the place, too – they couldn't leave home fast enough. I'm the baby – and they abandoned me. I was a mistake, or probably more likely Mum wanting someone to talk to other than Dad, who's not there even when he is there, if you know what I mean.'

Like me? Addy shrugged and attempted a smile, staring into the foreign streetscape that unfolded past the blank brick walls of the University of New South Wales.

Dan continued as he drove: 'Dad couldn't function without her. Gee, who'd want to be a man like that? He's just turned sixty-four and won't stop. Anyway, when Mum's had enough, she chucks down the tea towel and says, "Richard, you can do what you bloody well like, but someone else is cooking my dinner tonight" – which usually means Chinese, at Souths Juniors, because the food really is pretty good, and it's only five minutes from the hospital.'

He seemed to laugh to himself then, and with such fondness for his parents Addy was grounded for a moment there, with an inkling that was more felt than thought: this was the kind of family she wanted for herself one day, with children who would impersonate her and laugh at her with love behind her back. Who wouldn't want that?

As they half-circled a roundabout, he pointed up a hill to the left through the streetlight-studded dark: 'Five-minute drive that way – that's home. Coogee, near the beach – and also five minutes from the hospital.' That fond laugh again, tossed across his shoulder, and suddenly, too suddenly, he was slowing the car and telling her: 'There's the club.'

It was a building shaped like a huge ship's prow, clad in grey-green tiles; an unholy shrine dedicated to the pursuit of sport, beer and boobs, in that order, and all subsidised by the poker machines that would certainly have filled one of the windowless floors inside, as they did at practically every other leagues club across the state.

And we're having our first date here? Is this a first date?

Don't be insane. He's only being kind, giving you a lift.

Yeah, really? Because guys do that all the time, don't they.

Why else would Dan the Man be seen with you anywhere? He's a doctor's son who went to Sydney Boys. He's a nice boy, and you're just —

Shut up.

You need a beer.

Fuck off.

'What's your favourite Chinese, anyway?' he asked her, swerving into a carpark.

She heard the question but couldn't form any other response apart from: 'Oh everything. Mmm.'

The car had stopped and they were getting out; she was so removed from herself, she could not have said how she got that seatbelt off, and here was Dan Ackerman holding out his hand to her before they crossed a broad, black road, oil slicks shimmering iridescent under the rising moon. She looked at his hand for a moment as though it were a foreign object. *Just take it, you stupid freak. What the hell is wrong with you?*

And at the first touch of her hand in his, at the first sense of his real-life actual warmth, she hoped she'd come back to earth at least a little. *Please.*

She didn't. The road seemed an ocean of blackness, impossible that she should be walking upon it, and once inside the leagues club, she thought the swirls in the gaudy carpet might rise up to clutch her ankles and drag her down; she almost hoped they would.

Please, stop.

'It's only on the first floor,' she heard him say, and she found it hard to believe he could still see her face, it felt so numb, so absent, but there he was, smiling at her, with that sweet smile and that tidied-up haircut, as though everything was fine.

She tried to focus on the people they passed on the staircase: two young women, about her age, shoulder to shoulder, whispering under the thump of distant music and the hum of the air-conditioning system; blue eyeshadow and crimped hair like fountains on their heads; white jeans and striped pastel shirts. They were generic club girls she'd seen a hundred times before; they all had boyfriends called Scott or Shaun, and were almost finished their hairdressing apprenticeships because it was the perfect job to combine with future family commitments. They were the kinds of white-bread Aussie girls that Addy had gone to high school with, in bulk, who said she'd be pretty if she did something with her hair, who told her that boys didn't like girls who read as much as she did. These girls were alien creatures from a planet far, far away, and Addy didn't need a stress-induced hallucination to think it. But they did return her from the brink: she could feel her feet upon the stairs – she wasn't going to take a tumble for their entertainment.

'I made a reservation,' Dan told the waiter at the door of the restaurant. 'Ackerman, for two.'

He made a reservation? A cold sadness swept through Addy at the fact: here was a boy – a man – beyond perfect. An everything man; an all-occasions man; a renaissance man of many talents. And Addy was in every way undeserving of his attention. She was mentally unstable. Aimless. Damaged.

Find a way to put him off gently. There would be no arguing with herself about that, and it was the most grounding reality of all. She couldn't lead this one on. She would not break this boy's heart or cause him the slightest grief; she would make herself forgettable. *Shouldn't be very hard.*

'It's like walking back into the womb, hey,' he said, a soft aside to her alone, as the waiter showed them to their table.

What? She looked up at him, wondering what she'd missed; and in that instant felt her hand in his, just as he let it go. *Oh.*

'All the red,' he said, gesturing at the walls. They were indeed all red, decorated everywhere with black and gold, and topped with internal roof awnings in the style of an ancient pagoda, but otherwise so red the place glowed.

'It's like being inside a Chinese lantern,' she said, gripping the metal frame beneath the dining chair as she sat, to stop herself from floating away.

He laughed, a happy, generous laugh, settling into the chair across from her, drawing her back to him: 'Yep. That's exactly what it's like.'

He did not stop smiling or agreeing with her from that point on, even when she asked for an orange fizzy – he only laughed again and ordered two.

'So, what are you going to do after uni, do you reckon?' he asked her as their dim sim entrée arrived.

'Oh, I don't know,' she replied, seeing an opportunity here to show him what a total screw-up she was. 'I've just dropped out of law.' Then she dropped her heart's desire onto the tablecloth like spilt soy sauce: 'Reckon I might want to be a writer, because I'm obviously out of my mind.'

But he said: 'Wow.' He sat forward over his plate, keener than ever: 'Lucky I stole those notes of yours, then, hey – they'll be worth a fortune one day.'

'Steady on.' She laughed now, too; how he drew and drew her to him. She said: 'I haven't even written anything yet, or at least nothing fit for human consumption.'

'You've started something, though?' He could not have been more interested or more sincere – or more right.

She looked away, forking a dim sim onto her plate: *Why the hell did I mention writing?* She tried to shove that subject back in its box: 'It's nothing – only rubbish.'

'What's it about?' He was only keener still.

Oh, please, shush. She wanted to bat it away again, telling him: 'I've really got no idea …' But he did genuinely seem to want to know, didn't he? She trusted Dan Ackerman; she took the risk and told him: 'It's strange. This morning I found out some things about my family, my grandparents, and when I started writing it all down, it was like it, whatever *it* is, wanted to write itself. Like I'd disappeared into the words or something.' She rolled her eyes at herself: 'See? *Crazy.*'

But he said: '*Wow.*' He leaned even further forward, elbows on the table, and she noted that he hadn't touched the food there, as he asked her: 'So, what's the story?'

And the question was like a door opening onto her soul, light flooding in; she let the story pour out between them: 'My grandfather was a lawyer in Nazi Germany, apparently. He'd been this small-town nobody who somehow distinguished himself during the First World War. Afterwards, he got political, the wrong kind of political, and the Gestapo …' Dan Ackerman did not move his eyes from hers; she felt the heat rise in her cheeks, not from embarrassment, but from the injustice, the cruelty: 'They killed him, beat him up in front of my dad, who was only a little kid at the time. I don't know what happened after that, except that they took my grandmother away and she died as well, I don't know how, except it was horrific. So horrific that Dad hasn't told me any of this. I found out by accident, long story, big coincidence – you couldn't write that bit.' Dan was frowning now, thoughtfully, quietly; maybe too quietly. 'Anyway,' she shrugged, 'when I started writing it down, it just sort of took over. I might not know what I'm doing, but it feels like something I should do, I suppose.' She shoved a hunk of dim sim into her mouth, mostly to stop herself from saying any more.

'Hm.' He nodded as she chewed, and after half a forever, he said: 'Sounds like something worth doing.' She wasn't sure if that was nothing more than a platitude, until he continued: 'My grandfather's an artist. He'd know what you're talking about. He was in the First World War as well, as an Australian, though – long story, too, but he was born here, to German parents – and when he came home, to Australia, he suddenly had to paint. He always says it was like he didn't have a choice. He ended up going back to Europe, back to Germany, to go to art school, dragged the whole family over when my dad was little, but that was in the 1930s and things got unpleasant, as you could guess, and they were only there a couple of years before they had to turn around and come home again. He didn't care about that, though, he never wanted to be famous or anything. Painting is just something he has to do – it's the way he talks to the world. He's a small-town nobody, a coal miner, originally. Just a tech-head, really, like me ...' Dan looked away, the blush to his cheeks matching hers, and he told the tablecloth: 'I'm sorry your family had such a hard time.'

'Sorry?' Addy was lost for a moment in the mesh of history she seemed to share with Dan Ackerman, the scribbly lines of their true stories intersecting and reflecting. It was unreal. It was also somehow right, that like should attract like. Wasn't it?

'I mean war is such a giant serve of bullshit, hey?' He smiled, pensive at the edges. 'Our grandfathers were on opposite sides, but only by a trick of chance. My granddad survived only by a trick of chance, too – he got pretty smashed up.' Dan's smile widened into something else, somehow half ironic and half daydreamy as he said: 'Who knows? Maybe your grandfather was the one that fired the shell that hit mine, and he's sent you to me to make amends. Gee,' he snorted, and stabbed a dim sim, 'there's some crazy for you.'

Addy's whole mind smiled as she stabbed the dim sim beside his: 'You'll have to do a lot better than that if you want to beat me for crazy.'

The special fried rice with prawns arrived, and the honey chicken, a platter of sizzling steak, too, and she allowed herself a small, warm moment to imagine that chance might be tricking her nicely this time, that maybe this thing with Dan Ackerman was really real and right and true – that maybe, just maybe, it was meant to be.

THE FIGHT &
ITS UNEXPECTED AFTERMATH

'Maybe' is a favourite word of chance – it's noncommittal. Maybe boxing matches at leagues clubs aren't the most conducive places for love.

Addy could smell the massed testosterone before they'd even reached the ring – before they'd left the restaurant.

As they got up from the table, she said to Dan: 'I think I need a drink, something alcoholic.'

'Sure.' He frown-smiled at the idea as they made their way out, with five minutes to spare before the fight. 'The bar shouldn't be too crowded yet – what would you like?'

She really would have preferred to hold his hand again, both to ground her balloon and to keep her mind inside their blossoming togetherness, but she couldn't do that; she didn't want to drag him with her, wherever she was going now. Outside, in the no-man's land between entertainment halls, with industrial levels of cigarette smoke swirling around them like it had been pumped from a fog machine, and the plucky, plunketty strains of 'Girls Just Wanna Have Fun' somehow radiating up through the concrete and the carpet beneath her feet, she said: 'Dan, it's really lovely you came with me tonight – you can't know how much I appreciate you giving me that lift here, and for dinner, and everything – but you don't have to come to the fight with me. I can get a cab home.'

He stopped, mid-stride, and then turned to her with a scrunched-up squint: 'Nah ... Unless ... You don't want me to hang around?' He looked uncertain: and she saw in that look the first glimpse of his heartbreak. Breathtaking.

'No!' She scrambled at it: 'I didn't mean *that*.' What did she mean? 'I mean, if it's not your scene, I don't want you to put yourself through it.'

She didn't want this wonderful guy to have to meet her meathead brother and his meathead coach, or any of her brother's or her father's mates that might be there – the whole boxing crowd. The whole sweaty, grunting festival of ug.

Dan's squint twisted so that he looked as though he had a toothache: 'I don't have a scene, Addy, and I'm not too thrilled at the thought of leaving you at a boxing match on your own. That might be sexist of me, but there it is. I'll make myself scarce if you want me to, though.'

'I don't want you to make yourself scarce.' *Fuck!* 'I don't want you to go. I just ... You know ...' *Say something:* 'Do you like boxing?'

'I don't have an opinion either way,' he said, hands in his pockets, curling over himself somehow, so that he didn't seem all that much taller than her. He hunched up his shoulders: 'I've never seen a match except on TV. I've never taken a swing at anyone myself except on a football field and I almost broke my hand on the other bloke's head – never been keen to do it a second time.'

She laughed despite herself; he'd pushed through her gathering anxiety yet again. She said, with a little too much surprise: 'You play football?'

He raised an eyebrow: 'That's funny?'

'No!' She scrambled and scrambled: 'I didn't mean that, either.' Even if she sort of did; he seemed too rangy, too lean. She clutched at a joke: 'I bet you play rugby union, don't you.' With the posh boys, the rich boys – the 'soft boys', as her father would call them, though she knew well enough union boys called league boys the exact same names – mostly 'dickhead'.

'I did,' he said, leaning further into his pockets. 'But not this season. My fitness is crap, from smoking dope and laying about. I didn't even turn up to the first training session, and I'm not very proud of that – don't tell Granddad. So,' he raised both eyebrows then, 'what would you like to drink?'

She wanted a schooner of Riesling, but she shoved down the craving with her own shame: 'Oh. Don't worry about it.' She glanced unseeing at her watch: 'We're running late.'

They weren't. Within thirty seconds, they'd found the door to the arena where the fight would take place. As expected, it was startlingly similar to the dozen or so other boxing venues Addy had seen over the past few years: a darkened barn, walls painted the colour of pallid flesh, tables ranged around the ring, which was raised above the punters, ropes strung around it like a toy farmyard for big boys; there was the judges' table at one side, and a gallery above, half filled. The noise of men everywhere else, sawn-off and raucous; and the smell of men: body odour, aftershave, and the burning stench of whatever gears were being ground in the effort to contain their rage. No matter how many times Addy tried to remind herself of the socially beneficial purpose of controlled violence, she always came up shocked. It always struck her as weird, too, that while boxing was probably the nation's most multicultural sport, with all the great fighters being either Aboriginal or next-generation post-war refugees of some sort, the audience was invariably dominated by doughy, middle-aged white-bread men with oily comb-overs. There was so much Brylcreem, polyester and alcohol in this room, it was a wonder the lighting of cigarettes wasn't banned.

'Hello, darlin' – lost, are ya?' some leery beer-breath said as she continued around and past the judges' table, to the far side of the ring, where she could see the unmistakable bear shape of Nick's coach – Max Kovacs – talking to some other man she recognised, though she couldn't think of his name.

Max Kovacs saw her straightaway: 'Addy.' He grabbed her around the shoulders with one huge, hairy arm and squeezed, not that he had any particular affection for her, it was simply the way he greeted people – hard up against his cast-iron Hungarian pecs. He dislodged one of her hairpins in the process and it bit into her skull. 'Your father told me he couldn't get here tonight,' he said with rushed disappointment. 'Shout out loud for your brother. It's a very important bout.' And with that instruction, he disappeared into the shadows at the very back of the room, no doubt returning to Nick, somewhere psyching himself up – *Ug. Ug. Ug.*

It'll be over within the hour, she told herself. Even if they went the distance of the full twelve rounds. It used to be fifteen, but the rules changed when someone died during a world championship match a couple of years ago, a Korean boxer, brain haemorrhage from one too many knocks to the head. *Sport of kings? Sport of world-champion idiots.*

'Hi, Addy, isn't it?' Another massive wall of a man was beside her: it was Dave, her brother's housemate, not a boxer, a weightlifter, and friendly enough, but she could barely say, 'Hello,' in return.

'Addy?' It was Dan now, suggesting they take an empty table just behind the front row; she nodded, though by this time, so close to the bell, she was barely there at all. She tried to tell him with her eyes: *I'm so sorry.*

They sat down either side of the small, square table, in plastic bucket chairs, just as the referee ducked through the ropes, followed by the boxers, and the announcement over the PA: 'In the blue corner, we have Nicky Loest of Wollongong.' The man had pronounced it 'Loast', and declared him from Wollongong rather than Port Kembla, but whatever, at least their dad wasn't here to be offended by it. 'And in the red corner, we have John Deloso of Penrith.' Whoever he was.

The first part of Nick she saw was his back, monstrous, the overhead lights enhancing the contours and ridges of all the muscles across his shoulders. He looked like he'd got bigger since she'd last seen him, and that was less than a month ago, when they'd both gone home for Easter. He was only twenty-two. How much bigger was he going to get?

'*That's* your brother?' Dan said, and she nodded, used to the incredulity. Addy was, by physical comparison, an actual wisp of nothing; and while all her features were fine, birdlike, Nick's had been brutally chiselled, his nose broken twice already. He was as fearless as she was frightened all the time.

Dan asked her: 'You worry for him?'

Addy made some kind of face that could have meant anything but in fact meant: *Worry is not the word – nowhere near it. I am paralysed with fear.* She clutched the edges of the plastic seat until they dug into her flesh.

'Round one,' the announcer called and the bell went: *DING!*

'Aaaand box!' The ref set them off, two young men, dancing at each other, bare-chested, bizarre, and at the first punch Nick threw, Addy left the room – mentally.

The thwacking of gloves; the squeaking of boots on canvas mat; she was watching and not watching; she could tell more or less how things were going from the sound of Nick's ugs, anyway. He was winning from the first round, chasing his opponent down and towering over him.

DING!

She heard Dan say: 'Wow. He's pretty full-on, your brother.'

'Yep.' Addy nodded. 'Full-on.'

Nick was as full-on in the next round and the next, and the more he belted into the other guy, the more Addy reeled, clinging to the edge of her chair, though she could no longer feel it there. The sixty-second countdowns between rounds were too short and too long; she would never remember what scraps of conversation were exchanged with Dan amid the rising din of the crowd: 'Smash him, Johnno!' 'Gloves down, Nicky!' 'Come on!' 'Get into it!' 'Go harder!' It wasn't unlike being drunk, she thought, this stuck-still dizziness she felt; it was also not uncommon for her to blank out much of it, either.

This time, however, she saw Nick's dogged ferocity in a new light. She saw the Gestapo officer beating their grandfather to death; she saw her family fighting back; she saw her father's desperate need to win it this time, too. She saw the noblest height and most murderous depths of every man. But these men ... what did they do to her grandmother? What did they do to Frieda Stevenson? Of course, Addy knew. Oh, she knew. She knew in her own bones: women couldn't fight; not like this. Nick weighed more than ninety kilos; Addy weighed somewhere less than fifty, give or take a hamburger. If Nick had wanted to, he could have thrown her across the room. Not all men were violent thugs, not all men were caveman rapists, but the fact that any were stained them all, so Addy's revelation told her now.

She looked across at Dan, who was himself engrossed in the contest, just like every other man here: flexing and flinching with the blows, imagining himself there in the ring, no doubt.

She had begun to tremble even before she returned her gaze to the match, where she saw the smaller man, Johnno Deloso, find the gap in Nick's gloves at last and land one – *CRACK* – to the side of his face. She watched her brother's head snap back, sweat flinging upwards from his hair, an arc of silver droplets under the harsh downlights. He stumbled backwards, to the ropes, but he only used them to his advantage, hurling himself straight at his opponent once more. Somewhere behind her, his mate, Dave, had leapt up out of his seat and was bellowing: 'Nail him, Nicky – nail him!'

Addy wanted to be sick, yet her stomach, so full from that very nice meal she'd enjoyed with a boy she might have begun to love, already seemed hollow again. And just as well, for when Nick turned at the next bell, to shake a fist at Dave from his corner, he looked right at Addy, the side of his face streaked with blood, his left eye already swelling, and he grinned around his mouthguard like the rampaging ape he was.

You are fucken demonic.

Max Kovacs had to yell at him and push him to sit down to have his face cleaned up, swabbed with adrenaline hydrochloride to stop the bleeding and greased with vaseline to try to keep the wound from worsening. The bout only lasted another two rounds, though, Johnno Deloso getting pounded and pounded to his knees, counted out at number eight.

Hooray, you win.

As Addy watched her brother's hand being raised by the ref, listened to the crowd cheering, stamping their feet in appreciation of the match, she knew her father would be above and beyond proud. Nick was one fight closer to Commonwealth Games team selection; barring some not inconceivable corruption of the process within the Amateur Boxing Association, Nick would be off to Edinburgh next year. In the meantime, Nick would be insufferably pumped up. She didn't want to go near him, but she would have to, to try to get him to call their dad before he got drunk, before appreciative punters started pouring beer all over his head. She had to find a phone and get him to it – the main point of her being here. Of course, she could call home herself; Max would almost certainly call within the next half-hour, too; it wouldn't be the same, though. Her dad would be at home now, sitting by the phone, lighting another cigarette: waiting for Nick to call.

Nicky. Nicky. Nicky.

Prick.

'Oh man.' Dan was shaking his head in admiration, hands gripping his knees, laughing: 'That was *sensational*.'

Addy frowned at him, unsure of what she was looking at, some rage of her own roiling in her glare. *Maybe you're not who I thought you were. How could I tell in any case? I'm a serial fantasist.* She didn't realise that the trembling she felt inside her bones was adrenaline of her own; she didn't yet understand how reasonable it was that she should want to smash her fist into the tabletop between them. All she knew was that she had to get to Nick, and that this would not be an easy thing to do.

She stood up.

Dan stood up, too; he said: 'That was great. Thanks for asking me to come.' Still shaking his head: 'Man, that was so full-on.'

She said: 'I'm probably going to be ages, waiting for Nick. Really, you don't have to hang around.' She could hear the flatness in her voice: rude, aloof: *Go away.*

'What?' He squinted at her now, and not in an endearing way; he was becoming annoyed.

I don't blame you. But even then, she could only say: 'It'll be boring. For you. Hanging around.' *I don't want you to see me here anymore, in this place – this place in my head. This place in my too-weird family. You won't understand. Please, go away.*

He touched her on the arm, on the back of her elbow, the lightest touch, probably only about to say something reassuring like, 'I won't be bored,' or, 'I don't mind that you're nuts, I really don't,' or, 'I'm going to find the bathroom, be back soon,' but she'd already recoiled, moving her arm away as though he'd just attempted to grab her; she couldn't help it.

'All right, Addy.' He straightened to his full height: 'I won't hang around.'

'Dan, I —' Her arm hurt where he'd barely touched her; it hurt with the longing to tell him everything she really meant, all her truths; so many truths they jammed in her throat.

'No worries, Addy.' He gave her a careful smile, a face-saving smile; he said: 'You're out of my league, anyway.' Then he left her; she watched him move through the crowd.

Out of your league? Mine is not any league you want to belong to, she told his back as he pushed his way through the door and disappeared. Addy's league was far too exclusive: it was a league of one. For a moment, she stood there as if all her joints had seized. She scanned the room for Nick, unthinking.

'The serious business of this evening is yet to come,' the announcer was saying over the PA. 'The ladies' jelly-wrestling tournament will commence in fifteen minutes …'

Someone wolf-whistled above the general hubbub; a blow-up pool was being wheeled into the arena, wobbling with red jelly, bouncers in black shirts rushing to reconfigure tables around it. The shutters rolled up on the bar at the back of the room; and the eerie opening notes of '99 Luftballons' began to play.

It wasn't an uncommon song, having been a number-one hit last year for several weeks; with the bell-like, ardent voice of its singer, Nena, and its boppy beats, it was the kind of song that might be heard anywhere, and especially at a people-pleasing venue like this. It was a pop-rock taste of something otherworldly; something political from a place where politics actually mattered; it was romantic: it was German. But here, now, for Addy, it seemed to draw a fat black texta line beneath her own absurdity. She knew all the words, of course, and had spent countless hours grappling with their meaning, and yet as they loomed out at her across this cavernous space – *Zeit*, *Lied*, *Krieg*; Time, Song, War – she couldn't understand any of them anymore. She couldn't understand anything that was happening around her.

Many of the older men were filing out, like a riptide; a younger mob was rushing at the bar; a group of girls in oversized bathrobes leaned against the platform of the boxing ring, smoking, fluffing out their fluffy feather-cut hair – the wrestlers, Addy supposed.

Nick, where are you? Panic rose and rose; she couldn't see Max Kovacs anywhere now, either. She had no idea where the dressing room might have been, but she guessed that's where he'd be – having his cheek looked at, she hoped, and probably getting a dressing-down from Max for whatever he might have done better.

I can't believe I let Dan Ackerman walk away.

Can't you? I can. And you've done him a favour.

Nick, where the fuck are you?

The hurdy-gurdy of the loose *luftballons* wound down into the twanging rubber-band bass of INXS – 'I Send a Message'. If only she could. She was sure the volume of the music had increased, amplifying her distress. She spun around and the room spun with her, but she found a familiar face, sort of – Dave – emerging from a door at the dark and as yet unpeopled edge of the jelly pool. She just about ran for him. Before she got there, though, she saw Nick hulking out after him, Max with them. They looked like a different species of human, Nick and Dave, with their overinflated torsos, incapable of walking side by side without bumping against each other; and the elder, Max, appearing as though some of his air had escaped, having been left out too long in the sun. Or the solarium, as the case was – Nick wouldn't attend his own funeral without a decent all-over tan.

As she neared, she saw Nick's face, his left eye almost completely closed by the swelling. She'd seen him in various states of beaten-up, but immediately she sensed this one was a bit worse than usual.

'Hey, Sprout,' he said to her. 'Get me a beer.'

He was joking, but only half, and the way he shouted it above the music pushed every nerve in her. The way he sounded so much like their dad, loading Addy up with expectations she couldn't fulfil. Her every cell screamed: *Get fucked and fuck off.* She would do as she was asked, though; much as she loathed her brother's oafishness, she loved him, too. She loved his stupid beaten-up face, now that she was forced to look at it with some care; and today she'd been gifted a window, a precious snippet of history, on why he was driven to this violence. It was a violence he'd never used for evil, she thought, remembering a moment of their more recent history, back in primary school, when he'd efficiently dispatched a playground bully for her: Craig Benson was the boy's name, and after tormenting her one too many times, Nick had snatched up Craig's peanut butter sandwich, filled it with a handful of dirt and made him eat it. Those were the days when they were close, before puberty and mutual disgust had set in; such was the glue of siblings. Besides, she also more than wanted a beer herself at this particular moment: *And I am fricken well going to have one. I am going to have half a dozen.*

But just as she was about to ask him what kind of beer he wanted, so she would make the right choice from whatever they had on tap here, he seemed to bump against Dave unnecessarily. His face slumped forward, his corn-coloured hair, still damp from the shower, fell across Dave's pale-blue shirtsleeve as his whole body slumped sideways.

Oh my God! Oh my God! Her arms reached out to him instinctively, though futilely; only someone with equal strength could have prevented him from crashing to the floor. Thank God for Dave; thank God for Max and his quick reflexes, too, catching Nick on the other side, and accidentally knocking Addy with his own shoulder in the process, sending her staggering into a table nearby.

'Oh, mate.' Dave was bearing the majority of the weight, almost crouching with the effort of holding Nick up, but just as quickly Nick came to again, dazed, raising a hand to his head.

Oh my God. Addy could do nothing as they sat him on a chair, the music blaring around them; her mind blaring: *If you die, you will kill Dad. Fuck, fuck, fuck, fuck, fuck.* That wasn't entirely irrational, either: the Korean boxer whose death had changed the rules met his end exactly like this, and Addy knew it, just as she'd known there'd been a huge all-in brawl inside the boxing fraternity about reducing the number of rounds from fifteen to twelve at the time. *Fucken idiots – all of you. What am I going to tell Dad?*

'Don't tell your father anything – not yet.' Max was beside her, of the same mind, growling into her ear: 'I've already called him to tell him Nick won. Don't tell him anything more until we know if there's a problem. Go and get some water. It's probably only dehydration.'

It was almost a shame that Addy would not remember how good she was in such a crisis; pushing her way determinedly through the crowd at the bar to demand a jug of iced water, calmly informing the barman of the emergency, anyone might have thought she'd been trained for the purpose. But as it was, all she'd ever remember was standing with her brother as he sat with his head in his hands, her small hand on his large back, waiting for the ambulance to come, rockabilly drums thumping out a 'Crazy Little Thing Called Love'.

'Mrs Loset?' A nurse appeared in the waiting room with a clipboard and a new variation on the surname theme; and yet another, before Addy had had the chance to interpret the first: 'Losest? Mrs Nicholas Losest?'

Addy might have found a laugh in that, if she hadn't been shredded of all good humour; she'd have been revolted at being mistaken for her brother's wife, too, if she hadn't been so sure she was going to be told he was bleeding on the brain.

'I will come with you,' Max said, beside her, getting up from the row of vomit-coloured vinyl seats they shared with an assortment of Friday-night walking wounded and diseased; and she shook her head – she'd rather have stabbed Max Kovacs to death with a biro. She exchanged a look of unmasked terror with Dave instead: poor Dave seemed as wrecked as she was; sweat beading on his brow, he'd hardly said a word since Nick had fainted again getting into the ambulance. *Dehydration? I think not*. And all Max seemed to have been worried about was making sure the paramedics took him out through the back of the club. 'So it will be quiet,' Max had said. *So no one will see what you've done*, Addy suspected.

She braced herself now as she stepped towards the nurse, as much as she could when it felt as though she was dragging her feet through molten tar.

'Mrs Losest.' The nurse, blank-faced with her own exhaustion, gestured with the clipboard for Addy to follow her down a corridor of curtained beds.

'It's Miss,' Addy said, her voice dull, the correction irrelevant. 'I'm Nick's sister,' she told the hopscotch squares of light on the ceiling.

'Really?' The nurse threw the question over her shoulder. 'You don't look alike.'

'Probably because I'm not a boxer,' Addy replied, her nerves so chewed up she couldn't hold back the rudeness.

'Whatever.' The nurse didn't turn or break her steady stride. 'Your *brother* has a concussion, a serious concussion. The X-rays appeared to be all right – there seems to be no cause for immediate concern – but the registrar wants a second opinion, wants another senior doctor to take a look before deciding whether or not to keep him in overnight, for observation.'

Addy could have fainted herself, with relief; she blurted: 'Where's the nearest telephone? Please. I need to call our dad – in Port Kembla.' He'd be a special Pete Loest blend of worried and furious now – two hours on from the event.

The nurse stopped then and turned to her; Addy was sure she'd earned directions along the lines of, 'Take yourself across the carpark, down a dark alley and boot yourself straight to hell,' but she said with stunning kindness: 'Once you've seen your brother, come to the nurses' station, just around the corner.' She pointed up towards the end of the corridor. 'You can ask to use the phone there, so long as you're brief – don't mention it's a long-distance call and I won't mention it, either.' She swept open the curtain at her side, 'Here he is,' and then she walked away.

Oh, Nick. There he was, holding an icepack to his face; and he grunted at her on sight. *Yes, ug to you, too. He must be okay.*

'How are you feeling?' she asked him.

He grunted again: 'Headache.'

Well, derr. She asked him: 'Can I get you anything?'

'No.' After a hundred years, he added: 'Thanks.'

'I'll call Dad,' she said; she had to call him before she could no longer function. Her knees were juddering with the full weight of the day: discovering the depths of their father's pain; possibly beginning what might be a serious attempt at writing something; pissing off probably the best guy she would ever meet; and her brother evading a catastrophic brain injury. All of it shattering, confusing: too much. Addy clutched the iron bar at the end of the bed, asking Nick by some remote, auto-recall: 'Is there anything you want me to tell him?'

'Just don't tell him I passed out.' Nick sounded worried himself; she guessed he'd had a scare as well, this impen-etrable fortress that was her brother. He'd been so out of it, even when he was conscious he'd been incoherent, slurring words, but he was all right now. Yes, she looked and looked at him, to test the truth: he was all right now.

She nodded. 'I'll just tell him we got a precautionary X-ray.'

Nick attempted to nod too, but that only hurt him more, and he grunted yet again: 'Fuck this.'

'Why did you go to the hospital?' the interrogation began. 'What happened, Adrianna? Tell me the truth.'

'He just had a bad knock, that's all. You'll see for yourself on Sunday. Please don't worry, Daddy.'

'Put him on the phone – I want to talk to him.'

'He's not here. He's – ah …' *Fuck!* 'He's talking to the doctor.'

'What's he talking to the doctor about?'

'I don't know!' she just about hissed into the phone, trying to keep her voice down, as several nurses went about their business around her.

'Adrianna, are you not telling me something?'

'No! Please, Dad.' *Have another beer and go to bed.* 'It's been a long night. You know what it's like, waiting around.' Waiting around for Nick to have X-rays had been a family leisure activity since 1979.

'Yes, I do. And if you aren't telling me the truth, you know I will find out from Max.'

I doubt that very much. 'I am telling you the truth. You will see for yourself on Sunday. I have to go now – I'm using the nurses' phone.'

'Don't you use that tone of voice with me.'

What tone of voice might that be? Barely supressed hysteria I learned straight from you? 'Daddy, please – I have to go.'

'Tell Nick to call me – tonight. I don't care how late.'

'I will.' The day crashed hard into her now, smashing over her shoulders, and she told him the most basic truth of her heart: 'I love you, Dad.'

'What? What are you saying that for?' Her father didn't know this language; it didn't feature in the usual Loest family argot. 'If you have bad news to tell me, I want to hear it now.'

Her heart imploded and sank through the linoleum beneath her feet: 'There's no bad news, Dad. It's just something people say to other people they love.' *It's just fricken normal. OH, DAD!*

Grunt: 'All right. You know I love you as well, Sprout. It's a permanent fact. You don't go around saying it all the time without causing people to wonder what the fuss is about.'

'Okay, Dad.' *I'll never say it again, I promise. Love is too upsetting. Whoa, ain't that the truth of truths.* 'I really have to go.'

'Addy, I —'

'Bye, Dad, see you Sunday.' She hung up.

On a wave of guilt, she returned to Nick, and by the time she got there she was such a wreck, so crushed and crumpled, she wasn't even aware she'd begun to cry, until her brother said: 'What's wrong with you?'

She turned away from him, trying to force it back down.

'Addy?'

'Hm.' *Breathe.* She leant against the end of the bed.

She heard her brother sit up. 'Did Dad lose his shit?'

'Not too badly,' she told the curtain, regaining control of her emotions, if control was what this could be called.

'Why are you crying?' he asked her, carefully.

'I'm not crying,' she said, on reflex. She supposed he didn't really want to know, but only wanted her to stop. She wanted to stop. She told him: 'I'm just so sick of lying all the time. I'm sick of not being able to have an honest conversation with Dad about anything. I'm sick of holding things in. It's fucking me up.'

'Tell me about it.' The grunt was sardonic, but a trace of weary sadness in those words made her turn around.

'What's your worst right now?' she asked him, and she scrounged up a laugh for her own least unspeakable offering. 'I've dropped out of law.'

'Yeah?' He gave her a pained smile: 'You'll never beat mine.'

'I'm sure.' She gave him the same pained smile in return. 'Come on, then, what is it?'

He paused for a long, wary moment, as if he was checking she was in fact his sister; finally, he said: 'You don't know?'

'No.' She absolutely didn't; couldn't think of a single thing number-one favourite progeny would be hiding from their father, apart from present circumstances. The words 'anabolic steroids' flitted through her head, but she dismissed that idea almost instantly: Nick prided himself on reaching peak physique through his punishing training regime and vitamin beer. Besides, while he might have been a spoilt, arrogant arse, he'd never been a cheat. Maybe he'd failed one of his uni subjects, or all of them? Or he'd lost his part-time job at the gym? None of that would be any big deal, though, not for him. She said: 'Haven't got the foggiest.'

He frowned, grunted at the actual pain that gave him, and then he asked her: 'You've never wondered why I haven't had a girlfriend in the last four years?'

'No.' She smirked, and as much at herself: she hadn't had a proper boyfriend, either – ever. She said to Nick: 'I've only supposed your natural charm has been keeping them away.'

'Yeah, hilarious.' Nick sighed heavily. 'You're the smartest person I know, Addy, but you're so thick sometimes.'

She frowned now, still not understanding what he was trying to tell her.

He said simply: 'Dave.'

'Dave,' she repeated his name and even then it took her several seconds to work it out. 'Oh?' she said at the first inkling, a vision of him quietly fretting in the waiting room where she'd left him. 'Oh. *Oh.* Are you saying what I think you're saying?'

'Probably.' Nick sounded matter-of-fact, but she could virtually feel his heart charging as he laid it out: 'It's been nearly a year. It's good. It's very fucken good. Would you like to have to tell Dad that, though? And no, I'm not going to. I'm only telling you because – fuck. Every day, day after day, I think I'll blow apart from not being able to say anything or let anything show.' He pointed at his face: 'It's worse than this. A lot worse.'

'Fuck.' That was the sound of all Addy's wonder. Her brother was gay? Almost a decade's worth of increasing distance suddenly made sense. He had a boyfriend? At the first pass, that cut her through with envy: Nick was a bigger freak than she was, in so many ways, and even he could manage to sustain a relationship with a nice guy – indeed, they were living together. But at the second pass, fear rushed at her: fear for him. That kind of love had only been decriminalised last year – not that the New South Wales police were overly interested in upholding the law, as gay men were regularly bashed, even killed, their attackers never brought to any justice. Some right-wing lunatic legislators wanted to have homosexuals charged with manslaughter for the spread of AIDS; gay sex was still illegal in half the country. Nazis would have sent her brother to the gas chambers. This was a big deal. A very big deal. At the slightest hint of anything like this getting out, there would be no way Nick would make the Commonwealth Games team. *Oh, Nicky.* She wanted to hug him, except the Loests didn't do things like that, either. She wanted to reassure him that their dad would never know, no one would ever know, not from her, not until Nick was ready, and when he was ready, she'd stand by him for all she was worth. But all that came out of her mouth was: 'Fuck.' Mostly because she'd run out of other words today; this was one life-changing revelation too many; she said it again: 'Fuck.'

Just as the curtain swished open: 'Right, then, Mr Loest, is it?' A tall, silver-haired man appeared, white-coated and impeccable pronunciation of the surname. He regarded Nick with undisguised approval as he said: 'You are a specimen, aren't you. I'm Doctor Ackerman, and I've had another look at your X-rays. Good news is, you're fine to go home. Bad news is, you have a slight hairline fracture to the cheekbone, and given the seriousness of the concussion, you will need to keep clear of the gloves for a little while. Any further significant dizziness or worsening of the headache, don't hesitate to come back in, or see your GP. I'd strongly recommend you have your GP write you a referral to ...'

Addy couldn't keep hold of the conversation; all she could hear was 'Dr Ackerman', and the withering remains of her last 'fuck' hanging in the air. She was looking at Dan forty years on, same crinkled, twinkling smile; same gentle affability.

Same message for Addy, from every corner and crack of the universe: *Fucken idiot.*

She had almost fallen asleep in the back of Dave's comfortable sedan, slouching on the armrest of the door as they drove her home to Flower Street.

'They'll have some tinned tomatoes at the petrol station – I'll make some minestrone, yeah?' Dave suggested, and Nick replied, 'Yeah, that'd be good.' He was being looked after; this was beautiful; it was also oddly devastating, for Addy.

'Which house is it, Add?' her brother asked her; he didn't even know where she lived. Why would he? She'd never invited him over.

'Just past that next streetlight,' she said, 'on the left.'

Dave pulled the car slowly over to the kerb, but she didn't want to get out; she wanted to stay with Nick, curl up tight and tiny on the seat of one of the rowing machines at his house. She'd be safe there; looked after. She couldn't ask anything like that of him, though; she wouldn't intrude on his life; it wasn't her place, after so long … She reached around the front seat of the car and touched his shoulder instead; she said: 'I've missed you.'

He touched the back of her hand: 'Missed you too, Sprout. See you Sunday.'

'Probably see you on the train.' *I love you.* 'Thanks for the lift, Dave.'

And she was out on the street, a thin mist mizzling through the dimness, chasing her into the house. Down the hall, all was dark and quiet; she turned on the tall black lamp by the brown couch; all was tidy, too. There'd been no one round tonight, obviously. The house was so lonely, Addy was so lonely, not even No Name appeared.

I should be walking into this house with Dan, putting on the kettle.

You screwed that up comprehensively, didn't you.

Yes, I did.

She heard the soft but insistent creak of bedsprings overhead: Roz and Kendall Drummer Boy.

For God's sake. Please.

She went into the kitchen to wait it out; found Roz's cigarettes on the bench by the stove and helped herself to one. There were two bottles of grog there as well, a half-empty flask of vodka and a ruby port, uncorked but only a glass or so down. Port wine wasn't a favourite, always gave her a sinus inflammation, yet it was preferable to vodka, the smell of which alone was enough to make her want to chuck. She glugged a good portion of the port into a coffee cup, and near skulled it down, shivering and gagging as she did so; the instant warmth seemed worth it, though. She felt all her muscles slacken and chorus as one: *Thank you.* A fuzzy, mellow buzz enfolded her – enough to knock her out, she hoped.

Upstairs, the shagging had blessedly ceased, and she drifted bedways now, too. She undressed, hung up her frock, avoided any glimpse of herself in the mirror, throwing her cosiest nightgown over her head: pretty Pollyanna rosebuds with a frill circling the neck. She took one of her small notebooks from her bedside chest, climbed under her quilt and began to write under the light of her little red lamp:

Dear lovely Dan,
I don't know how to apologise for the fuck-up I am,
and I don't know how I'm going to fix all that's wrong
with me. But I would like another chance, please, to
at least make amends for being so rude to you, and to
show you that I really am very fond

She broke off there: *Fond? Who are you writing to? Mr Darcy?* She tore off the page, intending to toss it, then changed her mind, folding it under her pillow instead.

Maybe, she thought, *the apology could burrow into her brain as she slept, and find her some better words for the morning.*

GARDEN-VARIETY
ACTS OF MISOGYNY

*B*LERT, *BLERT, BLERT.* She slept right through until the alarm went off, a dreamless sleep through which her only sense of the world beyond was a certainty that the ruby port had not been a good idea. Irrefutable on waking. The back of her nose throbbed as though someone had been in there with a pickaxe; her eyes screamed, 'No!' on opening.

But Nick will be feeling much worse, was the thought that got her out from under the quilt, to get herself together for work. *But Nick is probably having breakfast in bed, made by someone who loves him*, was the thought that brought all her heartache back, all its suffocating layers. *Dan is not going to want to hear from me – don't annoy him further by writing to him. Just leave it – and him – alone.*

Alone, dazed and aching, Addy washed, brushed, zipped up her uniform; she crept through the sleeping house and out the door. And it was blowing a gale out there: one of those Sydney winds whipped up off the ocean and funnelled through the streets at such velocity it hit the skin like it was carrying splinters of glass. Dodging an airborne cardboard box in the alley nearing Broadway, she decided to make a run for the bus stop, sprinting across six lanes of light early-Saturday traffic – just as a city-bound was pulling in. She made it – *Phew.* She paid the driver, and, still catching her breath, swung into the seat behind him.

'Morning, gorgeous.' A man across the aisle leaned towards her; a gravel-voice, a pervy weirdo of some sort. She heard him rustle a newspaper and shot a glance in his direction, only to check the threat, expecting him to be a sad old wino, but he wasn't anything like that: she noticed his shoes were shiny, black leather business shoes, below navy trousers, all decent quality. A man on his way to work, too, maybe a retail manager, or some other weekend office-type guy. Being careful not to make eye contact, she didn't look at his face. She turned the other way, as though she was looking out the window, except she was really looking over her shoulder, to make sure there were other passengers on the bus – and there were, about ten of them. She wasn't alone with him, at least.

But she screamed inside, her anger as immediate as it was useless: *For fuck's sake, I'm dressed like a tuckshop tea lady, sensible sandshoes, mouse-brown ponytail, and I look like I'm asking for your attention, do I? Fuck you.*

'Can't take a compliment, eh?' He gave her a nasty little laugh as if he'd heard her, and she heard the very real, very ordinary threat in that.

She stared into the back of the bus driver's head, where he sat within his compartment, and she balled her fists in preparation for getting off, silently promising the bastard beside her: *If you try to touch my arse when I stand up, I will smash your hand away from me.* Every unwanted touch she'd ever received came back to her: from dancefloors and crowded trains, and once even at work, when she was reaching up to stack a bunch of hula hoops – a man ran a finger up the back of her leg, a man with three little kids, walking on as if he hadn't done any such thing. Such was the banality of evil. She wasn't going to cop it this morning. *Don't you dare try it, Mr – don't you fucken dare.*

He didn't; she slipped off the bus at her stop, back out into the gale. But the damage had been done. The very worst of this damage had been done a long time ago – seventeen months and twenty-three days ago, to be precise. As she ran across the lights towards Town Hall Variety now, she touched the tail of an understanding, the dragon's tail of her terror, under all the terrors that made up her anxiety, before it roared away. The flash of memory: his hand tearing at her underwear; his breath on the back of her neck.

No!

You invited him.

No one invites that.

You did.

No!

She couldn't let her mind go there, into that locked box; she didn't have time, anyway – she had to find an antihistamine for her sinuses, before she was due in at work. It didn't matter, it really didn't matter, she told herself as she scanned the shelves of the chemist next door. It wasn't as though he'd beaten her up. It wasn't as though she'd been killed. Like her grandmother; like thousands and thousands of other less fortunate women. Addy supposed she'd just outrun it one day, leave it behind her forever. This strategy wasn't working, though, was it.

'That's two dollars ninety-nine, please.' The girl at the counter gave her the first fake smile of the day, and Addy gave no further thought to the basest failings of man.

She'd accidentally bought the tablets containing pseudo-ephedrine, and while her sinus headache vanished within minutes, she spent the next five hours speeding. The slightness of her person meant that it never took a great deal of any pharmaceutical for Addy to feel the effects, and in this instance she'd also accidentally given herself double the dose recommended for men. It wasn't an unpleasant effect, and it certainly made the morning go faster; a busy morning it was, too, despite the weather. *How many pointless, stupid blue gnomes can people want to buy?* Fourteen of them, she counted, making their way down to the ground-floor cash registers, with the usual run of plastic construction sets and grotesquely tizzy fashion dolls – all before lunch. On her break, she forced herself to eat a curried egg sandwich in the staffroom, though she wasn't hungry; and then, idly flicking through a pointless, stupid gossip magazine, its letters' page weeping and whining over bad perms and hubby's bad breath, she began to come back down; down and down she came – with a thump.

When she returned to the toy department, the customer rush had abated, leaving in its wake all kinds of mess for her to attend to. There was even a breakage to record: a little fairy ornament had been smashed, its head lopped off, its wings chipped and broken. This wouldn't have been an easy achievement, by any means; the ornament was made of that sturdy polymer stuff – it would have required some force to break it. Nothing short of a hammer or a stomping under the heel of a boot could have done this to the fairy.

People are disgusting. She turned the pieces over in her hand as she walked across the floor for the Damages Book, to note the detail of the stock loss, and she might have devoted the rest of the day to a contemplation of Schopenhauer's theory of the ultimate pointless stupidity of all human existence, but that the piped music sent her at that moment KC & The Sunshine Band's hymnal heartbeat, 'Please Don't Go'. Of course, Dan looked a little like the lead singer as well, didn't he, except that Dan played the guitar, not the piano, and was a baritone; nevertheless, Addy looked over at the top of the escalators to see if fate might send her another magical coincidence. It didn't; this wasn't Hollywood. In real life, the lead singer, KC, had had a car accident a couple of years ago and had become addicted to painkillers, and Addy had to go over to Kevin in Electricals to get a counter signature on the damaged goods.

'Hey, Addy.' Kevin was pleased to see her; ever cheerful, he seemed pleased to see anyone, and especially pleased if they loved gadgets as much as he did. He was nearing forty, but he was a big kid, and she always managed to find a smile for him.

'Hey, Kevin.' She held out her hand to show him the broken fairy: 'We have a casualty.'

'Oh.' He peered down at the small, sad collection of bits. 'Whackadee. Who'd do a thing like that?' He clicked his tongue. 'You know, I once found a condom in one of the display toasters? A used one.'

'Ew.' Delirium swooped through her.

'Yeah.' He nodded, signing the Damages Book as required. 'There are some kooky people around. Imagine buying that toaster and taking it home and finding a condom in it.'

'Terrible.' Addy could barely get the word out. 'Thanks, Kevin.' She scuttled back to her department, bursting, not with laughter, no, this wasn't laughter; it was a response more savage and desperate than that. She searched for something sobering, anchoring, in the words she'd just written in the Damages Book, under the 'reason' column: *Destroyed by customer (unobserved)*. One of her tears fell onto the bottom of the page; not a tear of sadness or distress – far more savage and desperate than that, too.

She looked at the top of the escalator again and willed Dan Ackerman not to appear. She threw the fairy bits in the bin. She threw herself there after them.

The sunset sky was orange, golden orange, as she walked, almost jogging against the evening chill, back towards Broadway and Mr Lim's takeaway. The air was still now, but she imagined the dust stirred up by this morning's wind hung there, painting the light.

That's not a pointless or stupid thought, she knew; and she wondered: *Maybe I'm meant to be alone. Maybe that's what minds like mine have to be. Maybe I've been trying to fight nature. Like Nick's gay, I'm just me.*

She imagined never having a boyfriend and the thought was unexpectedly comforting: like fried rice, eaten alone in her room. That's exactly what she'd planned to do from hereon into the night, too: fried rice, solitude, and read over what she'd written of her grandparents yesterday, to see if it really was the beginning of something: a new chapter in every sense.

But tonight was not going to pan out like this. She should have known from the moment she stepped into Mr Lim's. He wasn't there; some sour-faced, unhappy stand-in shouted at her from the counter: 'What you want?'

She got her rice, she took it home; took a fork from the kitchen drawer, ignoring the sounds of a gathering outside in the yard, a flickering of flames from the old rusted drum that passed for a firepit, by the back gate, HRH laughing, a trill of, 'Ha-ha-ha-ha-ha-ha-ha,' and some male-laden hubbub above which she thought she heard the crushing of a beer can and Chubs Keveney declaring: 'You'd better believe it.'

Nope. That was the most unbelievable thing Addy had heard all week. Harriet and Chubs toasting marshmallows? That was as plausible as Margaret Thatcher cracking a tinny with the National Secretary of the Shoppies Union: both right wing; very different world views. Addy supposed it was only a trick of dread and hyper-fatigue that she thought someone like Chubs might be in her house. She dismissed it and continued on her way upstairs, where she found that there were no prawns in her fried rice. This was far more disconcerting – Mr Lim always had her rice loaded up with extra goodies, generous chunks of chicken as well – but even still, Addy wasn't shaken all that badly by it. Perhaps she was past shaking. Post-shaken. Post-disappointment. Post-heartbreak. *How postmodern.*

She opened her notebook, with her scribbling from yesterday, and, munching a mouthful of her dinner, she read the last thing she wrote:

Anna lingered by the piano, pretending to find the men's conversation interesting. Her father and Mr Falke were discussing a contractual dispute concerning one of their clients, but it was the young man who'd arrived with Mr Falke that was Anna's prime concern. She'd never seen him before. Who was

That's where Addy had broken off, realising the time, panicking that Dan would soon arrive – and that only set the whole disaster replaying in her mind once more. What did she think she was doing, trying to write out her grandparents' love, when she didn't know anything about the subject? Or so she felt. What was she doing intruding on their tragedy? But then she'd felt so good yesterday, purposeful, when she was writing; she'd felt a door had not so much opened as flown off its hinges, never to be closed again. She had to get herself back there – to this place where maybe, *maybe* she truly belonged.

She opened her atlas, found Darmstadt there, and attempted to force her memories into rewind, into streets that wound back to medieval times, before brownshirts and bombs. She heard something smash outside, down in the yard – only a glass, but it instantly brought her Kristallnacht. What was it like for Adam and Anna? Somehow, she saw her grandfather arguing in the street, arguing for just laws, defending the rights of Jewish shopkeepers; her grandmother behind a lace curtain, not wanting to know. Addy had to know. She heard the brick sail through the window, through time. Did that happen to the Loests, at their house in the city? Did Anna cling to Adam, begging him, 'Please – please, don't go'? Even if Addy begged Frieda Stevenson for every detail, even if Frieda could say, these were things Addy herself could never know, except here: with her own heart, born of their hearts, writing life out on the page.

She found the house, in her heart, in her mind – a town-house, narrow yet elegant, a slate roof and powder-blue render, a few streets from the old square. She was there. She was *there*. And there was no other truth that mattered.

But then, on realising that she was, in the present world of 1985, becoming quite cold, sitting there in only her cotton uniform, she got up to get her warmest cardigan. It was a pukey olive green, with raggedy holes worn through both elbows – she looked like a homeless tea lady now as she wrapped it around herself – and it was a favourite thing, because it had been her father's. It was as old as she was, older, and she wore it to study, here at this desk; it kept her more than warm: it kept her close to him and his hopes for her, and to her mother, too, for she knew Elke's hands had touched this wool. Her mother had kissed her father while he wore it; she had brushed a speck of lint from his shoulder; she had washed —

Oh frick it.

Luke Neilson's jumper was still in the washing machine, downstairs. It had been there since lunchtime-ish yesterday, and would now be a heap of stinking mould, along with her jeans and flannelette shirt and sundry undies. No way would Roz or Harriet have hung out Addy's washing, thoughtfully or otherwise: Harriet took most of her own washing and dry-cleaning home for inclusion in the Rawley-Hogue laundry service; Roz only washed when she ran out of clothes, and only ever on a Sunday. Addy couldn't put it off now that she'd remembered; she'd have to put the load through again, and this time, hang it out. It wouldn't dry before she left for home, for Port, in the morning; it would have to hang out there in the yard all day; not ideal but not avoidable, either.

Oh well, maybe I'll scrounge a beer while I'm —

The stereo started up in the lounge – the techno-calypso of Talking Heads' 'Once in a Lifetime' jumping out of the speakers, turned up way too loud. It wasn't yet seven o'clock; strange for a Saturday night in this house: Roz didn't usually bring a party home until somewhere after eleven, as she didn't knock off wenching until at least ten. Addy could only suppose it might perhaps be Harriet's elder cousin Miles, and some of his friends, who occasionally dropped round to slum it, all law graduates newly dispersed through the city's preeminent firms.

It was, in fact, Chubs Keveney, though, and with him a girl she didn't know but vaguely recognised as maybe a First Year, a Sloane Ranger wannabe. The girl was wearing an oversized cardigan as well, only hers was cream mohair, sewn all over with tiny pearls, and she had a big velvet bow in her hair, a lolly-pink bow that was flopping on top of her head in time with the music. Chubs was still in his rugby gear, smeared all over with grot from the game; he had a graze on one of his knees, and he was dancing with the floppy Sloane bunny in his typical hip-thrusting, ape-brained way, smoke in one hand, can of beer in the other. The song was a sermon, convulsive and urgent, on the emptiness of the capitalist dream, and it was turned up so loud, they didn't hear Addy coming down the stairs, never mind the pertinence of the lyrics.

She couldn't understand how Chubs Keveney was in her house, but here indeed he was, waving as he saw her, bellowing over the music: 'Adddeeeee Lowwwest!' Sloane bunny waved too.

Addy went straight through to the kitchen and out the back door, looking for Harriet, looking to see if she hadn't fallen through the pages of her notebook and ended up in some alternative universe. This did not make sense at all.

Fear returned, like a hand on her shoulder from a man who wasn't there.

Harriet was by the fire drum, brandishing a sparkler, slashing it about in the air. She was off her face: drunk. Harriet never got drunk – not like this. Her poison of choice, if she was going to be bad, was cocaine and Pimm's, and even then, she never lost control. She never had more than one or two beers, because she was always counting her calories. But here she was, just about legless, being grabbed up around the waist by a guy Addy recognised only as a friend of Chubs', Terry someone – someone also wealthy and Catholic – and he spun her around as she twirled the sparkler.

'Harriet!' Addy shouted above the music. 'Harriet!'

'Addles!' The sparkler squiggled frantically. 'Helloooo!'

Don't you call me Addles. 'What's going on?' She peered around the yard to see who else was here, trying to find faces above the firelight leaping about in the drum, her vision still dazzled by sparkler trails; she counted four, maybe five others – at least three of them men, two of them in football jerseys.

'Going?' Harriet stood up, released by Terry whoever-he-was; she was swaying, regarding the sparkler in her hand as it sputtered out. 'My sparkle is going. Oh boohoo! Boohoo.' She twirled it around once more, a spent, charred twig, and then she fell backwards against the tin fence, laughing and laughing, higher and higher. It wasn't funny. Addy felt her stomach turn over as though it were filled with stones, all grinding shame: for Harriet, and for herself, for every time she'd been that drunk – dangerously drunk.

She asked Terry: 'What are you all doing here?'

'Not a lot,' he replied, lighting a cigarette, not overly drunk himself – not that it was easy to tell with guys inured to necking a whole slab every Saturday night. The record changed inside, a new band, staccato snare and bass, singer with a whiny voice; Terry whoever-he-was said over it: 'Kicked on at the Cricketers Arms after the game, meant to come back here to have a shower before kicking on further. Seems we got stuck, kicking on here.'

That was hardly an explanation. 'You just picked our house at random, did you?'

'Oooooh!' A chorus of apes, mocking her; another laugh with it, another girl – another Addy didn't recognise at all.

Harriet slumped down on one of the upturned milkcrates they used for outdoor furniture, as Terry replied: 'We were invited.' A shrug, a chuckle: he'd do as he pleased.

Addy was pinned for a moment by the derision that glittered in his eyes; she was unsure what to do. Her nerves sped past fear and into that other realm, that place of disconnection. The other girl had joined Harriet on the milkcrates: 'Darling, how about we get some Thai food for din-dins. There's a new place ...'

This is none of my business, Addy told herself. Heartbreak does odd things, she knew that from her own learnings, and Harriet was just letting off some steam of her own. For whatever reason, she'd hooked up with this girlfriend, whoever she was, and they'd brought some meatheads home. *Not my business at all*, Addy told herself again, even though she already knew this night would not end well.

She left them; she had washing to do.

'That chick has no sense of humour,' she heard one of the other guys say as she went back inside.

I'll put the wash on rapid spin cycle, hang it all up in my room until the coast is clear, she was deciding as she slid open the laundry door. *It'll be fine. Not ideal, but fine. Harriet will be fine – her father is a Justice of the Supreme Court. No one is going to harm a hair on her head – not any of those guys, anyway, wouldn't want to ruin their career chances. I'm just annoyed that they're making so much noise, when I want to be writing a novel. A novel? Is that really what I'm writing? Yes, I think it is.* She let herself smile as she felt the fresh, tender thrill of that, even as she smelt the damp, festy clothes on opening the lid of the washing machine. *Yuck.* The stereo was belting out a faster song, its lyrics an anthem to adolescent desperation, the whiny voice getting whinier, and angrier, wanting a fuck.

'Addy Lowest.' She felt the breath on the back of her neck first, more than she heard the voice.

I just want this week to end, was the last thought she had before she turned around, expecting to see Chubs, expecting to tell him to fuck off and leave her alone. It wasn't Chubs, though. It was someone whose face she knew – a face at

Manning Bar, or in the uni cafeteria line, a face passed on her way between tute rooms – but she couldn't think of his name. He wasn't in any way remarkable; just a guy. He wasn't particularly tall, and yet he filled the doorway. She could smell the grass stains in his jersey and the piss on his breath.

He said: 'What are *you* doing here?'

She said: 'A load of washing. Maybe you should go home and do a load of your own.'

'You've got a smart little mouth on you, don't you.' He smiled around his private-school vowels; his eyes were dull, grogged up. His face in her face.

'What do you want?' She tried to edge away, but the space was so small, there was nowhere to go; the top of the washing machine dug into her back; the shelf above, where the washing powder and pegs were kept, scraped against her head.

'I think you know what I want, nursey,' he said, pressing himself against her, one hand on the shelf, the other on the machine beside her, trapping her there. *Nursey?* He pushed his erection into her stomach; through his shorts and her uniform she could feel how hard he was. He grabbed her ponytail: 'I want your little mouth to suck my cock.'

'My little mouth might want to bite it off,' she snapped back at him, and instantly regretted it.

'Like to play rough, do you? All right, then.' He yanked her head back and held her by the throat against the lid of the machine, and then reached behind him with his other hand to slide the door across. Dark closed around her, except for one tiny sliver of light.

'No.' The protest was hopeless – no one would hear her with the music thrashing so loud. She tried to appeal to his senses with the little she had left of her own: 'If you rape me, I will go to the police.'

This time – this time, I will.

'And who is going to believe a little scrubber like you?' he snarled.

Scrubber? As though she was fair game because of her class, because she was from a lesser tribe. And she was, to him, and every man like him. But when she felt something brush the inside of her thigh – his cock, a knuckle, she couldn't know – she lost her shit entirely: *I don't care if I die. Not this time.*

Outside, in the lounge, she heard Chubs saying, 'This album is so shit from here.' The music stopped, and in the seconds she thought she might have before the record changed, she screamed for all she was worth; an incoherent stream of every terror she'd ever known. She bashed at the sliding door with her right foot. She bashed at his face; she dug her nails into his cheeks.

'You fucking bitch!' He staggered back, almost knocking the door off its track. 'You crazy, fucking bitch!'

She wasn't finished yet; she pulled the near-full one-kilo box of washing powder from the shelf and bashed that at him, too. The tiny room filled with soap dust, and although Addy hadn't intended it, the arsehole copped a lungful – and staggered back again, coughing and heaving, right through the door. The track splintered off the frame above, and the whole thing fell to the floor, where he lay sprawled for a moment, pulling up his shorts, with Chubs looking in from the lounge: 'Jesus, Rourkie – what the fuck?'

The girl with the bow and mohair cardigan laughed beside him: 'Oh, Chris, what have you done?'

Chris. Rourkie. The name came to her now: Christopher O'Rourke. She wouldn't forget it again. And it rang a deeper bell still: he wasn't Young Labor or any of Keveney's usual lot – that's why she couldn't place him straightaway; he was Young Liberal, someone important in the scheme, father owned a chain of hotels or caryards or something. Someone who pronounced the 'g' in 'fucking'. He *was* power: money. Lots of it.

She told floppy bunny girl: 'Your friend just tried to rape me.' Her breath was ragged, but her words were clear.

'You filthy little liar,' he shot straight back at her as he got to his feet; he told Chubs: 'I didn't touch her. She's fucking nuts. I thought it was the toilet in there, and she just – went fucking nuts. Look what she did to my face.' He pointed to where she'd scratched his cheeks – barely, as it turned out, for all the force she'd tried to unleash.

She looked at Chubs and floppy bunny girl: they seemed to believe him; the girl frowned at her, querying. And that's when the shock set in, in those few seconds of silence that sat between them, there in the kitchen. That's when she began to doubt herself. Had she overreacted? Had she misinterpreted —

'Hello?' She heard a knock at the front door, and footsteps following after it; the door was open, and she expected to see another football jersey or several crash in off the street. 'Hello? Addy? Are you home?'

It was Dan. She saw the scuffed toes of his work boots first, and then his grey canvas overalls. She could not have known what he saw when he looked at her, washing powder showered all over her dad's old cardigan, her ponytail half pulled out, her face drained of colour, eyes filled with terror and despair. She only knew he looked horrified.

'Addy?' He looked at the laundry door on the floor, con- fused, as anyone would have been: 'What happened?'

'Just a misunderstanding.' Chubs stepped in. 'Addy thought Rourkie was having a go at her.'

'Having a go? What do you mean?' Dan looked to Addy again. She couldn't respond, though; she'd lost the power of speech. She wanted to run, but he was blocking her way – Chubs was as well.

'She thought Rourkie was making advances.' Chubs tried to laugh it off; some laughter drifted in from the backyard, too, Harriet trilling above it all: 'Noooo! I don't want pizza – I want tom yum goong, I truly do!'

'Were you?' Dan stepped further into the kitchen; he stepped towards Christopher O'Rourke. 'Making advances?'

'As if,' Christopher O'Rourke replied, composed as though he'd done this a hundred times; perhaps he had. 'I was having a joke with her, but you know what a crazy bitch she is.'

'Who's crazy?' Dan wasn't buying any of it. 'You know who her brother is, don't you? You'd have to be fucken game.'

'And you know what a prick tease she is, don't you.' Christopher O'Rourke shot back, laying plain his legal defence.

'No, I don't,' said Dan, standing over him. 'Tell me all about it.' Dan pushed him in the chest, pushed him so hard he fell back against the stove, coffee cups rattling in the cupboard overhead.

'Dan – Dolly – don't.' Chubs tried to hose him off. 'There'll be a pile-on if you take this further. Settle down.'

Settle down? Addy couldn't settle down, and she didn't want to see how this would end; she found her way unblocked now, and darted out through the lounge, up the hall.

'Go on, call the cops – you'll find out what happens if you do,' Christopher O'Rourke called after her, but they all knew the answer to that: she could never win.

She just wanted to be free of him, all of them, and so she ran.

She ran out into the night like a crazy bitch – and Dan Ackerman was running after her.

THIS IS WHAT A HERO ACTUALLY LOOKS LIKE

'Addy!' He kept on after her, all the way up to the alley. 'Please stop, let me help.'

There's nothing you can do. Please, go away.

She couldn't outrun him, though, obviously. She might well have been a little fitter than he was, but his legs were far longer, and she was tiring. And yet, even when she could run no longer, she did not stop moving; she kept up a pace through the alley and around the winos' pub onto Broadway.

'Addy, where are you going?' He was almost by her side.

I don't know. The pedestrian lights here at the crossing were flashing red, so she kept on going straight ahead, towards the centre of town.

'Please, let me help.' He was not going to go away. 'Did he hurt you?'

She couldn't say at that moment; she was still fighting for the truth of just what had occurred. Christopher O'Rourke *had* attacked her. There had been no mistake; no misunderstanding. He had meant to hurt her. He had meant to assault her. He *did* assault her. Her scalp still ached where he'd pulled her hair; her ankle was throbbing from having kicked at the door; the middle of her back was sore where he'd pressed her against the washing machine: these were facts.

'Addy, let me call my dad. You don't have to go to the police if you don't want to. He can deal with it through the hospital. I know he'll help – he'd want to help.'

'No.' The word flew from her; that would be one more humiliation too far. She could only imagine Dr Ackerman remembering her as the foul-mouthed girl from last night, maybe even judging her; no matter how nice he'd seemed, she would be ashamed of herself. Besides, she couldn't bear the thought of the fuss, the questions, the doubt upon doubt upon doubt. But 'no' was all she could say about it right now.

'I'm sorry if I'm making a pest of myself,' Dan continued regardless. 'I can't let you walk alone through the streets like this. You'll just have to put up with me.'

This stretch of Broadway was its usual night-time wasteland of empty warehouses, boarded-up shops and old workers' pubs no one frequented anymore. The brewery that sat in the middle of the next block was belching out the stench of hops; a truck lumbered past with a rattling cough; and they walked on.

After a while, Dan said: 'I came over to apologise. To see if you might have wanted to talk. I don't know what I did last night to upset you, but whatever it was, I'm sorry. I've felt bad about it all day – the way I left – like I was shitty. I wasn't shitty – I was embarrassed. I meant to call you, from work, but I left your number at home. Then I got caught up – my uncle Evan needed me to help him with this big order, and I couldn't get away. I'm sorry.'

That broke through, a little: he sounded so regretful – as though he might have prevented Christopher O'Rourke from attacking her. As though he might have prevented his fellow men from being arseholes generally.

She said: 'You haven't done anything to upset me.'

He said: 'Do you want to go for a drive or something, and just talk?'

She nodded: 'Yep.'

Still, she didn't say a further word as they made a return loop through the backstreets; and he didn't press her to speak, either. By the time they got to his car, parked on the kerb opposite her house, a delivery driver carrying a stack of pizza boxes was knocking on the front door.

As though nothing has happened, except that they decided against Thai, after all.

The stereo was playing something more sedate, something she couldn't quite hear.

How civilised.

She didn't know how she was ever going to walk back into that house again.

Dan drove her through the city, past the movie-theatre crowds, past the black labyrinth of the business district and out beyond the tourist trap of Circular Quay, to a part of Sydney she'd never seen before, though it wouldn't have been five kilometres from Flower Street. The Harbour Bridge vaulted up above the road, its line of lights shooting out across the water like stars. It was quite a magnificent sight, solid steel floating in the blue-black night; it was deserted here, too, nothing but decommissioned wharves, and the smell of the sea.

He said: 'It's all right here, isn't it.'

She almost smiled: *You're such a poet.* But she knew there was a lot more than that going through his mind.

He said: 'I come here when I'm feeling out of sorts.'

And then they sat there together for a long time not saying anything at all, only listening to the steady hum of traffic across the bridge, the clacking of a train heading north. She began to come back into herself; more tired, more deeply sore, everywhere, but somehow normal, whatever normal might be. A yellow splash of graffiti on the warehouse wall outside the window of the car said: '*Wazza was here.*' She felt just like that: mad, wonky, but here. She looked at Dan; he looked at her. He was tired, too; but he was here, too.

Finally, she said: 'Thank you. Thank you for being such a good friend.'

He gave her a sad smile; he said: 'I wouldn't want to be anywhere else.'

And that was it for Addy. She didn't have time to hide her face, the rush of her own sadness; there was nowhere to hide anyway, inside this tiny car. They were so close.

'Hey …' The sound he made was warm; safe.

The sound she made was of her wounding, and it was no less tortured for the delay. A small sound, but so essential, so profound, it filled all time and space. She stared ahead into the chrome button of the glove box, tiny silver disc shining out of the black. She told herself, and the silence and the sea: *I'm safe. I'm safe.*

'Are you sure you don't want to see a doctor?' Dan made the sensible suggestion again. 'Maybe a woman? Or maybe I can drive you home to Mum – she can sort it out. She'll understand – she really will. And she will want to see O'Rourke pay for this as much as I do. He should pay.'

Yes, he should, but not tonight and not with Addy's dignity, or the little she felt she had left. Revenge wasn't what she wanted in any case; she wanted the truth, and she wanted to tell it – now.

She told Dan: 'He didn't rape me. He wanted to. He pushed me down and pulled my hair. He rubbed himself against me. But that's not what it's really about. It's not the *doing*. It's the fear. The fear has got into me, inside every part of me, so that I'm frightened all the time. I'm frightened of men. I'm frightened of love. I'm frightened of myself. I *am* a crazy bitch. Every day, I am frightened and mad and ashamed.'

Dan frowned, not quite following: 'Ashamed? But —'

'Yes.' Now Addy let it flood from her: 'Ashamed. Damaged. Dirty. Fucked up. Fair game. Smile, missy. Have a sense of humour. Can't you take a compliment? Can't you not be a freak? It's all on me, and I don't know how to fix it – how to fix me. I don't think I can. And the one who really did do it, the one who really did hurt me – I'm pretty certain he's not given me a second thought since. It's too late now to try to make him pay, and the law wouldn't make him pay, anyway. The charge would get laughed out of court. In fact, it wouldn't get past Wollongong police station.'

'What wouldn't?' Dan asked her, with the same urgency; she still wasn't making sense to him. She was only making him upset, on her account; she could see his frown darkening; she could see him holding it back as fiercely: 'It's not my right to know, Addy, I'm sorry if I'm pressuring you, but —'

'No, it's all right,' she told him. 'I want to say it. I want to tell you.' *I trust you.* How she did. She'd come this far; even her tears were certain, thick and plain on her cheeks for this witness of a friend, not ashamed in this at least, inside this now, this here. 'His name is Alan Hadley,' she said, a name released like something rotten, something diseased. 'Not that he's anyone in particular.'

Dan nodded, speaking only with his eyes: *Go on.*

'He's the son of a real estate agent, in Wollongong,' she told him. 'Family business, upstanding members of the community, his dad's a part-time minister, holy rollers and all that. His older brother is a policeman.' She would tell Dan Ackerman everything; she would banish her silence to the sea: 'He was in Nick's year at school. They weren't *mates* mates, but they'd played football together. I'd been studying for my exams, had my head down so much that I'd forgotten about the Year Twelve formal. I didn't have a date – had a dress, of course.' She remembered that dress as though she held it in her hands right now: baby-blue Chantilly lace over white satin, simple but unusual, and handmade, ageless; she would wear it with strappy white sandals and a white mesh purse, all got for under ten dollars from three different charity shops; her only adornment would be the single-pearl pendant her father had given her for her eighteenth birthday, under advice from a lady at the local jewellers. 'But I hadn't got around to asking anyone,' she explained to Dan. 'I wasn't interested in anyone. I was working too hard, to make sure I got the marks to get into law – I didn't want to disappoint Dad by stuffing it up, missing out. If I wasn't studying, I was cooking fish and chips, doing Saturday shifts at a takeaway. I didn't have time to look at any boys other than those in my Maths class, just friends who were helping me get through calculus, my weakest link – that was all I was freaking out about then.

'Anyway, Alan wasn't exactly academic. After he'd finished school, he'd got into renovating old properties – his father would buy a crumbling bomb of a place and Alan would do it up, then sell it on at a profit. He'd been doing really well, had plenty to be happy about – he drove a brand-new car. For weeks I'd seen him almost every day, as he'd been working on a house right across the road from the school. I knew him enough to say hello, how're you going, how's Nick, blah blah for five minutes while I waited for the late bus home. He was all right to look at, hair bleached from the surf and fit from hard work, always in paint-spattered shorts, dusty boots. He seemed normal. Just a guy. He liked a chat. He'd ask me what I was studying, seemed impressed I wanted to enrol in arts and law. "Oh yeah?" he'd say. "You've got some brains, haven't you." He was funny in that sort of smart-arsy way, making cracks about the teachers and what have you. It was all small talk. Nothing in it, so I thought. I'll ask him to the formal, I decided – why not? And when I did, he gave me that same smart-arsy smile, saying, "Far be it from me to pass up the opportunity for free alcohol and perving at all your girlfriends." I didn't think he thought anything of me except that I was Nick's nerdy little sister. It didn't occur to me that anything would happen.

'The formal was pretty boring, all drinking and Top-40 dancing. I was still tired from the exams, stressing that I could have done better, not sleeping properly. My stomach was still upset, so I didn't even drink that much, probably half a glass of wine the whole night. I just couldn't relax. But I went down to the beach with everyone afterwards. I didn't want to be the dag that went home early, like all the other migrant kids. Alan was having a good time, or that's how it looked. I don't know how drunk he was. Drunk enough that the law would give it to him as an excuse, I have no doubt. There was a bonfire and bottles of el cheapo champagne being passed around with spliffs, and Alan said, "I'm a bit wasted. Come for a walk up to the lighthouse?" I said, "Sure," thinking I owed him a favour. I said, "A walk would be good, then I might get a cab home," thinking I'd save him the trouble of taking me – not that he was in any state to drive. We started walking up the dune at the back of the beach, where it's steep and scrubby, and once we'd got a little way beyond the crowd, not far, he grabbed my arm and said, "I'm not good enough for you, am I?" I didn't know what he was talking about. He shifted so suddenly, I didn't know what was going on. I said, "I don't know what you mean." He didn't answer. He just kept pulling me by the arm, through the scrub. All I could think was that he was going to kill me. I thought he was going to strangle me, bash me, smash me into the lighthouse rocks. I was so terrified, I'd have done anything he said. I don't remember much from then on, though. He pushed me onto the sandy grass, and he held me facedown there. I don't think it took very long. I only remember how much it hurt. How shocked I was that he was tearing me apart.'

Dan muttered something she didn't hear; she wasn't quite finished telling: 'I don't think I made a sound the whole time, I was too frightened. All I could hear was the pounding of my heart. When he stopped, he shoved me around and pushed twenty dollars into the top of my dress, into my bra. He said, "That's for your university fund. Don't tell anyone I didn't do the right thing by you." And he walked off, back down to the bonfire. I got up, tidied my dress, then I went and found a phone box and called a cab. I went home, had a wash, went to bed. I was in such shock, I didn't know what had happened. I'd never had sex before. I was pretty naïve about it all. I knew what he'd done, physically, but I didn't really know. I don't have a mother to talk to about those kinds of things, she died when I was small, and Dad – well, I don't say anything to upset Dad, he's had a hard enough time, and his idea of sex education has always been, "Stay away from boys," full stop. The next day, and every day afterwards, I just got on with things. I went straight into working full time for a couple of months, saving up for uni, for moving to Sydney. I had to get myself organised, find a place to live, with Roz, find a city job. I started to doubt myself straightaway. I wasn't sure if I'd made a mistake. I couldn't make sense of it – why he was so rough. Why he did it in the first place. Why he would terrorise me like that. What for? Only a week later, I heard he started going out with another girl from school, and I thought that was the end of it – I thought at least he wouldn't come after me and do it again. I thought I could forget about it. I put that dress in the garbage. I thought I could just leave it there, in the bin. Get over it.'

The realisation struck her then: the panic that had stalked her ever since, the sweeping dread, the loose ballooning, the drinking, poor lovely Luke Neilson, mucking him about the way she had, a clumsy attempt to fix the unfixable. The certainty she was having a heart attack; the certainty she was going mad. It was Alan Hadley all along who had caused this. Alan Hadley and a conspiracy of silence. Alan Hadley and possibly a genetic predisposition for bad shit happening. She would never know why so many men were arseholes, but she could know this: Alan Nobody Hadley had robbed her of joy for the past year and a half. He'd robbed her of the choice of sex – he'd robbed her of any love she might have had. He had hurt her. He had smashed her on the rocks. And his moral doppelganger had had another go tonight – in her own house.

She said to Dan Ackerman: 'I'll never be over it.'

'No.' He said the word so softly, she could almost hear the stitching together of their souls, bound forever now with this secret shared.

She said: 'At least all that might explain why I've been so weird – to you specifically, I mean. I'm not girlfriend material. I'm way too complicated. I should come with a warning label.'

She'd meant that as a joke, an acid one between mates, but he looked away, up at the bridge; probably disengaging from the remains of his own romantic fantasies, or so she presumed. She closed her eyes, rested her head on the back of the seat: relieved; scoured out, burnt out, devastated, and yet relieved. She told him again: 'Thank you for being such a good friend, Dan. I can't tell you how much you've helped, just by listening. I don't know what would've happened if you hadn't run after me tonight.'

He didn't reply. Several minutes went by before he asked her: 'What do you want to do now?'

That was a very good question. She didn't want to go back to Flower Street; she wished she could click her fingers and be home with her dad right now, pretending that none of this had happened, as per usual, resuming the snug confines of denial. She wished she was curled up on the couch at Gallipoli Street, watching a late-night movie, she and her dad passing a tub of Neapolitan ice-cream between them. But she had to go back to Flower Street whether she wanted to or not: she'd run out without purse or keys; she needed to change – she needed to shower. She needed to sleep. She needed to think about maybe packing a bag and going home for a week.

She asked Dan, and she was only joking again: 'You don't feel like driving to Port Kembla tonight, do you?'

'Where?' He turned to her, grim frown seeming confused once more.

She said: 'Port Kembla, home, as in Dad home – near Wollongong. And no, I'm not serious. I wouldn't ask you to drive for an hour and a half —'

'I know where Port Kembla is,' he said with the deepest reaches of that baritone, so gentle, so pensive. 'I've never been there myself, but that's where my grandfather was born – Mount Kembla, anyway, his father was a miner there, when he first arrived from Germany. They lived at Kembla until – doesn't matter. I just mean it's a bit strange, isn't it, like there's some kind of echo going on between us, you and me.'

Time seemed to tilt; her chest tightened not with anxiety but with those threads of gold thickening, though she was too post-fraught exhausted now to know them for what they were. The ancestral footsteps that had brought them here together were as real and ethereal as the lights on the bridge, a line of electric stars leading to this very spot on the globe, though she wasn't inclined to see them as such at this moment, either.

No. No more make-believe, she told herself.

'I'm happy enough with the coincidence that made you walk in on the ape brigade when you did,' she told Dan, words sharp from her aching throat; aching head. She steered back to practicalities: 'Is it okay if you drive me back to Flower Street, please? If they've moved on, I'll stay there. If not, I'll call my brother and see if I can stay with him.' Calling Nick was the last thing she wanted to do; though she was looking forward to seeing him tomorrow, to saying hello on the train without wanting to move carriages, she didn't want to explain to him what had happened tonight, never mind what had happened with Alan Hadley – Nick would make a fuss, he would tell their dad, and her brother and father would both end up in prison then. She didn't want to lie to him, either. She didn't want to confront any more of anything, not tonight. Her epiphany just now at the source of all her fear hadn't made her any less scared – of everything. She asked Dan: 'Is it okay if you come into the house with me?'

'Sure,' he said, turning the key in the ignition. 'Of course.'

He looked over his shoulder to check for non-existent traffic; she didn't see how upset he was; nor did she see the effort it took him to hide it from her.

From the street, she could see a light on at the front of the house – Harriet's room – lamplight soft through a crack in her curtains, but otherwise all was dark and hushed. It was only a little after half-past nine, yet it felt later, quieter, as if the police had just been through to break up a party.

She gave Dan a deep-breath shrug of, *Here goes*, and knocked on the door, calling out, 'Hello, Harriet? It's only Addy – forgot my key.' *When I ran from this house. How can I live in this house anymore?* She'd avoided pretty much the whole small city of Wollongong since the night of her school formal, except for the necessity of the train station; she wasn't going to be able to avoid the University of Sydney so easily, even if she did find somewhere else to live. She tapped on the window, too: 'Sorry!' Then she waited a few moments; if need be, she would get in the back way, ask Dan to give her a leg up onto the kitchen roof and break in via the dodgy lock on her bedroom window above, but she'd rather not do that if she didn't have to – it would mean dragging herself half a block around to the back lane and wrestling with the old gate. After a second tap on the window and an, 'Are you there, Harriet?' she finally heard a murmur inside: 'For God's sake.'

A thump and creak of floorboards and the door flew open: Harriet, not quite looking herself. With dishevelled bed hair but still wearing jeans and blouse, she had evidently retired early to pass out.

'Thanks,' Addy said, from the doorstep, Harriet standing in the way, perhaps grasping the edges of the door and the frame for balance, her face like melted wax.

'Hm.' She looked Addy up and down, eyes red, still drunk, but sober enough to know what she said next: 'You're going to have that laundry door repaired.' She humphed and glared: 'I'm not paying for it.'

'Yes, you are.' Addy was beyond too tired for this; she was five miles past petty anger and bitchy spats; she couldn't know it yet, but she'd never cop anything like this again. 'Excuse me.' She stepped forward, forcing Harriet to move back and let her through, as she added: 'You invited those animals into the house, you can clean up their mess.'

Halfway down the hall, she heard Harriet say to Dan, 'I don't know what you see in her.'

Dan said nothing; he'd barely said a word on the way back here – not that Addy had noticed. Her mind had been ticking over what she might do in this case or that case, backwards and forwards and round and round. And now, in the lounge, she saw a chaos of records and tapes scattered across the floor, half of them hers; her telephone book had been knocked off the top of the piano and its contents of takeaway menus, random notes and cards spilled everywhere – her last appointment reminder from the Women's Clinic looked up at her as a final violation of her person.

She bent down to gather it all together again, consumed by the idea that tonight must be a kind of goodbye, in every sense. She could not continue living here. *But where will I go? How will I move? How will I get my wardrobe back down the stairs? I don't want to leave Roz. Will she come with me? Or will I find a little flat by myself? With a writing window. And No Name. Can I do that? I'm too scared.* It was all too overwhelming to think about.

'I'll do this.' Dan began stacking the pizza boxes that were lying about open on the coffee table, half-eaten slices of garlic and mushroom, marinara, supreme – they were the best pizzas, piled high with topping, now a small, sad monument to uncaring, to waste. It looked like a neutron bomb had gone off midway through their feasting, vaporising all trace of humanity; rats scurrying off to destroy someone else's place after running out of grog, she thought more reasonably. 'You do what you need to do, Addy,' Dan said, somehow gentle and firm about it at the same time. 'I'll stay here. At least until Roz gets in.'

Was there a more decent guy on earth? Indeed, what on this earth did he see in her? This used-up, screwed-up thing that was all she could see of herself. He was still in his work clothes, and under the harsh light of the overhead bulb she could see now how grubby he was from his day; how washed out he looked, near as grey as his overalls.

She said: 'You're having a fun Saturday night, aren't you.' *I'm so, so sorry.* 'Thank you for caring, but you really don't have to stay.'

He said: 'If it bothers you that I'm here, I'll go. It wouldn't seem right to leave you alone, though. I'd prefer to stay.' The tone said he wasn't going to argue about it.

She almost gasped at his kindness: 'That's the nicest thing anyone's ever done for me.'

'Yep. Nice.' He took the load of pizza boxes out to the kitchen. 'Do you want a cup of tea?' he asked her as he went; she could hear his boots crunching through the soap powder on the floor there.

'No thanks,' she said. Although she'd have eaten live spiders for a warm, milky tea right then, she needed a shower more; she told him, already turning for the stairs: 'I'm going to get myself cleaned up.'

She felt mean as she left him, but she couldn't help it. The soap powder that had gone down the neck of her uniform had begun to irritate her skin – she had to wash it off this minute. She needed the heat and thrum of the water on her back, its arms around her, predictable, steady – clean, clean, clean. She couldn't have said how long she stood there – as long as it took – she didn't care. She scrubbed and sudsed every inch of herself; she shampooed and conditioned her hair. If she could have fallen asleep inside this warm-ball cocoon of steam she'd made of the bathroom, she would have. But she wanted that cup of tea, too. And she needed to get that damn washing done – it was still growing a new life form down there in the machine.

Back in her room, she stood dumbly for a moment, wrapped in her towel, her damp skin slapped by the cold, wondering what she should wear. It didn't seem appropriate to put on a nightgown – she never wore a nightie of any sort beyond bedroom or bathroom – but her mind had turned to such mush she couldn't make sense of the other options. She opened her wardrobe doors and all her frocks stared back at her, each one a historical document, of a woman and her time. She saw them more clearly for what they really were now, though: a longing for her mother, a need to have her near somehow. A need to know the unknowableness of her. Not since Addy was fifteen and earning enough at part-time work to buy her own clothes, had she bought any frock off the rack. True, the cheaper dresses in places like Town Hall Variety and other department stores were so repulsive she wouldn't want to wear them, anyway, but that wasn't why she had obsessively collected so much apparel from the decades, the days, of her mother's existence.

How she wanted real arms around her. Loving arms. The last person to hug her had been Max Kovacs, half a hug with one huge arm, crushing her at the boxing last night, the same pulverising hug he gave everyone. Before that, Roz had hugged her drunkenly on their way to the winos' bottle shop the Saturday night before last, and that was really only because Addy had tripped up the gutter in the dark and stubbed her toe.

The chill had no more time for idle melancholy, though, and it forced Addy to find what she needed more immediately: some warm clothes. She chose thick black tights and a skivvy – her favourite skivvy, a purple one. Then she found the hair dryer as well, where she'd left it, in Roz's room; she flicked the switch to give her wet head a quick blast. The whine of the hair dryer brought a soothing ordinariness, of doing the simple things that needed to be done, and she hummed along tunelessly with it – *wrrrrrrrrrr, wrrrrrrrrrr, wrrrrrrrrrr*. After a minute or two, she imagined she could hear a piano accompaniment: the bass notes of the *Moonlight Sonata*, the sorrow-tinted wistfulness of the first movement in particular. And she did allow herself a smile at that: madness had its compensations, didn't it?

But when she turned off the hair dryer, the music continued. Someone was actually playing the piano. It couldn't have been Harriet, who was no doubt at present still incapable of the hand–eye coordination required; and she never played Beethoven. *Is it a record?* Addy wondered. No, it surely wasn't – she knew every note and every whisper of her own copy, and hers was the only copy in the house. It was either Dan, or No Name, or someone Addy didn't want to converse with, whoever it might have been. She lingered on the landing, half annoyed at the intrusion, half comforted by the music. While it wasn't the happiest piece ever written, it was so perfectly formed; a wordless essay on beauty that always brought her butterflies, it was impossible not to be lifted by it. And whoever was playing, they were good at the job; these were practised hands.

She took a few steps down the stairs; she had to know who it was. And she saw it was Dan. At the piano seat. Playing with no music on the stand.

What? But he plays the guitar, in a post-punk jingle-jangle band, she thought. *Rhythm guitar – the workmanlike jangle to the jingle ...* Evidently, not this night.

She looked at her own hands, touched her still slightly damp hair, looked at her toes curled round the edge of the stair: she was here.

He played on, slowly, deliberately, letting those final chords of the movement drift; and before she could even think to make any sound of appreciation for it, he was into the second, a kaleidoscope shift, butterflies dancing, beginning to break free. She realised she'd heard him play this sonata before – sometime in the early hours of Wednesday morning. *Oh, please – really?* She let the delight of it take her for a moment, a laugh escaping. He kept going a few bars more, but he fumbled, laughing too: 'And I jiggered that up, didn't I.' Then he turned in the seat to look at her: 'Hi.'

'Hello.' Her head swam off with her heart: who would *not* be in love with him? Playing Beethoven in grey overalls. After tidying up the lounge room. For real. But it was the wrong, wrong time. She reached out for the bannister, dizzy.

'You okay?' he asked, getting up, moving towards the stairs, towards her, concerned.

'I'm all right.' *Liar.* She felt her balloon loosening; she sat straight down, on the step. *Breathe.*

'You don't look all right,' he said, moving closer, leaning a hand on the step below her. She tried to focus on his eyes: they weren't completely brown but flecked with gold and blue; unusual.

'I just need that cup of tea, I think.' Her voice had sounded far away, trapped in a bottle at the bottom of the ocean. *I will never be free of this.*

'Sure. I'll put the kettle on. Stay there.' He left for the kitchen; she listened to the clank of cup on bench, the pop of the lid on the teabag tin; the swift whistle of the kettle boiled not long ago. 'How do you have it, Addy?'

'Just milk, please.' *Don't care.*

He brought it up to her, there on the step; he even gave it to her handle outwards: so thoughtful. He said: 'Maybe you want to take it up to your bed?'

She shook her head: 'I'm all right. Really.' *I am only a small load of multiple disasters. Load?* 'I've got to get a load of washing on.'

'I don't think so,' the smile-frown said. 'Not now. It's past ten o'clock.'

'I can't leave it as it is,' she told him, panic regrouping around this nearest triviality. 'It's already stinking – I left it in the machine yesterday. And I've got to get up early in the morning, for the train home. I have to do it now.'

'I'll deal with the washing,' he said, so mildly, but in that same no-argument way.

Why are you so kind to me? She was just like a stray cat being coaxed to trust; like No Name had been when she'd first met him, hiding in the tall tin-fence shadows of the back yard. She couldn't yet see herself for what she was: how worthy she was of kindness. And love.

His loveliness did calm her, though; he helped her tether that balloon again just by holding her there with his eyes, wanting to help. He said: 'You can have a sleep-in in the morning, anyway.'

'No, I can't.' That brought her back with a jolt; she wanted to touch his face, to touch something of his many sweet thoughts. But she wouldn't do that; she gave him the nuts and bolts of it: 'I've got to get the eight o'clock train.'

'No, you don't. I'm driving,' he said, eyebrows raised somehow smugly, before he explained: 'Your brother called, when you were in the shower. He wanted to check the train time or something. We got talking and, I don't know, I just offered to drive. I said I'd pick him up on the way through.'

'My brother called?' Addy didn't know what was more unbelievable: that Nick had actually picked up a phone to call her; that he would need to check the time of the train they always caught; or that he and Dan had had a chat. That last seemed so out of the realms, she had to ask: 'What did you talk about?'

'Not much, not for long,' he said quickly, a little awkward about it. 'Just the fight last night, said he'd cracked his cheekbone, had a concussion and all that. And that's when I offered to drive.'

She did not believe that at all, but she couldn't have said exactly why. It was just beyond odd – like the front door was about to burst open with men in white coats come to take her away, papers signed by a Dr Ackerman, charging in on a zebra. *Maybe that wouldn't be a bad idea.* She sipped her tea: that was real enough; in fact, it was excellent, just the way she liked it, though he'd never made her a cup of tea before. She asked him, testing: 'And you play the piano, too?'

'Ah. Hm.' He blushed; he was so beautiful, the way his cheeks filled with rose-coloured gorgeousness. 'Yeah. Bit of fancy maths, that is. I'll do anything to try to impress a girl.'

The tenderness he sent with that gave her another jolt; she caught a glimpse of her own power, its wayward tail; she couldn't decide or dismiss whatever it was he felt for her. And she couldn't deny what she felt for him, either. That wasn't fancy maths. It was quite simple, really.

She said: 'Dan. I want to love you. I think I already do. But I'm not ready.' As she said it, some knot within her unwound, a tension gave way; even as she added: 'I'd be worried I might break us both.'

'It's all right, Addy.' He sat on the step below her, his shoulders straight against the wall, his eyes still holding her. 'I can wait. It's taken me two months to get here, since the first time I saw you. I'm not a fast mover.'

'Two months?' She was surprised; she hadn't really registered his being at all until this Monday night just passed.

'Yeah.' His smile curled crookedly, wry: 'Remember that band comp night? At Manning Bar? First week of term?'

'No.' She'd have been too drunk, of course, so she had to presume – she had no idea what he was talking about.

He said: 'When I walked in, to set up the sound desk for the comp, you were playing darts with Roz. You had on a bright orange dress and you were shouting some poem at her – I don't know what it was, Shakespeare or something.'

I do. Memory deluged: it wasn't Shakespeare she'd been shouting into the near-empty early-evening bar; it was John Donne:

And now good-morrow to our waking souls,
Which watch not one another out of fear —

THWACK – she'd smacked a dart into the board. She'd made a wish as she'd done it, too, a wish that she could stop being so fearful. The pictures strobed from there: an Indian meal; her laughter high and harsh; a club on the North Shore, all disco pop; waking up at Luke's place, back in the city, in Glebe, her soreness the only evidence of her attempts at love, at courage, scuttling out before the sun rose, leaving a note, another lie:

Great night ☺X

She said now, to Dan, to everything: 'I'm so ashamed.'

'Addy.' He clasped her right foot in his hand, solid, assuring: 'If I could make one thing happen, tonight, or sometime soon, it wouldn't be for you to love me, but for you to not be ashamed. You've got no reason to be ashamed.' He squeezed her toes and she looked at his hand on her foot as though it contained there the meaning of life – because it did. All love, all reason, sat in the atoms that lay between them, skin to skin, soul to soul. Moving his hand away, giving her the time, the space she needed, he told her, with that smile wry and shy together: 'You want shame, I've got a whole drawer full of really, really bad poetry, all dedicated to you.'

'You do not.' She smiled back, a smile that reached into her hollow centre with such everywhere, all-over sunshine she could almost hear the seagulls of home, smell the lemon and salt sprinkled on fresh-cooked chips.

'I do.' He nodded, standing up. 'Why don't you go to bed? Try not to worry anymore tonight.' *Yes.* More than sensible, that idea. He said: 'Tomorrow will be a good day.' His jaw clenched, something emphatic in it. 'Don't you worry about anything,' he assured her again, and it sounded like a threat this time – because it was. She was far too beyond weary to know it, though; too almost obliviated to perceive the darkness that crossed his face as he turned away.

She virtually crawled back up the stairs and into bed, with only a vague concern that her dad might not have enough chicken for an extra person at lunch, and that this would annoy him. She'd call him in the morning, to warn him, though perhaps Nick would have let him know already. So strange, so very strange, to think of her brother and Dan

Ackerman chatting. Whatever, if there wasn't enough chicken, Nick could forgo and make an extra mountain of pasta for himself. Technically, Nick had invited Dan, hadn't he? *What? How crazy is that?* Whatever, whatever, they could pick up a nice cake from some Sunday-opening café along the way, and that would make her father happy. *Cheesecake …*

Go to sleep.

She closed her eyes, but all she could see then was Christopher O'Rourke calling her a crazy bitch; she could still feel, deep in her scalp, where he'd pulled her hair. Her ankle throbbed. Did men know, she wondered, when they did things like this, a woman could never escape? She was trapped there forever, for that moment could never be erased. Time was the trickiest fish of all, wasn't it? Most of it evaporated, unmarked; what was left, what was extracted in the limbeck of the mind, were the grains of our truths, pinches of highs and lows, of joy, wonder, grief and distress.

She switched on the bedside lamp, stretched across it for the paperback there, her copy of *The Fire Flight*, her eyes falling straight upon the line: '"We're going to do it for Australia!" he yelled above the thrashing propeller blades …'

She couldn't recollect who 'he' was at this moment, or anything much about the story so far, except that the war which would soon be declared would probably require a lot of mutton from the sheep station, Rowallan's Run, and that the complex moral dilemma separating the lovers was about to get gratuitously convoluted. The story wasn't the point, not tonight. She fell into the words, holding the book in her hands as the hero flew above the wide, brown land; holding the book tight to her body, with the wordless, everywhere, all-over prayer, that one day her thoughts would make a book of their own – make one great crazily courageous flight. She thought perhaps she heard Kathleen McAllister laugh at that from somewhere not too far away, throaty and affectionate. Probably mad. Two mad people, author and reader, their spirits whispering together over these pages, between these lines, inside the stamp of the printer's ink, inside the tiny carbon-black particles of the realest and truest of all life ...

And then, at last, to the tumbling drum of the washing machine downstairs, she gave herself to sleep.

THE ANSWER IS ALWAYS LOVE & QUANTUM PHYSICS

'There is not enough cheese on this sandwich,' Frieda Stevenson was talking to someone – someone wearing that stunning chiffon frock, pale gold, rain-spot speckled with tiny sequins. She had her hair pinned up, a neat twist of boring brown, just the way Addy wore her —

Elke? Mum? Mummy?

Addy knew she was dreaming, not least because that frock wasn't old enough for her mother to be wearing in real life. The chiffon was nylon and the drape of the skirt was definitely 1970s, more ballroom-dancing gown than mid-century cocktail. It was also impossible that Frieda and Elke could have known each other to be talking about cheese sandwiches at all.

Are you me? she asked, but the woman didn't respond.

She said something to Frieda in German, too quick for Addy to catch a single word.

Then Frieda replied in English: 'I agree. She should wear it. She probably thinks it's too beautiful, though. I don't know if we can trust her to keep her promises.'

You can trust me! Addy tried to shout, but the audio system in this dreamland wouldn't let her be heard. She wanted to know what promise she should keep. *Please!*

The zebra snorted at her shoulder; he said: 'Don't mind them. You're perfect and important, just the way you are. Remember?'

She reached out and stroked the tufted mane between his ears; it was soft, yet stood firm, like an old-fashioned clothes brush. *You're alive?* she asked him.

'We're all alive,' the zebra said. 'And I'm the one who bought the dress, remember that as well. So you just do what you want to do. Be … Just be …'

Yeah … Guitars. Drums. Piano. Somewhere …

'You're the real thing, Addy Loest.' The zebra laughed and she felt his breath on the back of her hand. 'Be the best thing, for us. For all of us.'

Light filled the shop window now, like sun bursting through thick cloud, obscuring her sight, but it was glorious and warm, warm, warm.

'I have some more cheese in the storeroom,' she heard Frieda say, as she moved away.

Addy smiled, slipping between the dream and the day. She sensed a steady pulse under her hand, under the touch of fur; a small face nudging hers: it was No Name, stretching in the crook of her arm, his tiger-striped head at her chin.

The sun was high, blasting through the grime of her own window: she had indeed slept in – and odder still, the realisation brought her no impulse to panic or dash out of bed. She shifted around to look at her clock: it was eight thirty-seven, and even the red Doomsday glow of the numbers seemed to say in some gentler way, *Good morning, Addy.* She smiled: someone must have switched off her alarm in the night. Dan? The warmest thought, not a thought at all, but a feeling. Or maybe it was Roz? Love, in any case: it whispered, just beyond hearing, everywhere around her.

As she curled back around No Name, she felt the faint throb at her ankle, the remains of yesterday's terror, and even that had changed: *I fought back.* She had got away from the one who'd meant to hurt her, and in a great spray of washing powder: soap flakes hung like crystal mist over that memory. She had given that ape-brain O'Rourke a deserving serve, hadn't she? And in front of his ape-mates. Yes, she had. That was no dream.

'I agree, she should wear it …' Fragments of the actual dream she'd just now been inside returned as she lay there, waking, wondering at the promise she was supposed to keep. She could only remember that she'd promised Frieda Stevenson she'd visit her, and of course she would, only not today, though – obviously. Sundays were for going home, and she didn't know if The Curiosity Shop would be open on a Sunday, anyway. *Then again, if Dan is going to drive*, was her next thought, *maybe —*

Dan was going to drive her home, to Port? That still seemed the least believable thing that had ever happened to her – that, and his apparent chat with Nick. But it was true, too – wasn't it? And yet —

'I don't know if we can trust her,' Frieda had said. But to whom had she said it? Who *was* that other woman in the shop? What did it all mean? These wonders began to crowd and whirl, one on top of the other.

Stop it, Addy – it was only a dream. Really. There was a talking zebra in it. And you're just not used to waking up on a Sunday without a pounding hangover, are you? Not used to having ordinary, actual dreams as opposed to blackouts.

No. That was too true.

Still, she decided to hedge bets: she'd get up and get dressed, just in case she had imagined the whole thing with Dan, so she'd have time to make the ten o'clock train if need be. *I'll be late – and no more or less mad.* She'd ring her dad; he'd understand; he always did – he'd drive back into Wollongong to pick her up, grumbling that she'd thrown out his cooking schedule.

Either way, what would she wear? The garden dress sprang first to mind, not unsurprisingly but most inappropriately: it was a party frock, and summery, not something to be worn mid-autumn, however sunny the day. Not something to be worn to lunch at her dad's, where she'd probably end up going for a walk along the beach and maybe fishing if she stayed late. Even still, the notion lingered with an insistence that she should wear that dress today: it tugged at her in the same way the dream had – like a promise she couldn't quite recall. She couldn't wear that dress, though, not today; it would be too silly. In all honesty, it was one of those dresses she would probably not wear very often anywhere, simply because it was a bit too beautiful. It was precisely the kind of investment dress one bought with every intention of making every day beautiful, and then —

But every day is *beautiful.* The epiphany hit her as she stood at the wardrobe doors: *I am alive. That's pretty fricken beautiful.* She suddenly realised that to consider life as anything less than marvellous was a dishonour to those who were no longer here. To those who had made her own being possible. To those who had survived, carrying burdens of all kinds.

She would wear the garden dress today – she would wear it for them, all of them. She would wear it for her dad. She would wear it for herself. Why not? She might die in a car crash on the way there or the way home, she might choke to death on a chicken bone, in which case she'd die without having worn the most beautiful dress she owned. That would just be too stupid.

She looked at all her frocks now, all her colours, all her stories there, and promised them that she would wear every one of them, each in turn: she would be beautiful every day, in one way or another. Even when she didn't feel like it. Especially when she didn't feel like it. No one would ever take this beauty from her again. *This* joy.

Here, right where she left her, carefully pressed, the garden dress seemed to shout: '*Yes!*' Poppies and cornflowers and tiny white camomile stars, all tumbling endlessly through limitless sky, she would let herself fall as these flowers fell: into their field of infinite possibility. Into life.

And into Dan.

But could she?

I think I want to. I think I really do.

She washed and dressed quickly, forbidding further equivocation in the rush of doing, of choosing jacket and boots, both black – *too black* – and rummaging for her flame-red scarf for contrast. *There*: and she liked what she saw in the mirror. For the first time in her small forever, she liked all of it. The teaming was a little eccentric, perhaps, but it was honest. It was one-hundred percent Addy Loest. It was her best foot forward into the future, an immediate future in which she was determined not to worry about where Dan Ackerman might be, or if he might be, or how long she should wait for him before making her way to Central Station for that ten o'clock South Coast train.

Except that some neuroses were too ingrained for any resolution, weren't they? She thought she should maybe call Nick first, to confirm that all arrangements were true and correct, but that thought was interrupted by a flash of guilt at the very idea: *I don't call my brother. Ever. Because I'm a terrible sister. And that's why I didn't know he was gay, isn't it. How could your own sister not know you're gay? I should call him now, absolutely – right away. Then again, if I have made up everything that I thought might have happened with Dan, Nick won't be at home, will he? He'll be on the train already. Fuck. How am I going to get through life with my brain like this? Without alcohol?*

She was halfway down the stairs, halfway back to that more familiar place of crippling uncertainty, when she saw exactly where Dan Ackerman was: just where he'd been last Tuesday morning as she'd crept down the stairs desperate for a hamburger, except this time he wasn't asleep on the brown couch – he was reading a book. He looked up from it and followed her with his eyes as she stepped around the end of the bannister: 'Wow.'

'Wow.' She thought the same thing, all uncertainty vanishing at the sight of him. He'd gone home and got changed at some stage, into impeccably perfect Sunday-lunch jeans, not too dressed up, not too dressed down, and he'd shaved so cleanly she wanted to kiss the roses in his cheeks – not that she could have allowed herself to do anything quite as mad as that. She glanced at the paperback on his knee instead: it was that cultish space-farce thing, *The Hitchhiker's Guide to the Galaxy*; she wasn't at all interested in science fiction, but she had a feeling she soon would be.

Every atom she owned was a smile; she said: 'Hello. Would you like a cup of tea?'

'Sure —'

'Addles!' Roz appeared at the doorway to the kitchen, wrapped in a crimson kimono, kettle in hand: 'Look at you. Look at that *dress* – hubba hubba, hooley dooley.' But the look on her face was saying, *Get over here*, and with some urgency.

Addy did as she was bid; she made her way into the kitchen and stood with Roz by the stove as she lit the gas – *whoomp* – with the question: 'What the holy fucken hell happened here last night?' Roz flicked her eyes at the laundry door, now upright against the side of the fridge; while the soap powder had been swept up, there was no disguising the damage done to the wall where the track had come away from it: the plasterboard was torn and a great chunk of paint sheared off, exposing a layer of wallpaper, shit-brown ground with ick-yellow tulips on it – gaggingly hideous.

'Um. Well …' Addy didn't know where to begin. She should have just come out and said it: *Christopher O'Rourke tried to rape me in there and I fought him off.* But shame had a mind of its own; she couldn't get the words out, not even to her best friend. She couldn't one-hundred percent trust that Roz would take her side against the Fine Young Liberal: because shaming women works precisely this way – doubt worms and worms through even the sanest brains. She glanced again at the wallpaper: *Someone was paid to design that …*

'Addles?' Roz blinked at her insistently.

I don't want to be Addles anymore – and I definitely don't want to live here anymore. She didn't want Roz to be stuck with contributing to the cost of repairs, though, either – and most definitely didn't trust Harriet not to make an issue of it, if she hadn't already – so, with a sigh of resignation, Addy said: 'Don't worry, I'll get the door fixed.' *Somehow.* Maybe she could ask Nick – he'd always been pretty good with a hammer. And it wasn't as if it needed to be a fabulous job: the place was just about derelict, waiting to be condemned.

'The door?' Roz squinted at her, uncomprehending for a second, before lowering her voice again: 'I know what happened to the *door* – fucken fuckers – Dan told me everything when I got in last night. You poor darling. Are *you* all right?'

'Oh.' Addy shuddered with all of her relief. 'Yes,' she said. 'I'm all right. Now.' And she was, remarkably.

Roz clicked her tongue with a little grunt of contempt: 'O'Rourke will get what's coming to him – I'll see to that.' She gave Addy a squeeze around the waist: 'I have the photographic evidence, to make sure of it.'

'Photographic evidence?'

'Of Chubs and Rourkie – you know.'

Addy shook her head: 'No idea.'

'Remember that night Chubs fell asleep in his own vomit out the back of Jane Buckingham's parents' house – you know, on the garden furniture?'

Addy shook-nodded, remembering the vomit but not the house, apart from its very posh garden furniture, Chubs lying there with an empty chip packet on his head, like Satan's favourite cherub crashed to earth.

'Well,' Roz explained, 'I had my camera with me that night, didn't I. Jane was after images of male–female body language for this assignment thing we had to do, blah blah, and so I just happened to take a couple of happy snaps of Chubs in repose – with Rourkie pretending to take him clerically from behind, dick out, swinging it, the whole revolting show. You never know when these things will come in handy, do you? I'll have some copies made up tomorrow.' She winked, reaching for the teabag tin, as she added: 'The revenge will be a pleasure shared, don't you worry about that.'

Addy wanted to ask her to elaborate on what she meant, if that piece of garbage O'Rourke had hurt her as well, or anyone else, but Roz had moved on: 'Anyway, when you get back tonight, let's start making plans to get out of this dump, hm?'

'Hm.' *Fricken oath.*

'Please don't say anything to Harriet,' Roz went on. 'I'm sure she won't want to come with us, I'm sure she's making her own escape plan right now. I don't want her to think I don't love her, though, even if I don't love her all the time – you know how it is.'

Addy nodded, thinking: *Not exactly, but I'm not going to argue with your change of tune. No more Harriet! Yippee! Yahoo!*

'Besides, Kendall's stereo is even better.' Roz looked like the cat that ate the cream with chocolate topping. 'Ah yes, in other news, I've been deciding maybe I'll be wanting to shack up with Drummer Boy, maybe he's a keeper.'

Addy tried not to look too shocked at this: that Roz wasn't going to turf him after her five minutes of fun, per the usual routine, and that her eyes were sparkling all their shades of hazelly green with the truth of it.

'He's heard there's a whole top floor of a warehouse coming up for rent, in Camperdown,' she mused. 'You know, one of those old factory buildings out the back of Newtown. It's got a bodgied-up shower and a loo, couple of office boxes, and that's about it, not even sure it's got a stove – whatever, it's so cheap it'd be virtually squatting. Big windows over-looking the city, space to paint. Space to *be*.'

'Sounds rather excellent to me.' Addy closed her eyes and made a wish for it, at the same time thanking whoever had cranked the wheel of fate to give her this friend. A writing window with a view high above the rooftops of Sydney: that'd do. And they could take No Name with them.

But Roz lowered her voice once more, as the kettle began to gather steam: 'Whatever happens now, you have to know, when I got in last night, Dan was guarding the bottom of the stairs like a lion. He was pretty angry.'

'Angry?' Addy couldn't quite imagine him angry, mild-mannered Dan.

'Yeah. Seething, quietly, that way he does.'

Does he?

'Hm. Not saying very much about his feelings for you, but saying everything in his actions.' And Roz warned her once more then, too: 'So don't you break his heart. He's a good guy, Add – such a good guy.'

'I'm not going to break his heart,' Addy promised with all of her own. *Please, not if I can help it.* She looked over her shoulder through the kitchen door, saw him leaning over his book, reading, or maybe pretending to; she called out to him, she called out with every promise: 'How do you have your tea?'

'Where am I going?' Dan asked her, hands on the steering wheel of his beloved old Imp, his smile so mild Addy didn't hear the question for the wonder of where or how anger might reside on such a good-guy face.

'Pardon?'

'Your brother's house – where is it?' he said, and they were so close she could smell that last gulp of tea on his breath: white with one sugar. She could still hear him saying, 'We should probably go now,' swigging that tea, pulling out his car keys. He was mesmerising. He had become so suddenly all her thoughts, she'd almost forgotten to call her dad on the way out, to warn him of the extra guest: 'Who is this boy, Adrianna?' he'd said; 'Just a friend from uni, Dad,' she'd replied; 'Is he a good driv—'; 'See you soon, Daddy – bye.'

And Dan wanted to know what? Where Nick lived, to pick him up. 'Yes,' she said, but she couldn't think of the name of the street, could she; his house was right on the south-west, Erskineville edge of Newtown, about equidistant between the train stations of those two suburbs, and not far from the back end of a big pub; she knew exactly where it was; she knew it was number 104 – neither a prime nor a number she liked the look of, as she wasn't much of a fan of any number that ended in four, because it always looked uncomfortably lonely, like someone standing interminably on one leg, leaning against a wall. *ADDY! You fricken loon. Just answer him. Just tell him the truth.* 'I'll have to give you directions,' she said, at last. 'His house is in Erskineville, but I can't remember the name of the street.'

'Okay.' He smiled with those warm, kind eyes. Because everything was okay.

Except: 'I've got to get a cake on the way, though, for Dad,' she remembered. A surprise cake was always a mood improver; while it wouldn't make her dad any less intimidatingly weird, it would go some way to making up for the surprise guest, throwing out his routine, mucking up the schedule. She knew the Olympia Café wouldn't have anything apart from unnaturally firm vanilla slices and iced donuts sprinkled with hundreds and thousands, hangover food, but she couldn't think of any alternative in the general King Street direction they'd be heading; she asked Dan: 'Do you know anywhere that might do a nice cheesecake?' And on a Sunday morning, it did seem a bit of a longshot.

'Um …' Dan thought about it for a moment, turning the key in the ignition; then he said, 'Yeah,' like he might have been enjoying the sound of the car engine, before he turned his smile back to her: 'There's a great café up past the supermarket that does cakes – all kinds. And their baklava is amazing – let's get some of that for the road, hey?'

'Okay,' she replied, barely. How epically wonderful was this? She never went past the supermarket on King Street, not in the day. And she'd never fallen in love before, but how brave she was this day.

On they drove, through the Sunday-hushed streets, up to Newtown, where the shopping strip was more alive than she'd expected it to be: people going in and out of the bookshop and the record store; a girl in a tutu carrying a pizza box, skipping along still in party mode, probably still drunk; an old woman shuffling past in the opposite direction, past caring, irreparably smashed by the same cup and whatever bundle of tragedies she was carrying, so alone and —

And they'd just sailed past The Curiosity Shop, Addy realised. Was it open? She couldn't see, they were too far past it now.

'Dan.' She almost grabbed his arm. 'Can we go back? I just want to see if that shop is open – you know, The Curiosity Shop, with the zebra?'

'The zebra?' he asked, looking over his shoulder, slowing the car.

'Yeah – where I saw you, Tuesday morning. The second-hand shop.' *Where I ran away from you.*

'Oh – sure.' He tossed her a frown: 'We're getting on for time, though.'

'I know,' she said. 'I won't be long. I just want to see if it's open – see the lady there, Frieda. I got this dress from her. I just want to say hello, show her I'm wearing it.' *Show you a bit more of what a freak I am to test your keenness while I'm there.*

'Okay.' He turned the car around, a casual shrug over the no-U-turn lines; it was only a few doors down —

Only, it wasn't there at all.

'What?'

She stared from the car window. The shop they had pulled up outside was a second-hand place, but it wasn't Frieda's. It was open, the lights were on, bare bulbs illuminating a jumble of furniture: lounge suites, lamps, tables, chests of drawers, chairs hanging from the ceiling; there was a counter at the front displaying teacups and other crockery oddments, beyond that, a few racks of clothes, and at the very back, there was a wall of wardrobes, not a bookshelf in sight. She looked around the other way, across the road: yes, there was Ali's felafel shop. She looked up at the bricks above the awning of this whatever-it-was, and they were dark pink, plum-coloured, old: this was the right shop. And it wasn't. She blinked and shook her head: 'No.'

A cold, black dread swooped, silent, rushing.

'What's wrong, Addy?' Dan asked her, his voice far too far away and far too close.

All she could say was: 'I'm going mad. I really am.'

'What do you mean?' He leaned towards her, closer still, as he peered out with her, his face almost touching hers in the tiny car.

'This was a different shop,' she said, fixed on it and disbelieving. 'There was a zebra in the window. A red curtain. A tiffany lamp. Gold lettering. And Frieda – didn't you see her? On Tuesday? A lady, an old German lady with white hair.'

'Maybe – I wasn't really looking,' he said, somewhere behind her ear, shifting, a sigh of seat-leather: 'I don't think I noticed anyone except you when I was in there.'

'But how ...' She turned to him now, as much to assure herself that he was still there, still Dan Ackerman; she gripped the edge of her seat, clutching for sense. For non-sense. 'I came here three times – on Tuesday, Wednesday and Friday. I bought a shirt. I bought a book. I put this dress on lay-by. I talked with Frieda – we talked for ages. She was friends with my grandmother – she *gave* me this dress. She told me what happened to my — oh!' *I made it all up in my broken head? I can't believe that any more than* — 'How can she not be there?'

'Maybe she was,' Dan said, unflinchingly reasonable. 'I mean, obviously she was, or you wouldn't have seen her – and you wouldn't have the dress, would you.'

'But – no. How can that be?' *I can't cope with myself anymore. You should drive me to the nearest hospital. This is the end.*

'Nothing we see is really here,' he said, no less reasonably. 'I mean, it is, and it isn't.'

She stared at him: no idea.

He said: 'No, I'm not stoned.' Then he looked out the front windscreen at the slow Sunday traffic. 'It's just more fancy maths. Quantum physics – really. You can't trust anything you see. And at the same time, you can trust everything.'

She could only keep staring: *Go on.*

'Well, it's complicated,' he began, 'and I'm not saying I understand it, but it's the most amazing thing you'll ever think about. It's like something you can just see out of the corner of your eye, and when you try to look right at it, it's gone. Blows my mind.' He looked at her again, and he held her in his eyes, inside his own wonder: 'The time we're in now is only a slice of all time that's ever happened or ever will happen – we can't see beyond it either backwards or forwards. We're sort of stuck, but all time is happening all the time around us, in every direction. In the quantum world, inside all our atoms – and every atom everywhere – the rules we think of as rules, like time and gravity and matter, don't apply. Things can exist in different places at the same time, or not be where you expect them to be. We get a glimpse of it, we know time isn't a straight line, that it doesn't move at the same speed in every circumstance – that's Einstein's theory of relativity – the faster you move, the slower time goes, it's relative to the speed of light, and at the speed of light, time stops altogether, and then beyond the speed of light, time starts travelling backwards. It's nuts. In the quantum world, it's even more nuts. And not nuts at all. We see all kinds of shit that's there, and not there. I don't know, Addy. Maybe you just needed to see that lady at that time. The window opened, and then it closed.'

A shiver of something like recognition shimmered up Addy's spine, but still she quipped: 'Maybe you read too much science fiction.'

'Maybe,' he laughed, 'or maybe I am madder than you. The thing is, we don't know. We're almost completely made out of space – at a percentage of ninety-nine point nine, nine, nine repeating. Each one of us, we're almost a hundred percent nothing. That's not science fiction – that's just a fact. We're nothing, but we're huge – we *are* space. And we'll never know the end of truth – it isn't a destination. It's a ride. A magical ride, hey?'

God, she wanted to kiss him; she looked down at the flowers of her garden dress, and touched the falling poppies at her knees: *Please.* How she wanted to fall and fall for him, be mad *with* him. How she wanted to believe – everything.

'Or maybe the old lady and the zebra just had to move in a hurry,' he added with another light, anything-is-possible laugh. But that seemed somehow the least plausible of all to Addy. He glanced at the clock on the dash then: 'We really should get going – if you want to get this cake.'

'Yeah,' she breathed out the word, wondering at the atoms she'd just sent whirling through the air: was Frieda Stevenson somehow, somewhere there?

She was still caught up in the conundrum two minutes later, running into this café she'd never seemed to have seen before either, even as she asked for the price of the sole but rather perfect cheesecake she saw there among the array of tortes and tarts, slices and pastries, trays of baklava and Turkish delight. Was *this* real? Was it just that Addy had been tearing about in such a distracted daze she could never quite tell where she was?

'Eight dollars fifty, darling,' the nice café guy smiled a pleasant Sunday-morning smile, leaning out from his steaming espresso machine, and Addy could tell very clearly this cheesecake cost more than she'd been hoping to spend. The baklava was expensive here as well, at four dollars a box of ten. This was a yuppie hang-out, a place where law graduates and other cashed-up trendies came to drink real coffee. She glanced out the door at Dan, where he was making space for cake in the boot of the car, looking just like a doctor's son, and the nasty thought crept up behind her: *You can't be good enough for him – seriously. He's way too cool and interesting and lovely for you.*

Stop it – seriously. She was quick to dismiss this crap now, and not only because she didn't have the time to waste. She looked back to the cheesecake in the counter: it was a baked one, Continental-style, a gorgeously golden circle of sweetened cheesy goodness. It was her father's favourite kind. He deserved this cheesecake as much as she deserved a bit of self-respect. Whatever the story was, she saw him and would always see him as that little boy so lonely, hurt and lost; and it didn't matter what that cheesecake cost. He was worth it, and so was she; she promised to be kinder to herself, and at the same time knew she would have to break that other promise to that same self she'd made: that she was going to tell him she'd dropped out of law. That would not be happening today: unexpected guest plus unexpected and possibly devastating disappointment that his daughter wanted to be a writer? Way too much. She would wait a little longer for that, maybe save up to buy him a bottle of Scotch for the event.

She told the café guy: 'I'll take it, thanks – and a box of baklava.' Because she knew Nick would also like at least half a dozen of them. And, *What the hell*: 'One of those chocolate éclairs as well, please.' *For me.*

Back on the footpath, arms full of enough dessert to kill them all, Dan took the box full of cheesecake from her and laid it down in the boot, wrapping a rug around it to keep it safe for the trip, settling it snug up against the toolbox there. *He has a toolbox in his boot*, she noted: her father would be impressed. Real men carried toolboxes in their boots, and Dan Ackerman was a real man. He knew things about quantum physics, important, essential things that she wanted to know about now herself. All her heartstrings sang, nerves spinning into a warm, fizzing ball of light as she considered, yes, maybe she had imagined Frieda and the zebra; maybe she'd bought her garden dress in that ordinary second-hand furniture store for a few bucks and had made up a story around it, an extraordinary story for a broken head and heart. Elfriede – Elfie? Didn't Frieda say that's what she'd been called once upon a time? Didn't that sound quite a lot like Elke? Didn't that sound a huge lot like a fraught imagination missing her mum? Wishing she could know her. Maybe she'd also dreamt Dan could play the *Moonlight Sonata*; maybe he'd been playing 'Chopsticks' instead. Did shifting facts make her feelings any less true? No. *Truth is a magical ride*, so he'd just said – and she wanted a tattoo of that, as soon as she could organise it.

One hand on the wheel, he ate a diamond wedge of baklava as he drove, a pistachio crumb sparkling golden on his lip. And it was here, now, within that tiny glint she felt at last the goldenness thick in the air between them, these atoms that had already spun their thread and by this alchemy made a metal all their own. There was a fantasy, yes, but it was real, too. This madness. This daring and daring to fall.

'Where do I turn off?' he asked her, and after giving him directions, just like anyone would give another person directions, she found that Erskineville was where it had always been.

Nick was waiting on his front step for them, black eye in full bloom, the tiny terrace tinier for the shape of him. He waved back into the house, through the door as he closed it, and as she imagined Dave in there, lifting a barbell, grunting a farewell, happiness seemed to chinkle everywhere, from each gleaming leaf of the camelia at the gate and into the clear, bright sky.

'How's your head?' she asked as her brother squashed his massiveness into the back of the Imp.

'Ug,' he replied, and as she laughed, he said: 'How's yours?'

She laughed some more, handing over the box of baklava to him, and a bit more at the way his t-shirt sleeves strained around his shoulders: *that* was unreal.

She didn't notice the silence between him and Dan, though, their exchange of glances in the rear-view mirror. As she turned back around, she saw only Dan's fine, long fingers tuning the radio dial to Triple J, Sydney's only decent music station, and off they went, listening to bands no one had ever heard of and probably never would again, as the rickety outer-reaches of King Street gave in to concrete highway.

After twenty kilometres or so, past the turn-off to Roz's folks, the radio sputtered out of range with the tall gumtrees and wide rolling scrub of the National Park; she looked over her shoulder at Nick: he'd closed his eyes, dozing, filling the whole backseat. The swelling at the top of his cheek had almost completely gone down, but the bruising still made her wince; the whole concept of boxing was beyond her. She wondered if affection transmitted through atoms to heal wounds, and supposed it did; she supposed it helped, at least.

She looked at Dan, lost in his own thoughts, focused on the road; she said to him, to the neat triangle-tip of his nose: 'Thank you, for driving. I hope you haven't given up a better deal for this.'

'Heh.' He gave her a quick grin. 'No. I can do without a Sunday jam session today.'

'Oh? Band practice?' Immediate jab of guilt that she'd taken him from a pleasure.

He chuckled: 'Yeah, band practice.' She wanted to capture that chuckle in a jar, so she could spread it on toast. He said: 'Paul will be annoyed, but he's always annoyed.'

'Who's Paul?' She had not the slightest.

Dan gave her a quick squint, a little surprised she didn't know: 'The bass player.' Didn't mean anything to Addy; she didn't know the name of the other guitarist, either, the jingle to Dan's jangle. She shrugged an apology, and he continued: 'Paul's just arranged a weekly studio booking for us, but I don't know if I want to keep going with the band, anyway.'

'Really?' She found that oddly relieving; not that Elbow were *that* bad, she just wasn't super keen to be one of those girls who went out with a boy in a band.

'Yeah.' Dan explained: 'He's got us an audition for that new TV show – *Star Search*. Have you seen it?'

'No.' She'd seen the ads for it on TV, flicking around the channels during attempts to watch the afternoon soapie serials through their snow-storm reception: it was a talent quest type of thing, but she hadn't had a couch-slouching evening opportunity or inclination to watch the show.

'It's terrible,' Dan told her. 'I don't want to do it. I *couldn't* do it unless I was triple-fried – and I'm not doing that on national TV. I'm a coward, no doubt about it, but some things shouldn't be turned into competitions. I don't like the idea of it. Any kind of art – music, writing, painting, whatever – how do you choose who wins? Not that Elbow is art, and not that I'm really a musician. You know what I mean ...'

'No.' She snorted: even if her imagination had inflated his talents, he was a musician. She said: 'You play two instruments, sing and write bad poetry. I think that makes you an artist.'

'I'm glad you think so.' He smiled at the road. 'Art is for everyone, hey? Like sport. Soon as it's professionalised, soon as you put money on the table – bam – all the love goes sliding. It's just a job. One of my brothers – Dunc – he's a violinist with the London Philharmonic – sounds great, hey, and it is, it's fantastic, but he still hates his boss sometimes, and he'd rather be at home with his family instead of travelling all over the place. He'd rather be working on his own music. I don't ever want to not love playing music. I don't know what I'm talking about really. Anyway, they want to change the name of the band – the TV people. Though they haven't even seen us play yet, they've decided. "Elbow" is just too weird, apparently. They can shove their weird up their shiny TV arses.'

She laughed, another layer of fear slipping from her like a fast-food wrapper flattened and forgotten under the wheel of the car, but she had to admit: '*Elbow* is pretty weird. What's the story with that name?'

'Oh.' A soft groan, eyes still on the road: 'I suppose it does seem a bit dumb now. Last footy season, in the semi-finals, I landed awkwardly in a tackle and twisted my elbow. It wasn't a big deal, but Dad wouldn't let me play in the finals, carried on about it like you wouldn't believe – like I'm a five-year-old. I wasn't very happy about it, had a bit of a sulk, like a five-year-old, went and got monumentally fried and then I wrote a song about it – no, you'll never hear that one, it's so bad. That's how the band started, though – in part to piss Dad off. And also, I don't know … Granddad's always had this bunged-up elbow, on the arm he draws with, always bandaged and smelling of liniment and sort of "fuck you" determination. Just about every part of him was smashed up during the war, inside and out, and I'll never know anything like it – I'll never know that hardship or sacrifice or that daily grind of pain. So, I named the band after him, in a way. A bit of fuck you, that probably doesn't make sense at all. Just me being a wanker.'

'No,' said Addy, falling and falling and falling. 'I don't think you're a wanker.' *I don't think you could be a wanker if you tried your hardest.* He was quite possibly the most sincere person she'd ever met.

He ignored the vote of confidence; he told her, through a streak of shade: 'I'm turning twenty-two on Tuesday. When Granddad was twenty-two he was sitting in a trench on the Western Front. It's time for me to stop frigging around. Granddad's not going to be with us much longer. It's more than amazing he's gone on this long – Grandma checked out three years ago, and everyone thought that'd be the end of him. I'll never be ready to see him go, but I don't think I could hack it if his last sight of me was on the revolving stage of *Star Search*.'

His laughter was a loud song, and she joined him there: the best sound ever, clashing around the car. He kept his eyes on the road; she kept her eyes on him. She saw him swipe off a tear with the heel of his hand, smiling again – and it was there, right there, she finally let herself fall completely and irretrievably. She fell right to the garden floor, she landed softly on the tender grass, inside that loving, laughing tear.

At the first salt-tingle of the ocean, she smelt home; she seemed to smell the wholeness of time; grandfathers breathing the same air across a battleline; those atoms somewhere now, all of them, in the earth, in the sea, in the sky; and out of the corner of her eye she saw something of the deepest and most never-ending truth of all – there, there.

But in the next breath it was gone; a gull sailing in the wind above the sand-blown stretch of Wollongong's northerly suburbs.

'Turn left up here,' she told Dan, hard-wired to the way as they neared a set of lights just gone green under the sign that pointed to Port Kembla.

'No – go straight through.' Nick stirred in the back, with the first words he'd spoken in over an hour and they were rasp-edged. 'Go into the Gong – I've gotta drop something off.'

'What?' Addy looked around at him: 'It's nearly twelve. Dad'll be —'

'Don't worry about it, Add.' Nick looked at Dan in the mirror again and she saw the exchange this time. *What's that about?* she wondered, but she didn't ask, unsure if it might merely have been a glance of acknowledgement. On through the centre of town they went, shut-up shopping malls straddling the road like abandoned plague ships, oozing loneliness and regret. Addy hadn't been here since sometime just before her final high school exams, looking for a new pair of swimming cossies to distract herself from the stress, and not finding any that weren't too expensive or too daggy;

she'd wandered around empty-handed, cold, and caught the bus back to Port. She shivered now with the memory, as Nick said: 'Drop me here – I'll see you at home.'

'Nick!' Addy called after him, but he was already half out of the car. 'Where are you going?'

'Don't worry about it, Add,' he said, from the footpath. 'I won't be long – five minutes.' And off he walked, towards the cab rank above the railway station, where he got into the solo Sunday cab that was idling there.

Addy clicked her tongue and shook her head: 'Well, there's my brother for you.' *Arseface – always something better to do.* 'Ug.' She looked at Dan, and winced apologetically: 'He didn't happen to mention to you where he might be going, did he? When you were talking last night?'

'Nah, I don't know.' Dan shook his head, too, pulling away from the kerb. 'Where to now?'

She directed him down the next left, and back on the road home, a niggling suspicion that she'd just missed something. *What's Nick up to?* All she could think was that he was off to square a bet with one of his old school mates, and wanting to hide the evidence of gambling from their dad, who didn't much approve of that sort of thing – Nick had done that a few times before. *Whatever*, she put it behind her with the last of central Wollongong.

At the first glimpse of the great long sheds of the steelworks, her heart was truly home: this was the closest thing to chest-swelling pride she ever felt, hailing from this place, but it was a pride she could never quite articulate. The towering stacks, chugging away, rusted onto the sky, the sheer extent of the site – seven hundred football fields' worth of nonstop solid industry – and her father worked in there. He was an important man in there: king of a shed that spanned a whole kilometre.

'Wow.' Dan hunched at the wheel, taking it in, the mountains of the Illawarra escarpment to the west, rising above it all. She felt his thoughts: this was the place where his grandfather was born. She wanted to take him up there, hiking the trails: she would one day. He looked back over at the steelworks to the east, rolling on, and on; he said, 'Wow,' again, and again.

'You don't think it's ugly?' she asked him; she'd grown up with the smudge of that word all her life, its breath laced with lead and sulphur dioxide, toxic smog wafting over the clothes line, over her primary school playground, the heady tang of it on a hot day, like some strange sherbet lingering under her tongue.

'Ugly? No,' he said. 'Well, it's not an oil painting, is it. But it's where stuff is made. Steel. The stuff I make gates out of for my uncle Evan comes from this place. Amazing. I'd love to have a look in there, hey ...'

She'd arrange that one day, too. She took him around the Old Port Road now, so that he could see the harbour view: this shore that had called in thousands, the hopeful and the heartbroken, with the promise of new beginnings across this boundless Pacific blue. The world met itself here and made its three-bedroom monuments to peace from red brick and pastel-palette fibro.

Two more left turns and a right, and Peter Loest was pruning the rangy tips off his iceberg roses out the front on Gallipoli Street, cigarette in one hand, shears in the other. She always loved her dad at first sight, his frown of concentration overlaying a lifetime of concern, his crisply ironed shirt – today's a honeyed butter colour almost perfectly matching the house, which was a pristine time capsule itself, cut straight from the everyman's architectural catalogue of 1964 with its groovy low-line roof extending on the right-hand side over her dad's beige and beloved three-year-old Holden Commodore. He looked up and saw the unfamiliar car that approached him now, frowned deeper still and waved; then he smiled on seeing her: and there, in all his joyful creases, *there* was all that was beautiful in man.

'Dad!' She leapt out of the car, suddenly bursting with happiness, so excited to be about to introduce him to Dan, so excited to be about to give him a cheesecake, she was dancing on the spot as Dan retrieved it for her from the boot.

Peter Loest extinguished his cigarette in the spin-lidded outdoor ashtray on the front verandah table, placing his garden shears beside it; then he wiped his hands with his handkerchief before meeting his daughter just inside the gate. All within the moment that followed, he blinked at her as if in some surprise, opened his mouth to speak, changed his mind, gave Dan the once-over with a typically unreadable glare, which he then returned to Addy with a flash of high-voltage alarm: 'Where's Nicky?'

No wonder I've never had a boyfriend. 'Hello, Dad.'

ANYTHING IS POSSIBLE,
BUT SOME THINGS ARE MORE
POSSIBLE THAN OTHERS

'What do you mean you don't know where he is?' Her father wouldn't let her finish the sentence, his black-cloud dread suspended over them on the front path.

'He said he'd be here, Dad.' *Be calm, think of rainbows, don't start lunch with an argument.* She made an attempt at levity, for Dan's sake more than anything else: 'Funnily enough, Nicholas doesn't ask my permission before he goes to visit his friends.'

Her father did not find that amusing: 'Who is he visiting?'

'I don't know! Dad – please.' *You'd better not be cheating on Dave or anything like that,* she inwardly frowned, wondering, as she outwardly smiled, thrusting the white bakery box at her father: 'We've got cheesecake, here —'

'Aren't you going to introduce me to your friend?'

Just as well I love you. 'Of course. Dad, this is Dan, Dan Ackerman. Dan this is —'

'Ackerman?' Peter Loest gave the young pretender before him another inscrutable up-and-down: 'Are you German?' More accusation than question.

'No, not really. Ah – hi, Mr Loest.' Dan thrust out his hand, evidently not too bothered by the business of over-bearing father, and as they shook under the cheesecake, Addy saw the trace of an approving smile on her dear dad's lips: must have been a good, firm shake, and doubtless another point for correct pronunciation of their name.

'Are we allowed to go inside now, Dad?' She kissed him on the cheek, stepping past him, another admonishment following her up the front step: 'Don't be rude,' he said.

Inside, beyond the tiny foyer panelled with mustard-tinted glass, the house smelt of apricot chicken simmering in the electric frypan, a pot of rice beside it on the stovetop, around the corner in the kitchen that lay at the end of their roomy living space. The place was white-walled and sparsely furnished in shades of walnut and burnt orange, but it was comfortable, made to last, and always preternaturally clean. Not that any of those details mattered much when their almost floor-to-ceiling picture window was filled with such a scape of the sea: deep blue, unfathomable, hovering above the back paling fence to the horizon, to infinity.

'You would like a beer,' her dad was saying to Dan, behind her, and again it wasn't a question.

Dan declined, of course, 'No thanks.'

Addy turned and caught her father's dubious glance; she could almost hear the wheels turning: *What is wrong with this boy?* Everyone drank in Port Kembla – *everyone* – unless they had a terrible illness or personality disorder, as far as the functionally alcoholic consensus was concerned.

'You are at university,' the interrogation continued across the breakfast bench, her father checking under the lid of the rice pot.

'Yes, electrical engineering, final year.' Dan seemed to be undeterred.

And Addy could feel her father's sigh of relief that it wasn't a fine arts or basket-weaving student he'd let into his house; he asked: 'In what field will you work when you finish your degree?'

'Um, I haven't decided,' Dan replied, awkward for a second, stooping, then straightening to his full height, which was a good couple of inches taller than her dad, who wasn't short himself. 'Realistically,' Dan explained to him, 'I'll probably go into sonography, medical ultrasound, on the design side of things, if I can. I'm interested in acoustic technology, too – micro-acoustics in hearing aids and all that. Or maybe music production, if an opportunity came up. But yeah,' his shoulders folded around the question again, 'I don't know yet.'

But yeah wow. Nice answer, Dan the Man. She'd never know just how much he was shitting himself at that moment – but yeah, anxiety was like that, wasn't it?

'Sprout.' Her father's sudden command was short and sharp, and he cocked his head towards the dining room that lay to the far side of the kitchen through a set of louvred doors: he wanted a word.

'Won't be a sec,' she said to Dan, following her father, a clockwork daughter. The table was set, the good placemats laid out on the crisp white cloth, the way they always were for visitors, but, she supposed, he'd found cause for disappointment with this visitor today, cause to stop the show. It had happened before: most notably, the one and only time she'd brought Roz home to Port, to help her pack for the move to Flower Street. He'd called Addy into the dining room and said: 'She will leave tomorrow.' Why? 'She is too loud.' He hadn't liked the sound of her large, unbridled laughter: it had upset his need to remain permanently on edge. Addy stared into the pattern of the placemat nearest: fawn-lace daisy chains, round and round and round.

'Where did you get that dress?' he asked her, an urgent whisper.

'What?' That was the last thing she expected to hear; she took a moment to absorb the question, looking from table to frock, at the blooms cascading down the tulle; too loud? 'This dress?' she said. 'A shop in Newtown.' Whatever that shop might have been; it didn't matter where she'd actually got it: she looked up at her father and found the grief in his eyes – the grief that was always there, waiting to ambush and overwhelm him.

'Your mother had a dress like that,' he said, letting her see how bereft he was at the thought. And he was one-hundred percent sober: he never drank before lunch.

'*This* dress?' Addy felt every quantum dot of her being stop still, listening.

'No.' He shook his head, the lines on his brow whole valleys of lost love. 'It couldn't be. I think the colours were different – I can't remember. She would decorate dresses and blouses this way – with flowers, like these. She made them herself, from silk scraps she got from the factory. Ah, what do I know about dresses? It's just that —' His knuckles were white, fist tight around the top of a dining chair.

'Dad, I'm sorry.' Addy tried to think what she might get changed into – all she had here these days was an old netball skirt, tracksuit pants and some pyjamas. She wanted to turn the frock inside out, so he couldn't see the flowers at all. She wanted to bring him new love, a love to break this spell of loss, but that was never going to happen: it had been almost seventeen and a half years; he was trapped inside his mourning, held fast in a tangle of snapped strings, as if Elke had left him yesterday; as if to love again would only risk a further loss and one he could not bear.

He smiled now, though, and touched the side of Addy's face with the back of those knuckles. 'You shouldn't be sorry,' he said, a gentle growl. 'You look very beautiful, that's all I wanted to say. You look just like your mother.' He cocked his head again, back at the kitchen: 'You like this boy, hm?'

'I think so.' She swallowed her own emotions under a shrug, scrunching her nose as if she were happily noncommittal: 'We've only just met.'

Her father grunted: 'Is that so?' As if he didn't believe her.

'It's true.' She laughed as her father's compliment began to sink into her centre, warming her from the inside out: he'd never called her beautiful before; he'd never said it so plainly, out and out and in the absence of wine: *You look just like your mother.* She said to him now: 'I didn't know Dan existed a week ago.'

The front door opened and closed. 'There's Nicky,' her father said, already gone.

She smiled at Dan, standing by the picture window, hands in his pockets; she smiled at her dad, watching as he grabbed Nick by the chin in the lounge, inspecting the damage to his cheek. She saw the glance Nick threw at Dan and the glance Dan threw back at him.

'Dad, lay off.' Nick grabbed their father's arm by the wrist. And then she saw her brother's knuckles: red, grazed, as though he'd freshly decked someone.

Her brother met her gaze now, too, and she could see it in the post-fight glaze of his eyes: *You have, haven't you.*

Of course, Addy would never learn just what Nick had done to Alan Hadley that Sunday afternoon. It wasn't as though she and that filthy bastard were ever going to mix in any of the same circles in future for her to hear the faintest word.

No, she'd never find out that her brother had taken that cab straight to the Hadley's place, to their big, fuck-off house in the highest heights of the Wollongong suburb of Figtree, knowing that the whole holy-rolling family would be gathered there post-church for their own lunch.

'Hey, Nick!' It was Alan who had opened the door to him. 'Long time, no see. Come in, mate, come in. We heard about your win on Friday night. Have a beer.'

'Nah.' Nick shook his head, as Alan's father appeared behind him at the door.

'Nick, great to see you,' his father had said. 'Come in and join us, please, pull up a pew.'

'Nah.' Nick shook his head again. 'Don't have time, Mr Hadley. But thanks.' Alan's father was quite a nice bloke, and Mrs Hadley was quite nice, too, except that they'd managed to turn both their sons into spoilt pricks – takes one to know one, as Nick well knew, but he drew the line at anyone hurting his sister.

He said to Alan now: 'You raped Addy, I just found out.'

'What?' Both Alan and his father took a step back.

'You heard me,' Nick said, right at the same moment Alan's brother, Scott, the police constable, stepped in.

'Watch your mouth,' Scott said, muscling up like he'd just learned how to do it at cop school. 'What's this about, then?'

'Your brother raped my sister,' Nick repeated the reason for his visit, and explained: 'At her school formal, he took her into the bushes and raped her. As a fair thing, I'm going to hit Alan once for it now, just the once, and we won't say another word about it – right?'

'Shit – Al?' Scott turned to his brother, and the looks all round said the charge was true: Alan Hadley was guilty as sin, and suitably mute with terror as Nick grabbed him by the front of his shirt. Nick dropped that dirty fucker there and then on the patio, one very hard crack that smashed his jaw off its hinge, leaving him whimpering, with his mother racing out from the kitchen: 'What's going on?'

'Sorry, Mrs Hadley,' Nick said, with some genuine remorse. He looked over at Mr Hadley: 'I reckon that's the end of the matter. Unless you want to get legal over it, but I don't reckon anyone would come out of that looking too clean. My word is as good as yours.' It was, and as well, Dave's father happened to be a criminal barrister – not that anyone needed to know that right now. Nick bent over Alan, who was moaning and clutching at his broken face, and he whispered in his ear: 'If I hear you've done the wrong thing with that dick of yours again, I'll come back and rip it off, and then I will make you eat it.'

At that, Nick had walked back across the yard and out to the waiting cab, with the sounds of Alan's girlfriend screaming, 'Oh my God!' ringing all the way up to the lilly-pilly hedge. No one came after him, though; even Scott knew the ultimate score, at least in this town: while the Hadleys might have been upstanding members of the community, none of them were up for Commonwealth Games selection. This was Wollongong: sport came first. Alan Hadley had just lost a contest, that was all. Boohoo. Nick was more concerned by then for how late he was for his own lunch; although he'd been less than five minutes at this business, it would take him another ten or fifteen yet to get home to Port.

And when he got there, the look of revulsion on Addy's face was enough to keep his mouth shut, the way she'd seemed to guess. She hated violence; he'd never let her know any had been committed in her name – he wouldn't even tell her when he'd hear the good goss a few weeks later that Alan and his girlfriend had split up while he was still sucking jelly through a straw; he'd never let their dad know he'd just put his entire future in jeopardy, either. He knew this Dan bloke felt the same way, too: protective. He was all right, Dan Ackerman, calling him like that last night, looking up his number in Addy's telephone book: 'You don't know me, I'm a friend of your sister's ...' Nick had always found that sister of his a bit hard to read, but things got a lot simpler between them from that point on.

'How is Dave?' their father asked, bringing out the chicken and rice, and Nick replied, 'Yeah, good,' but Addy saw the light return to his eyes at that second, the instant spark of love, before he sidestepped further chat, getting up from the table to go back out to the kitchen himself: 'Gunna put some pasta on. I'm hungry.'

'You? Hungry?' Addy teased him, even as her heart stung for her brother's most tender and dangerous secret; it made her think that it was none of her business who he might have just flattened or why, that he'd have had his reasons, and they were probably decent ones. She wondered if it was best to leave some things unsaid, to let some revelations unfold in their own time, when everyone was ready – especially their father. It wasn't as though either she or Nick weren't always thinking of him in their own ways, and trying to work out how they might best be able to bring him joy. Nick would do everything humanly possible to impress the Amateur Boxing Association board of selectors to get onto the Games team; he'd do everything he could to pass his final exams this year as well, despite his lack of interest in economics – or indeed in any academic thing. And Addy, she had now firmly decided, would go on to do Honours in English and everything humanly and metaphysically possible to be awarded First Class; and she would write a novel one day: she would place the printed pages in her father's hands, her name emblazoned on the cover: their name. *To be mispronounced by millions for all time*, she smiled to herself around a plump, piping-hot apricot.

'You were at the bout?' her father asked Dan Ackerman, and all the talk over the next half-hour was of boxing, the match, blow by blow, only a fleeting moment of unease when Dan confessed he'd never played rugby league. Addy couldn't remember ever feeling so contented, looking at these three men, feeling something was complete now that Dan was here, some good and right thing. *Such wilt thou be to me ...* Donne joined them now too:

> *Thy firmness makes my circle just,*
> *And makes me end where I begun.*

Or, at least, nearly.

She rose to put the kettle on for coffee, and to slide the cheesecake onto a plate. As she did so, looking into its plainness, she thought the cake needed a candle. She'd say they should celebrate Dan's forthcoming birthday, but really, she just wanted to mark this day as special, first day of the rest of her real, true, magical life, or something like that. She had a stash of candles somewhere, and she rummaged through her mind for them, through kitchen drawers and linen cupboard shelves, sensing all the while that they were somewhere more obscure. Then, yes, she remembered: they were in a white paper bag in her old school case, where she kept all sorts of odds and ends, under her bed. Memory can be funny like that, can't it? Capable of extraordinary detail when we need it to be. Or when we're ready for it to be.

Her old bedspread said hello as she opened the door of her room: soft chenille stripes of purple and green, immediately comforting. What a haven this little room had been over her growing years, a refuge, whether from a school bully, the steelworks' stink or that forgettable jerk Hadley, she'd shut the world out here, and hadn't realised until now how much she'd missed it, sitting at her little desk, staring out to sea. She retrieved the school case from under the bed, a dear battered thing of brown cardboard, bestickered with hearts and butterflies all creased and peeling around the brooding cartoon face of David Bowie; she wondered what David Bowie might think of his image stuck forever in such an unglamorous place, and supposed he'd like it – she'd put it there with such adoration in the summer at the end of Sixth Class.

She popped the locks with her thumbs, an action which always made her feel like a gunslinging cowgirl for some reason absolutely vanished to the mists; she imagined the first exquisite tinkling piano bars of superfreak Bowie's 'Life on Mars', felt a pang for glitter eyeshadow and a long-lost desire to learn the cello, just to be near him. How precious this little case was: it's where she kept the photographs of her mother, the three of them.

Elke and Peter dressed for dinner, smiling for the restaurant camera, and – yes! There was an appliqued rose on her bodice, unnoticed before in the black and white, but there it was indeed, a flower, a flower her mother had doubtless made, peeping out from where she pressed her heart to her husband's coat sleeve.

And there was Elke by the caravan they'd lived in before they built this house, snowy-haired Nick on her hip. She looked tired and happy, her reassuringly boring hair a mess, slipping from its pins. Nick just looked fat.

And there was Elke with Addy: they are laughing into each other's eyes as mother places a frangipani flower behind baby's left ear: forever. Addy could smell that frangipani even now; she could see the surf-bleached midnight-indigo of her mother's swimming costume.

There were other bits and pieces in the little case: her mother's fox-fur ear muffs; a fine china cup with rabbits dancing around the rim; an empty perfume bottle, clear-cut and heavy in her hand – Joy by Jean Patou, still faintly trailing its floral bouquet. How Addy came to have these treasures, she never knew; they simply were: undiscussed and hers. They lived in this case with all her birthday cards from her father, old academic reports and awards, the small yet dignified laurel-wreath trophy for that German prize, half-filled notebooks of sketched vignettes and poems, a short story published in the high school magazine. Two tins as well: a large round biscuit tin with parrots on the lid and her crochet things in it, hooks and scraps of wool; and another lunchbox-sized one containing a home set of important utilities she liked to keep handy, including scissors, nail clippers, compass and pro-tractor set, needle and thread, thimble, two pencil sharpeners, a roll of sticky-tape – and, under all that, the packet of cake candles inside their white paper bag. There were four different colours – blue, red, yellow and green – all candy-striped with white spirals, and she'd only used one, a yellow one, for her father's birthday last year.

Candles in hand, she was just about to close the case and return to the kitchen, when another photograph caught her eye, on its side at the back, as if it had been dislodged from behind her stack of notebooks – she glimpsed some sort of parkland scene, big trees and a wide lawn, and it wasn't a photo she'd recalled ever having seen before. At first, she thought it must have been a picture she'd cut out of a magazine for some long-ago school project; when she picked it up to take a closer look, though, she saw it was sepia-toned and printed on thick card. It *was* a photograph: a very old one. Beneath the trees, and in front of a formal, flower-filled garden bed, it showed a picture of two girls, one taller than the other, both in light summery dresses, white socks and black buckle shoes. They were beaming for a bright, happy day, and between them was a donk—

No. Between them was a *zebra*.

She stared and blinked and stared and blinked again, yet the picture remained.

She turned it over, to see if there might be an inscription of some kind – such as, *Ha-ha! Got you a beauty this time*. But the faded-pencil words here only said:

Anna und Elfie. Zoologischer Garten Frankfurt am 11 August 1919.

Perhaps it was the psychic overload delivered by the long week's shocks and slings, but Addy took this one calmly.

She sat back on her heels, with the photograph in her hands, taking in the face of her grandmother, the taller of the two, searching for a resemblance; her face, though, both their faces, were too small to see much more than their sunshiny smiles. They were smiling at her, at Addy, from their eternal holiday, framed on her lap by the full-colour European blooms of her garden dress, giant around them here, now. *Had* she seen this photograph before? She looked over her shoulder, out the door into the empty hall, as if someone might tell her. She wanted to run out to her father: *Dad! Dad! Where did this photo come from?* Could he have slipped it into her school case? Why would he have done that? *How* could he have done that when there were no photographs of anyone from that generation in the house? She'd snooped more than a few times, and she'd asked – years ago. 'No, Adrianna, there is nothing,' she was told, and she knew not to ask a second time. Maybe he'd lied, just because he didn't want to talk about it – couldn't talk about it.

Whatever the story was, it had sent her this: a silent gift of permission that she should, beyond all doubt, continue with her own. She held her own future in this sweet whisper of the past: she could hear their laughter, she could smell the sun-warmed dust in the zebra's soft tufted mane. The light before the dark, the right before the wrong, the peace before the war, all the way backwards and forwards again. This was her story to tell, however it came.

The kettle whistled in the kitchen; it was time for cake.

They stayed late, walking, just the two of them, Addy and Dan. They went down to the rocks of Fisherman's Beach at the end of Gallipoli Street, then up over the Hill 60 Lookout, past the old concrete bunkers of World War Two, past the public swimming pool, to Port's best treasure: a crescent shore of sparkling sands six and a half kilometres long, glowing softly gold in the lowering sun.

They talked and talked, of all kinds of things, where they'd been, where they wanted to go, what they'd known, and what they wanted to know. They exchanged thoughts on the strangeness that so many Australian streets and other suburban features were named after battlefields: Gallipoli, Hill 60, Tobruk, Suvla, Marne, Somme. There were flowers among them, of course, native and not, a sprinkling of Aboriginal words, too, and memorials to long-forgotten explorers, but war was the prevailing trend. They decided that peace was expensive, and that no one could ever know if it was worth the price.

They weren't travelling at the speed of light, and yet perhaps those strings that drew them tight together made wings so that all time had seemed to cease, even as the sun sank towards the dusk, and they walked on and on, bootless, toes delighting in the cool, silken sand.

She asked him, looking out at the deep blue horizon: 'If the universe is unimaginably enormous and everything is happening all at once, all the time, everything in its separate slice-moment of being, could it really be possible to speak to someone from the past?' As much as the inexplicable glitch of Frieda and The Curiosity Shop had seemed gifted, even tantalisingly romantic, the illogicalities snagged like beached seaweed. *Could I really have spoken to Frieda? Could she really have told me what happened to my dad, to my grandparents? Or did I make it all up, after all? If I did make it up, though, how on earth did I buy that copy of* The Fire Flight *from the second-hand furniture place when that shop most likely doesn't even sell books? Or did I buy it somewhere else? Or did I not buy it at all and I'll find a completely different book sitting on my bedside when I get back? Was Dan just humouring me about quantum whatevers? I don't want to be anyone's crazy girlfriend. I want to be me – but usefully me, brain-more-or-less-intact me. Please. I want some kind of explanation I can understand.*

'Well, I don't know …' Dan stopped walking, and squinted out at the sea: 'We're all fundamentally connected to each other, aren't we? Like water, sort of.'

'Hm?' *No idea what you're talking about.* She scrunched her toes into the sand, feeling its realness, whatever real might mean; she watched the gentle breeze lift a lock of his hair from his forehead: *yep, real enough for me.*

'Hm.' He was still squinting at the water, thinking about her question; he said: 'The sea can seem like one whole, big thing, can't it? It's not, though – obviously. It's made up of molecules – hydrogen and oxygen bonded together, yeah?'

'Yeah.' She knew that much from Year Ten chemistry. H_2O: two hydrogen atoms, Hs, linked to their oxygen O with lines that looked like outstretched arms.

'Yeah.' Dan went on: 'Well, the molecules themselves aren't bonded to each other, are they. They're attracted, they want to be together, but they're not stuck to one another. When they need to, they break apart – like when it rains, or when the surf washes up on the shore, or when water drips from wet hair. It's still all water – every bit of it – it's all one, and it's not one, either. It's just a heap of fancy electricity, going on inside every atom, all the time, and this water, all of this water, every molecule of it across the whole world, in one way or another has been here for all time – forever in all directions. So, every water molecule you can see has, conceivably, been everywhere in the world at some time – in the sea, in a cloud, in a tear – and *is* everywhere in the world right now. They're all constantly in existence. You see what I mean?'

'No, not really.' She wanted to kiss the tip of his nose for his enthusiasm for water molecules; she'd almost forgotten her question.

Nevertheless, he continued: 'The important thing is, we think we know water, this thing we see every day, but we only know a small bit about it. And it's the same with life, with people. Of the less than tiny fraction of us that isn't space, about sixty percent of the matter we're made of is water, and the rest is stardust – basically, the same stuff that everything in the world is made of, and we hardly know about any of it. So, if someone really needed to, and under the right circumstances was able to, what's to say they, or something of them, couldn't break from where they were and be somewhere else for a time – and then return to wherever they'd come from? Nothing. Unless you could prove absolutely it was impossible, then it's possible. And it's only by imagining that something *might* be possible that it can ever *be* possible at all. Yeah?'

'I'll have to take your word for that.' She smiled inside his smile as he turned to her. *You are quite a bit madder than I am, aren't you?*

'Yeah, well, anyway.' He brushed the back of her hand with his, a deliberate accident. 'If you imagined you spoke to someone from the past, maybe you really did. Trust me, I'll tell you if you start talking to someone who's not here.'

'Phew.' She shared the laugh, but doubt's grey tendrils swept over her, too: 'You're not just saying that, are you?'

'No.' He held her steadier than ever in his eyes, with all his perfect loveliness. 'The truest thing is, Addy, I don't know, and no one else does either, so you might as well err on the side of the amazing – my dad says that. It stops him from losing his mind. You know, he sees a lot of terrible things, like any emergency doctor does. He's seen people dying in the most awful pain and fear, but he says, in almost every case, there's this quietness that takes over right at the end. He calls it grace, not in any religious way or anything. He says it's like that person is more than just leaving their body, they're going somewhere, to be somewhere else. To be something else maybe. Where do they go? Where does all their electricity go? The thing is, no one knows.'

She saw it wholly then, this deepest truth she'd ever met. She saw it in the love that shone in Dan Ackerman's eyes, the knowledge that she belonged somewhere outside herself for the first time. The knowledge that there was no such thing as death in love. And it transformed her, irreversibly, there on the sands of Port Kembla Beach.

She reached for his hand, curled her fingers around the edge of his palm and she let the warmth rush through her; she let the fear and pain fall away, a carapace to the most luscious of bloomings: freedom.

A pelican stood in the shallows nearby, long, white feathers ruffling as it watched the hauling of a catch further out, the motor of the fishing boat a steady purr; and she kissed him then. She raised her face to his; she tasted the trace of cake on his lips; she tasted his saltwater and let it be one with hers, as the full moon rose over the ocean, bright and silver and round.

And hand in hand, on the edge of the sand,
They danced by the light of the moon,
The moon,
The moon,
They danced by the light of the moon.

Edward Lear, 'The Owl and the Pussy-Cat', 1871

AUTHOR NOTE

Addy Loest is a girl magicked up from the soup of my own soul. Her experiences of university and growing into herself in the 1980s in so many ways reflect mine, but she is not me. I couldn't possibly have written a true memoir of those times – we're all very respectable people these days. And what is the real truth, anyway?

Real truth, for me, whispers through all our bonds of family, friendship, the threads of history, recent and distant, that make our hearts beat and make all kinds of tangles in our minds. Real truth is that winding path you take, through and around uncertainties, anxieties and the boot-stamps of distress, to find at last what treasures you hold inside you: what you're really good at and passionate about. What makes all your atoms sing.

While the setting of the story is absolutely the Sydney I knew, eagle-eyed readers familiar with the city will spot that I've invented Flower Street and the Hairy Egg, and blurred some elements of the university itself, in order to avoid the real truth incriminating any real-life person, and also because my memory has become naturally blurry after all these years. It's important, too, to stress that none of the characters in the story represent anyone I've ever known; my university days came a few years post-85, and I was never a participant at WoCo or the SRC, so any resemblance to any real-life person really, truly would be accidental. All of Addy's descriptions of her mental unsteadiness are, however, taken directly from my own songbook of long personal struggle with the beasts in my brain.

Those for whom the name Ackerman has rung a bell: yes, Dan is the grandson of Daniel from my very first novel, *Black Diamonds*. The whole Ackerman family still lives very large in my imagination – as if they might be real people – and I never know where or when one of them is going to reappear on the page.

For those who might be wondering, the paperback Addy reads, Kathleen McAllister's *The Fire Flight*, is a fictional novel; some might recognise that it's also a coded homage to the work and spirit of the timelessly marvellous Colleen McCullough.

The John Donne quotes that appear in the chapters, 'Addy Loest Is Probably Not Going to Die Today' and 'Anything Is Possible, but Some Things Are More Possible than Others', are from 'A Valediction Forbidding Mourning'; and those which appear in the chapters, 'English Literature & Other Forms of Middle-Class Indulgence' and 'This Is What a Hero Actually Looks Like', are from 'The Good-Morrow'.

Quotes from Donald Horne's 1964 classic, *The Lucky Country*, which appear in the chapter, 'Best Intentions & the Art of Self-Sabotage', can be found in the Penguin Books Australia edition (2005, pp.10-11), and have been reproduced here with kind permission of Penguin Random House Australia, and the author's family.

The quotes from and paraphrasing of *Tacitus on Germany* in the chapter, 'Not German Enough, Heart Too Broken', are taken from Thomas Gordon's translation of the monograph (P.F. Collier & Son, New York, 1910).

Special thanks to the following irrefutably real people for sharing your own memories of our Sydney: Mark Swivel, David Anderson, Damien McDonald, Mick Meehan, Sarah Bunn, Narelle Woodberry-Daniels, Anna Broinowski, Kate Broadhurst, Donna Meadows, Louise Briffa, Helen Mountford, Adam Long, Matt Drewett, Caleb Cluff, Mick Walsh, Greg Johnston, Jason Roweth, Lucy Halliday, Anthony Porthouse, Elisabeth Storrs and Rachael Vincent. Not all of you witnessed my personal capacity for green ginger wine, but to those who did, chin-chin!

An extra special thank you to Linda and Dirk Visman as well, for photographs and recollections that helped me imagine Port Kembla and the steelworks as it was in those days.

Thank you, always, to my ever-magical agent, Selwa Anthony, for your unwavering belief in the power of stories, and to Linda Anthony for your sparkling enthusiasm for this one. Thank you, Alexandra Nahlous, my editor, for caring not only for my words but for my characters – and for this writer's heart. Thanks once again to designer Alissa Dinallo for making this book look beautiful, and to Joel Naoum for making its publication possible. To the team at Bolinda Publishing, who have produced the audiobook edition, thank you for believing in my work, too.

To my sons, Tom and Cal, I hope you find this semi-historical document useful as time goes by – bulk mamma thanks, Cal, for your very useful thoughts on the first draft. And to my darling Deano, ex-Port metallurgist and best-ever nice guy, I couldn't do the maths without you, *mein Schatz*, but I'll always be a bit glad I'd done just a little more growing up by the time I took you home.

HER LAST WORDS

From the gritty glamour of Bondi Beach to the cold streets of London, *Her Last Words* is the story of a murder, a missing manuscript, and an undying love – one which lays bare the truth that words themselves have a way of enduring, and exacting a justice all their own.

WALKING

Set across two wars and two great romances, *Walking* is inspired by a true story of medical genius and betrayal. A crisply told tale of bigotry and obsession, love and loss, that charts the path of a woman finding her feet in a man's world – and discovering, above all, the power of kindness.

SUNSHINE

Three wounded veterans of the Great War find themselves sharing a patch of farmland, and not much else – until one battle-hardened nurse changes everything. *Sunshine* is a tale of home, hope and healing, of growing life and love, and discovering that we are each other's greatest gifts.

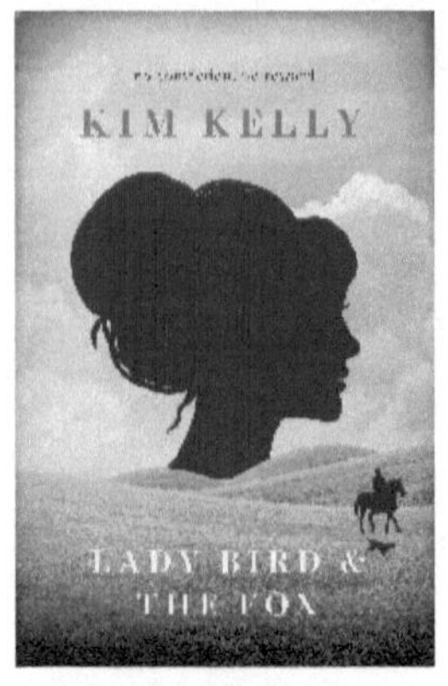

LADY BIRD & THE FOX

At a breakneck gallop through the wild colonial Australian goldrush, *Lady Bird & The Fox* untangles a tale of true identity and blind bigotry, of two headstrong opposites thrown together by fate, bushranging, and the irresistible forces of love.

JEWEL SEA

Based on the true story of the loss of the luxury steamship *Koombana* to a vicious cyclone off the coast of North-Western Australia in 1912, *Jewel Sea* is a tale of fatal desire, theft and greed – of kindred spirits searching for each other, and for redemption.

WILD CHICORY

A journey from Ireland to Australia in the early 1900s, along threads of love, family, war and peace, *Wild Chicory* is a slice of ordinary life rich in history, folklore and fairy tale, and a portrait of the precious bond between a granddaughter, Brigid, and her grandmother, Nell.

PAPER DAISIES

A haunting story of love, murder and misogyny. Unfolding at the dawn of 1901, as Australia at last becomes a nation and her women rally for the right to vote, *Paper Daisies* tells of the dangerous path one woman must tread to see justice done – and the man who lights her way.

THE BLUE MILE

Against the glittering backdrop of Sydney Harbour, *The Blue Mile* is a story of the cruelties of Great Depression poverty, the wild gamble a city took to build a bridge – a wonder of the world – and the risks only the brave will take for a chance to truly live and love.

THIS RED EARTH

It's 1939 and the girl next door wants adventure before she settles down – but war gives her more than she's asked for. From Australia's sparkling coastline to her dusty, desert heart, *This Red Earth* charts a fight for home, and a quest to tell the truth about love – before it's too late.

BLACK DIAMONDS

From the foothills of the Blue Mountains to the battlefields of France, comes a story of war and coal. Told with freshness, verve and wit, *Black Diamonds* is the tale of a fierce young nation – Australia – and two fierce hearts who dare to discover what courage really means.

Available at all major online retailers worldwide, in paperback, ebook and audiobook.

KIM KELLY

Kim Kelly is the author of eleven novels, including the acclaimed *Wild Chicory* and perennial bestseller *The Blue Mile*. With distinctive warmth and lyrical charm, her work explores Australia, its history and people, its quirks and contradictions, from colonial invasion times to the present, and from the red-dirt roads of the outback to its glittering cities.

An editor, reviewer and literary consultant by trade, stories fill her everyday – most nights, too – and it's love that fuels her intellectual engine. In fact, she takes love so seriously she once donated a kidney to her husband to prove it, and also to save his life.

Originally from Sydney, today Kim lives on a small rural property in central New South Wales just outside the tiny gold-rush village of Millthorpe, where the ghosts are mostly friendly and her grown sons regularly come home to graze.

PRAISE FOR KIM KELLY

'Consummate storytelling. A deeply satisfying page-turner ...' – Tracy Sorensen, *The Lucky Galah*

'alive, full-hearted and shimmering with hope' – Belinda Castles, *Bluebottle*

'Kelly is a masterful creator of character and voice.' – Julian Leatherdale, *Palace of Tears*

'makes you think as well as feel' – Wendy James, *The Golden Child*

'an author who writes with such a striking sense of atmosphere and sublime instinct' – *Theresa Smith Writes*

'storytelling is clearly encoded in her DNA' – *Writerful Books*

'It is uplifting to know that there are people who can write like this, with clarity, a bit of devilment and a hint of a smile.' – *Canberra Times*

'marvellous depth and authenticity based on some impressive research, and her characters, plot and fluid prose draw the reader into this world' – *Daily Telegraph*

'colourful, evocative and energetic' – *Sydney Morning Herald*

'storytelling that breaks the rules so beautifully' – Jenn J McLeod, *A Place to Remember*

'Kim Kelly's writing is magnificent' – *With Love for Books*

'told with wit, warmth and courage' – Kylie Mason, *The Newtown Review of Books*

'vivid and enthralling' – Lisa Walker, *The Girl with the Gold Bikini*

'simply superb' – Karen Brooks, *The Darkest Shore*

'Kim writes like no one else, with a depth of skill few authors achieve' – Kelly Rimmer, *The Things We Cannot Say*

'a literary page-turner... Kim Kelly is a talented and courageous story-teller' – Cassie Hamer, *The End of Cuthbert Close*